Lewis Hough

Dr. Joliffe's Boys

A Tale of Weston School

Lewis Hough

Dr. Joliffe's Boys
A Tale of Weston School

ISBN/EAN: 9783337025762

Printed in Europe, USA, Canada, Australia, Japan

Cover: Foto ©Andreas Hilbeck / pixelio.de

More available books at **www.hansebooks.com**

DR. JOLLIFFE'S BOYS.

DR. JOLLIFFE'S BOYS:

A TALE OF WESTON SCHOOL.

BY

LEWIS HOUGH,

Author of "Phil Crawford," &c.

LONDON:

BLACKIE & SON, 49 & 50 OLD BAILEY, E.C.;

GLASGOW, EDINBURGH, AND DUBLIN.

CONTENTS.

ILLUSTRATIONS.

"CAN'T YOU GIVE HIM A SCIENTIFIC WRINKLE?"

"HE WENT SULLENLY TO HIS TUTOR'S HOUSE."

"I HAVE A GOOD MIND TO HAVE YOU FLOGGED."

"HERE IS YOUR MONEY BACK."

DRIVING FROM THE STATION.

THE THEFT.

DR. JOLLIFFE'S BOYS:

A TALE OF WESTON SCHOOL.

CHAPTER I.

WESTON *v.* HILLSBOROUGH.

"WELL cut, Saurin, well cut! Run it out! Four!" The ball was delivered again to the bowler, who meditated a shooter, but being a little tired, failed in his amiable intention, and gave the chance of a half-volley, which the batsman timed accurately, and caught on the right inch of the bat, with the whole swing of his arms and body thrown into the drive, so that the ball went clean into the scorer's tent, as if desirous of marking the runs for itself.

"Well hit indeed! Well hit!"

The Westonians roared with delight, and their voices were fresh, for they had had little opportunity of exercising them hitherto. Crawley, the captain of their eleven, the hero in whom they delighted, had been declared out, leg before wicket, when he had only contributed five to the score. Only two of the Westonians believed that the decision was just, Crawley himself, and the youth who had taken his place, and was now so triumphant. But he hated Crawley, and rejoiced in his discomfiture, even though it told against his own side, so his opinion went for nothing.

Well, no more did anybody's else except the umpire's, who after all is the only person capable of judging.

"Saurin has got his eye in; we may put together a respectable score yet."

"He is the best player we have got, when he only takes the trouble; don't you think so?" said Edwards, who believed in Saurin with a faith which would have been quite touching if it had not been so irritating.

"He thinks so himself at anyrate," replied the boy addressed, "and we are a shocking bad lot if he is right. Anyhow he seems to be in form to-day, and I only hope that it will last."

The batsman under discussion hoped so too. If he could only make an unprecedented score, restore the fortunes of the day, and show the world what a mistake it was to think Crawley his superior in anything whatever, it would be a glorious triumph. He was not of a patriotic disposition, and did not care for the success of his school except as it might minister to his own personal vanity and gain, for he had a bet of half-a-crown on his own side. But his egotism was quite strong enough to rival the public spirit of the others, and raise his interest to the general pitch.

The match between Weston and Hillsborough was an annual affair, and excited great emulation, being for each school the principal event of the cricketing season. One year it was played at Weston and the next at Hillsborough, and it was the Westonians' turn to play on their own ground on this occasion.

Hillsborough went in first and put together 94 runs. Then Weston went to the wickets and could make nothing of it. There was a certain left-handed Hillsburian bowler who proved very fatal to them; it was one of his twists which found Crawley's leg where his bat should have been. Result, eight wickets down for twenty, and then Saurin went in and made the 9 we have witnessed.

Between ourselves the cut was a fluke, but the half-volley was a genuine well-played hit, which deserved the applause it got. The next ball came straight for the middle stump, but was blocked back half-way between the creases, and another run was stolen.

"Over!"

The new bowler went in for slows. The first, a very tempting ball, Saurin played forward at, and hit it straight and hard into the hands of long field on, who fumbled and dropped it, amidst groans and derisive cheers.

Warned by this narrow shave he played back next time, and seemed to himself to have missed a really good chance. This feeling induced hesitation when the next ball was delivered, and the result of hesitation was that the insidious missile curled in somehow over his bat and toppled his bails off. Saurin was so much mortified as he walked back to the tent that he could not even pretend to assume a jaunty careless air, but scowled and carried his bat as if he would like to hit someone over the head with it. Which, indeed, he would.

There was one consolation for him, he had made ten, and that proved to be the top score.

For the first time within living memory Weston had to follow its innings!

Now when you consider that the presidents of Oxford and Cambridge Clubs kept an eye on this match with a view to promising colts, you may imagine the elation of the Hillsburians and the dejection of the Westonians when Crawley and Robarts walked once more to the wickets. Their schoolmates clapped their hands vigorously indeed, and some of them talked about the uncertainty of cricket, but the amount of hope they had would not have taken the room of a pair of socks in Pandora's box.

But Crawley was a bowler as well as a batsman, and Robarts was the Westonian wicket-keeper, so that both were somewhat fagged when they first went in, whereas they were now quite fresh. Again, the Hillsburian bowling champion found his dangerous left arm a little stiff, and his eyesight not so keen as it had been an hour before. One is bound to find a cause for everything, so these may be the reasons why the pair, after defending their wickets cautiously for an over or two, began to knock the bowling about in great style.

"What a jealous brute that Crawley is!" said Saurin, sitting down by Edwards.

"Awful!" replied Edwards, not at all knowing why, but following Saurin blindfold, as he always did.

"I was the only one who made any stand in the first innings, and yet he does not send me in early. He will keep me to the last, I daresay."

The wonderful stand spoken of had not lasted two overs, but Edwards only observed:

" It's mean."

" Not that I care," said Saurin.

" Of course not."

" Only I do hate spite and jealousy."

" He ought not to be captain."

" Bah! the soft-spoken humbug; it's a wonder to me that fellows don't see through him."

" It *is* strange," echoed the complacent Edwards.

The number 30 went up amidst a storm of clapping, and Saurin relapsed into prudent silence, but he thought " hapes," like the Irishman's dumb parrot. The dinner-bell rang, the pair were not separated, and the score stood at 50.

" It will be a match yet," was the general opinion on the Weston side, and their opponents also thought that the affair did not look quite such a certainty, and agreed that they must not throw a chance away, though they hoped much from dinner, which sometimes puts a batsman off his play, the process of digestion inducing, especially in hot weather, a certain heaviness which impairs that clearness of brain necessary for timing a ball accurately. At the same time the bowlers would get a good rest, and the left-handed artist, who had been acting as long-stop, might reasonably be expected to regain his cunning. True that the midday meal tells most upon the field, which very generally grows sluggish after eating: but the Hillsborough boys fancied that would not matter so much, if they could only separate those two.

But "those two" had a due sense of their responsibilities, and ate a very moderate meal, which they washed down with nothing stronger than water. They also played very careful cricket on first going in again, and risked nothing until they had got their hands in. *Item*, Crawley had mastered the left-handed bowler's favourite ball, and by playing very forward hit it away before it took the dangerous twist. It looked very risky, and the Hillsborough wicket-keeper was in constant hope of stumping him, but he never missed, and scored off every ball of that sort which came to him. When the same twisters came to Robarts he played back, contenting himself with simply guarding his wickets with an upright bat.

Altogether the two put 85 together before Robarts was caught at point.

As they were going in to dinner Crawley had said to Saurin:

"You go in the first wicket down. You showed good form in the first innings, and it was a very unlucky ball that settled you so soon. But you will have a good chance again presently." Which speech had the unintended effect of making Saurin more exasperated than ever. "Confound his patronizing!" he said to himself; but he could not find any excuse for any audible utterance except the conventional "All right," and he now drew on his gloves, took up his bat, and issued from the tent.

"Play careful cricket, Saurin," said Robarts as he passed him; "the great thing is to keep Crawley at the wicket as long as we can."

"A likely story!" he thought to himself as he strode across the turf, "to make myself a mere foil and stop-gap for that conceited brute! Not I." Far from practising the abstinence of the other two, he had eaten as much as he could stuff and drunk all the beer he could get, and this, combined with resentment at Robarts' words, caused him to go in for slogging just to show that he was not to be dictated to.

The first ball he got he hit as hard as he could, and well on to the ground, but it was cleverly stopped before a run could be made. The second he sent into the hands of the fielder standing at mid-wicket, who stuck to it, fast as it came, and threw it up amidst the cheers of his friends. Saurin stalked away with his duck's egg.

Four more wickets fell before Crawley was run out, by which time he had scored 90 off his own bat, the total standing at 150. Thirty more was added before the Westonians were all out, and the score stood—first innings, 40; second, 180; total, 220, against 94. So that Hillsborough now had to make 126 to tie, and 127 to win.

It was a good match; anybody's game. During the remainder of the afternoon Saurin behaved disgracefully. His temper had completely mastered him, and he was sulky and careless to an extent which made even Edwards ashamed for him. He let balls pass with hardly an attempt to stop them, picked them up and threw them in in a leisurely manner, which gave more than one run to the other side, and showed such indifference that he was hissed.

For every run was of importance. The fact was that Weston that year was decidedly weak in the bowling, Crawley being the only one to be depended upon, and he could not be kept at it for ever; and, though the fielding generally was good, the Hillsburians scored fast. At seven o'clock they were 100 for seven wickets, and the excitement was very great when Crawley, who had had an hour's interval, went on once more to bowl.

His first ball was cut for five. His second took the middle stump clean. His third came back into his hands. His fourth, the nastiest of shooters, glided under the bat into the wicket. Three wickets in three consecutive balls—something like a sensational over!

The match was over, and Weston had won by 21 runs.

There could be no doubt to whom the victory was due, and Crawley was pounced upon, hoisted, and carried home in triumph amidst the most enthusiastic cheering.

"All right!" he said, colouring and laughing as they put him down; "I am glad we won, but that last ball was the most awful fluke I ever made in my life. I lost my balance as I delivered it, and nearly came down. To tell the truth, I feared it would be wide, and could hardly believe my eyes when I saw the bails off."

One would have imagined that Saurin's evil genius was taking part in the events of the day, and piling success upon the rival he hated in order to exasperate him to madness. His state of mind, indeed, was little short of that as he went sullenly to his tutor's house, with the sight of Crawley, raised on his comrades' shoulders, in his eyes, their cheers ringing in his ears, and the thoughts of Cain in his heart.

"I shall give up cricket," he said to Edwards next day; "it's a beastly game."

"I don't care for it myself," replied his friend; "only, what is one to do?"

"Lots of things; you don't know Slam's. I tell you what—I'll take you there."

"Thank you; that will be very jolly; only don't you think if one were caught, you know—eh?"

"We should get into a jolly row, no doubt; but there is no fear of being caught. And, as you say, if one does not play cricket, what is one to do?"

One thing which induced Saurin to relinquish the game which he had at one time practised with some hope of success, was that he shrewdly suspected that, after what occurred, he would no longer be retained in the eleven. And he was right, for at the very next meeting of the committee it was unanimously agreed that a fellow who failed so utterly to keep his temper was of no use at all, even if he were a much better player than Saurin; and this opinion was intimated to him without any squeamishness in the choice of terms. Had Weston lost the match his conduct on the occasion might have resulted in his being sent to Coventry; but success is the parent of magnanimity, and, since his lack of public spirit had not proved fatal, it was condoned. But it certainly did not increase his popularity. The whole affair was most unfortunate. Saurin was a disappointing sort of fellow. He was rather good-looking, and on ordinary occasions his manners were those of a gentleman. His abilities were

certainly above the average, and his eye and hand
worked together in a manner which was calculated
to ensure success in all games, especially as he was
fleet of foot and muscular. Thus he was always
giving promise of distinguishing himself, and
dying away to nothing. The explanation is that
he was very vain and very indolent, and his
vanity induced him to engage in different pursuits
which would excite admiration, while his indo-
lence prevented him from persevering long enough
for success. Directly anything bored him he
dropped it. Self-indulgence seemed to him the
only true wisdom. He never resisted the whim
of the moment except through fear of the consequences, and unfortunately many of his propensities were vicious.

He had taken up cricket rather warmly, and
seemed less inclined to get tired of it than of
most healthy and innocent diversions, and cricket
kept him out of mischief; so it was very unlucky
both for himself and for those over whom he had
influence that his jealousy of Crawley had led him
to make such an idiot of himself.

CHAPTER II.

BOUT a mile from Weston College there was a dilapidated old house with a large yard and an orchard. There had been a farm attached to it once, but the land had been taken into the next estate, and the old homestead let separately many years before. The landlord would gladly have got rid of the present tenant, but he had a long lease, and, while he paid his rent, he was secure, and could snap his fingers at the squire, the clergyman, the magistrates, and all other people who did not appreciate him. Not that he ever did so snap his fingers; on the contrary, Mr. Slam, though practically defiant, was remarkably civil, not to say obsequious, in his demeanour when he came into contact with the gentry. By profession he was a rat-catcher, and he had an intimate knowledge of the habits and frailties of all the small predatory animals of Great

Britain, and knew well how to lure them to their destruction. In a game-preserving community such talents ought, one would imagine, to have met with appreciative recognition; but unfortunately Slam was suspected of being far more fatal to pheasants, hares, and rabbits than to all the vermin he destroyed. He protested his innocence, and was never caught in the act of taking game; but if anyone wanted to stock his preserves, Slam could always procure him a supply of pheasants' eggs, and more than one village offender who had been sent to expiate his depredations in jail was known to have paid visits to Slam's yard.

Slam was a dog-fancier as well as a rat-catcher, and therefore doggy boys were attracted to his premises, which, however, were sternly interdicted. In the first place they were out of bounds, though this of itself did not go for very much. There was no town very near Weston, and so long as the boys made their appearance at the specified hours they were not overmuch interfered with. Paper chases, or hare and hounds as they are sometimes called, were openly arranged and encouraged; and if boys liked to take walks in the country, they could do so with a minimum of risk. If they were awkward enough to meet a master face to face when out of bounds, he could hardly help turning them back and giving them a slight imposition; but if they saw him coming, and got out of his way, he would not look in their direction.

But to enter an inn, or to visit Slam's, was a serious offence, entailing severe punishment, and even expulsion, if repeated.

Yet one beautiful warm summer's evening, when the birds were singing and the grasshoppers chirruping, and all nature invited mankind to play cricket or lawn tennis, if there were no river handy for boating, four youths might have been seen (but were not, luckily for them) approaching the forbidden establishment. A lane with high banks, now covered with ferns and wild flowers, and furrowed with ruts which were more like crevasses, ran up to the house; but they left this and went round the orchard to the back of the yard, in the wall of which there was a little door with a bell-handle beside it. On this being pulled there was a faint tinkle, followed by a canine uproar of the most miscellaneous description, the deep-mouthed bay of the blood-hound, the sharp yap-yap of the toy terrier, and a chorus of intermediate undistinguishable barkings, some fierce, some frolicsome, some expectant, being mixed up with the rattling of chains. Then an angry voice was heard amidst the hubbub commanding silence, and a sudden whine or two seemed to imply that he had shown some practical intention of being obeyed. A bolt was drawn, the door opened, and a short wiry man, dressed in fustian and velveteen, with a fur cap on his head and a short pipe in his mouth, stood before them.

"Come in, gents," said he. "Your dawg's at the other end of the yard, Mr. Stubbs, that's why you don't see him. He's had an orkardness with Sayres, Mr. Robarts' dog, as was in the next kennel, and I thought they'd have strangled themselves a-trying to get at one another, and so I had to separate them."

"Will it be safe to let him loose?" asked Stubbs.

"No fear; he will never go near the other while he's loose and the other one chained up; besides, he'll be took up with seeing you, he will."

It was very pleasant to the feelings of Stubbs that his dog knew him, which he evidently did, for he danced on his hind-legs, and wagged his tail, and whimpered, and did all that a bull-terrier can do in the way of smiling, when his proprietor approached for the purpose of freeing him from his chain. Their interviews were not as frequent as either dog or boy would have desired, but then they were very pleasant, for they brought the former a short spell of liberty, a meal of biscuit or paunch, and sometimes— oh, ecstasy!—the worrying of a rat, while Stubbs enjoyed the sense of proprietorship, and the knowledge that he was doing what was forbidden. He had dreams of leaving school and taking Topper home with him, and owning him as his friend before all the world, and he talked to Topper of that happy prospect, and Topper really quite seemed to understand that Stubbs was his master, who had paid money for him, and was now put to considerable expense for his board and lodging, let alone the danger he ran in coming to visit him. To an outsider, calmly reflecting, it did not seem a very good bargain for Stubbs, but still very much better than that of Perry, his friend and present companion, who kept a hawk, and vainly endeavoured to teach the bird to know him and perch on his wrist. But Perry was fond of hawks, and much regretted that the days were gone by when hawking was a favourite pastime.

The other two visitors at Slam's that evening were Saurin and Edwards. Edwards had never been there before, and consequently his feelings were curiously compounded of fear and pleasurable expectation. He had looked from a distance at the place, the entrance to which was so sternly forbidden, and imagined all sorts of delightful wickedness—how delightful or why wicked he had no idea—going on inside. He was considerably disappointed to find himself in a dirty yard full of kennels to which dogs of all sorts and sizes were attached, none of whom looked as if it would be safe to pat them. There were a good many pigeons flying about, but he did not care for pigeons except in a pie. Perry's hawk was only interesting to Perry. There was a monkey on a pole in a corner, but he was a melancholy monkey, who did nothing but raise and lower his eyebrows.

"Does the gentleman want a dawg?" asked Slam.

"He will see," replied Saurin; "if there is a real good one that takes his fancy he may buy him. It's all right; he's a friend of mine. Have you got that tobacco for me?"

"To be sure; you will find it in your drawer."

Saurin went to a little wooden outhouse which contained a table, a chest of drawers, a cask of dog-biscuits, cages of rats, and other miscellaneous articles, and opening a locker which seemed to be appropriated to him, he took out a meerschaum pipe and a tobacco-pouch, and came out presently, emitting columns of blue fragrant smoke from his mouth. Edwards looked at his friend with increased respect, the idea of being intimate with a fellow who could smoke like that made him feel an inch taller.

"I think it's beginning to colour, eh?" asked Saurin.

"Beautifully, I should say," replied Edwards.

"Won't you try?"

"Thanks; I think I should rather like," said Edwards, who began to feel ambitious, "but I have not got anything to smoke."

"Oh, Slam will let you have a pipe, or a cigar if you like it better."

Edwards, calling to mind that cigars smelt nicer than pipes, thought he should prefer one.

"Slam, my friend wants a cigar."

"Well, sir, as you know, I can't sell such things without a license; but if the gent likes to have a few rats for one of the dawgs to show a bit of sport, I'll *give* him a cigar with pleasure. It's sixpence for half a dozen."

"And, by the by, Edwards, it is usual to stand some beer to pay your footing. A couple of quarts of sixpenny will do."

"That will make eighteenpence altogether," responded Edwards cheerfully, producing that sum.

"I'll send out for the beer at once," said Mr. Slam, taking the money and going towards the house.

Where he sent to is a mystery, for there was no public-house within a mile, and yet the can of beer arrived in about five minutes. It is much to be feared that Slam set the excise law at defiance when he felt perfectly safe from being informed against.

"Rats for Topper!" exclaimed Stubbs. "Oh, I say, Edwards, you *are* a brick, you know. I have been hard up lately, and he has not had a rat for ever so long. You won't mind my letting them out for him, will you? You see, I should like him to think it was I who gave him the treat, if you don't mind."

Edwards had no objection to become a party to this innocent deception, and the cage of rats was brought out from some mysterious place where there was an unlimited supply of those vermin. Whereupon every individual dog in the establishment went off his head with excitement, and began barking and tearing at his chain in a manner to soften the hardest heart. That rats should be so near and yet so far! The building, which was once a stable, had been fitted up expressly as an arena, where dogs might exhibit their prowess, and thither the cage was now carried by Stubbs, Topper going almost the whole way on his hind-legs, with his nose close to the wires. Considering the amount of excitement the entertainment did not last long; the rats were turned out into the arena, where Topper pounced upon them one after the other with a nip and a shake which was

at once fatal. In a couple of minutes there were
six fewer rats in the world, and Topper was extremely anxious to diminish the number still
further. Doctor Johnson, the compiler of the
dictionary, said he had never in his life had as
many peaches and nectarines as he could eat, and
that was Topper's feelings with regard to rats.
Edwards did not enjoy the spectacle quite as much
as he felt that he ought. Besides, he was engaged
in desperate efforts to light his cigar. Match
after match did he burn, sucking away all the
time like a leech, but no smoke came into his
mouth.

"Let us go into the orchard and finish the
beer," said Saurin.

The orchard was surrounded by so thick a
hedge that it was just as private as the yard. A
cobby horse was cropping the grass, an ungroomed,
untrimmed animal, very much better than he
looked, his master, for reasons of his own, being
as anxious to disguise his merits as most proprie-
tors of the noble animal are to enhance them as
much as possible. There were possibilities of
recreation here, though they were somewhat of a
low order. Quoits hung up on several large nails
driven into a wall, and there was a covered skittle
alley. For there were a good many small farmers
of the class just above that of the labourer in the

neighbourhood, and some of them frequented Slam's, and were partial to skittles.

The four boys and the proprietor of the establishment seated themselves on benches in this orchard and gulped the beer.

"Your cigar does not seem to draw well," said Saurin.

"No," replied Edwards; "I can't think what is the matter with it; I never smoked a cigar like this before."

Which was perfectly true, as it was the first he had ever put into his mouth.

"Let me look at it. Why, you have not bitten the end off! You might as well expect smoke to go up a chimney that is bricked up at the top. Here, I'll cut it for you with my penknife; now you will find it go all right. What a row that hawk of yours makes, Perry!"

"Yes, he ought to be hooded, you know. Hateful times we live in, don't we! How jolly it must have been when education meant learning to ride, fly a hawk, train a hound, shoot with the bow, and use the sword and buckler, instead of mugging at abominable lessons."

"Right you are, sir," said Mr. Slam; "why, even when I was a lad a fight or a bit of cocking could be brought off without much trouble, but nowadays the beaks and perlice are that prying

and interfering there's no chance hardly. And as
for them times Mr. Perry was speaking of, why,
I've heard tell that the princes and all the nobs
used to go to see a prize-fight in a big building
all comfortable, just as they goes now to a theayter.
And every parish had to find a bull or a bear to
be bated every Sunday. Ah! them was the good
old times, them was."

Edwards did not find his cigar very nice. The
smoke got down his throat and made him cough
till his eyes watered, and the taste was not so
pleasant as the smell. However, Saurin seemed
to like it, so there must be some pleasure about it
if he only persevered.

He laboured under a delusion here, for Saurin
would rather not have smoked, as a matter of fact,
though he had a great object in view, the colouring of his pipe, which supported him. His real
motive in this, as in all other matters, was vanity.
Other boys would admire him for smoking like a
full-grown man, and so he smoked. He would
never have done it alone, without anyone to see
him, being too fond of himself to persevere in anything he did not like out of whim, or for the
sake of some possible future gratification, of the
reality of which he was not very well assured.

"Did you ever play at quoits, Edwards?" asked
Saurin presently.

"Yes, I have played at home; we have some."

"Suppose we have a game, then. Why, hulloa, how pale you look! don't smoke any more of that cigar."

"I do fee—feel a little queer," said Edwards, who certainly did not exaggerate his sensations. A cold sweat burst out on his forehead, his hands were moist and clammy, and though it was a warm evening he shivered from head to foot, while he had a violent pain in his stomach which prevented his standing upright.

"Come, man alive, don't give way. We must be getting back soon," said Saurin, who was rather dismayed at the idea of taking his friend to his tutor's in that condition, and the consequent risk of drawing suspicion on himself. "Would not a drop of brandy be a good thing, Slam?"

"Well, no, not in this here case," said Slam. "The missus shall mix him a little mustard and warm water; that's what he wants."

"You are sure it's only the cigar," groaned Edwards. "I am not poisoned or anything?"

"Poisoned! how can you be? You have taken nothing but the beer, and we have all drunk that. No, it's the tobacco; it always makes fellows rather seedy at first, and I expect you swallowed a lot of the smoke."

"I did."

"Well, then, drink this and you will be all right presently."

Edwards took the emetic, which had the effect peculiar to that description of beverage. It was not a pleasant one; indeed, he thought he was going to die; but after a while the worst symptoms passed off, and he was able to walk home.

Saurin and Edwards lodged at the same tutor's, and they went up to the room of the latter without attracting attention. Here Edwards, under the other's directions, washed his face, cleaned his teeth, changed his jacket and neck-tie, and put some scented pomatum on his hair, and then lay down on his bed till the supper-bell should ring.

"I shall not be able to eat," he remonstrated. "Do you think I need go down?"

"Oh, yes; come and have a try, or else it will excite suspicion. You would have to show at prayers directly afterwards, you know, so it will not make much difference. You have nothing to do with old Cookson between this and supper— no exercise or anything?"

"No, thank goodness!"

"That's all right. You have a good hour for a nap, and your head will be better then. I must go and sweeten myself now."

I regret to say that "old Cookson" was the shockingly disrespectful way in which this flagitious youth spoke of his reverend and learned tutor.

CHAPTER III.

WESTON COLLEGE was a polishing-up establishment. Boys were not admitted under the age of fourteen, or unless they showed a certain proficiency in Greek and Latin, in the first book of Euclid, in arithmetic and algebra up to simple equations. And the entrance examination, mind you, was no farce. If a candidate was not well grounded they would not have him; and it was necessary to be particular, because the first or lowest form assumed a certain amount of knowledge in the commencement of that course which proposed to land the neophyte in the Indian Civil Service, the army, or a good scholarship at one of the universities.

Though fourteen was the age of possible admission, very few boys were qualified until they were at least a year older, and consequently there was no organized system of fagging, and flogging was

a very rare and extreme measure; but otherwise
the system somewhat resembled that of the large
public schools. The head-master and three other
masters each had a house full of boarders, whose
preparation of lessons on certain subjects he
superintended; and every boy had a separate
apartment, which was his study and bed-
room.

It was an expensive school, and the discipline
of Dr. Jolliffe was more lax than many parents
and guardians quite liked; and yet few of the
boys who went there were rich. It was very
rarely, that is, that one of them had not to make
his own way in the world. And the number,
which was limited, was always complete. For
results speak for themselves, and the examination
lists showed triumphant successes for Weston. It
is true that if they only took boys of considerable
proficiency, and got rid of all who made no progress, they might be expected to show a good
average; but then, on the other hand, there was
no cramming, and every encouragement was given
to healthy athletic exercise. Three or four years
were taken to do the work which is too often
jammed into a few months. That was the secret;
and, though of course there were failures, it
answered well on the whole.

This is an explanatory digression, just to let

you know what sort of stage our characters are acting upon.

It was Saturday afternoon, and a half-holiday, and there was only one boy left in Dr. Jolliffe's house. His name was Buller, and he was neither sick nor under punishment. His window was wide open, for it was very hot and stuffy in his little room, into which the sun poured, and on the other side of a lane which ran underneath was the cricket-field, from which the thud of balls struck by the bat, voices, and laughter resounded in a way to tempt any fellow out of his hole. But there he stuck with his elbows on the table and his head in his hands, forcing himself to concentrate his attention upon a book which lay open before him.

"Because $\frac{a}{b} = \frac{c}{d}$," he murmured, "the first quotients m m are equal. Yes, I see that; again, since $\frac{a}{b} = m + \frac{x}{b}$, and $\frac{c}{d} = m + \frac{r}{d}$, hum, hum, why, in the name of all that's blue—oh, yes! I see. But then—oh, a thousand blisters on the idiot who invented this rot! But I won't be licked."

And he began again and again, sticking to it for another half-hour, when he suddenly cried out, " I have it! What a double-distilled ass I am! Of course it is simple enough. If $\frac{a}{b} = \frac{c}{d}$, and a and b be prime to each other, c and d are equimultiples

of a and b. Of course they are; how could they
be anything else? The other fellows saw it at
once, no doubt. What a lot of trouble it gives
one to be a fool! Now, I'll go and practise
bowling."

Buller was no fool; indeed he would not have
thought himself one if he had been; but he was
slow at everything—learning, games, accomplishments—though he had this compensation, no
slight one either, that when he had once mastered
a thing he had got it for ever. His school-fellows
called him a duffer, but it did not vex him in the
least, for he considered it a mere statement of a
patent fact, and was no more offended than if they
had said that he had two legs. But he had a
strong belief that perseverance, *sticking*, he called
it, could make up in a great measure for want of
natural ability. The fable of the hare and tortoise
had given him great encouragement, and, finding
in practice that he passed boys who had far more
brilliant parts than himself, he never gave way to
despair, however hopeless the task before him
might seem.

His ambition—never expressed, however, to
anyone—was to get into the eleven. Had it been
known it would have been thought the very height
of absurdity, and have become such a standing
joke that its realization would have been rendered

well nigh impossible. It proved that Buller had sound sense that he was able to see this. He did not much expect to succeed, but he meant to try all he knew ever since the day he was called "old butter-fingers" in a game in which he showed especial incapacity to catch the ball. He began by mastering that; whenever he could he got fellows to give him catches. He practised throwing the ball up in the air and catching it again. When he went home for the holidays he would carry a tennis-ball in his pocket, and take every opportunity of throwing it against a wall and taking it at the rebound with both hands, with the right hand, and with the left. At last he got quite dexterous—and sinistrous, too, for that matter.

But the mere fact of being able to manipulate the ball smartly, though it is of supreme importance in cricket, would never gain him admission into the eleven of his house, let alone that of the school. For that, as he well knew, he must cultivate a speciality, and he decided upon bowling. Wicket-keeping could only be practised in a regular game, and no side would agree to let him fill the post—it was not likely. Batting everyone wanted to practise, and it would be very rarely that he would be able to get a good bowler to bowl for him. There was a professional, indeed, who was always in the cricket-fields during the season, but his services were generally in request, and, besides, they were expensive, and Tom Buller had not much pocket-money. But there was almost always some fellow who was glad to get balls given to him, and, if not, you can set a stump up in front of a net and bowl at that.

To have worked all this out in his mind did not look like lack of intelligence or observation, and to act upon it steadily, without saying a word about it to anybody, showed considerable steadfastness and resolution. He now put his algebra and papers into his bureau, took out his cricket-ball and ran down-stairs and round to the fields. At first it seemed as if he would be obliged to have recourse to his solitary stump, for, it being the Saturday half-holiday, there were two matches going on, and those present not taking part in them were playing lawn-tennis. But presently he espied Robarts, who had been in and out again in the game he was engaged in, and was now waiting for the innings of his side to be over, standing in front of a net, bat in hand, with two boys bowling to him.

"May I give you a ball, Robarts?" he asked.

"Of course you may, Buller; the more the merrier," was the reply; "only, if you are so wide as to miss the net, you must go after the ball yourself." And Robarts raised his bat, prepared for a good swipe if the ball came within reach, which he did not much expect.

Buller measured his distance, took a short run, and sent the ball in with the energy begotten of long mugging at algebra on a fine afternoon. Every muscle in his body seemed to long for violent exertion; the pent-up strength in him, like steam, demanded an outlet, and, with his hand rather higher than the shoulder, he sent the ball in with a will.

"By Jove! that was straight enough, and a hot one too!" exclaimed Robarts, who had only just managed to block it. "It made my hands tingle."

The two others delivered their balls, which were hit away right and left, and then Buller came again with another which had to be blocked. The other bowlers who had been playing, and were going in again presently, were glad to stop and leave Buller to work away alone, which he did in a deliberate, determined manner, proving that his first attempts were not chance shots. Twice he sent the wickets down, and once, when the ball was driven back to him, he caught it with the left hand, high up.

"Well," said Robarts when he was called away to go and field, "and you are the fellow they called a duffer! Why, it is like magic! Were you playing dark last year, or what?"

"No; but I have been practising."

"You have practised to some purpose, then. If you could only vary your bowling a little more you would be very dangerous. You see, if you always send the same sort of ball, a fellow knows how to meet it after a bit."

Robarts as an all-round player was only reckoned inferior to Crawley, and his words of approval were very gratifying to Buller, who felt himself a step nearer one particular goal. He did not indulge in daydreams, however, not being of an imaginative disposition. The actual difficulty which he had to master at the time took up all his thoughts and energies, and the distant object to be attained, though never absolutely lost sight of, was never dwelt upon or brooded over.

He at once looked about for someone else to bowl for, and found his particular chum, Penryhn, who, after fagging out through the heat of the day, had gone to the wicket with the sun in his eyes, and been clean bowled the first ball.

"Will you really bowl for me?" he said eagerly in reply to Buller's offer. "What a good fellow you are!"

"Why? for doing what I want? That is laying in a stock of good works cheap. You won't mind a few wides, I hope; Robarts says there is too great a sameness about my bowling, so I want to practise twisters and shooters. You won't mind if I bowl at your legs?"

"Not a bit; *ignis via*—fire away."

The necessity for violent exertion had been taken out of Buller, indeed it was now oozing away from every pore of his skin. So he did not try fast bowling, except now and then when he attempted to put in a shooter, but concentrated his attention principally upon placing his ball, or on pitching it to leg with an inward twist towards the wicket. He constantly failed; sent easy ones which were hit about to the peril of neighbouring players; cut Penryhn over once on the knee-cap and once on the ankle. But he never once delivered the ball carelessly, or without a definite object. And when his arm got so tired that his mind could no longer direct it, he left off, and Penryhn bowled in turn to him, his great object then being to keep an upright bat rather than to hit.

"I'll tell you what, Tom, you have improved in your cricket awfully," said Penryhn as they strolled back in the dusk. "Why, you took Robarts' wickets twice."

"Yes, but I should not have done it in a game; fellows step out and hit recklessly in practice."

"No matter for that; you are quite a different bowler from what you were."

"The fact is it takes me all my time to learn to do what comes to other fellows naturally."

"That's a bit too deep for me; some fellows can do one thing easily and others another, and every fellow has to work hard to learn those things which belong, as it were, to the other fellows. There are chaps, I suppose, like the Admirable Crichton, who are born good all round, and can play the fiddle, polish off Euclid, ride, shoot, lick anyone at any game, all without the slightest trouble, but one does not come across them often, thank goodness. I say, do you know what genius is?"

"Not exactly; that is, I could not define it."

"Well, I have heard my father say that some very clever chap has said that it is 'an infinite capacity for taking pains;' and if that's true, by Jove, you must be a genius, Tom!"

And they both burst out laughing at the notion, and went in and changed their flannels. And Buller lit his candle and mugged at a German exercise till the supper-bell rang.

Half-holidays did not necessarily preclude work in the tutor's pupil-rooms, which was preparatory to that in school, though practically the hours of recreation were never interfered with in fine weather. But after the hour of "All In," as the local phrase went, when the roll was called, and every boy had to be in for the night, an hour which varied with the time of the year, it was different. And on this Saturday evening Mr. Cookson had some arrears of Historical Theme correction to make up. For since history plays a considerable part in modern competitive examinations, every boy had to read up a certain portion of some standard work every week, and write a theme upon it, without the book, in the pupil room. This theme was looked over with him by his tutor before being sent in to the head-master, and if it did not reach a certain standard it was torn up, and he had to read the subject again and write another one. Edwards was one of the essayists whose paper had not yet been examined, and he stood at his tutor's elbow while he read it over. "'After he had been some years in England Sir Elijah Impey was tried by Doctors' Commons—'" "*House* of Commons, boy," said Mr. Cookson, "people are not impeached at Doctors' Commons, that's where wills are proved," and he made a correction,—"'and proved he hadn't murdered the rajah. And so Sir Philip Francis, the author of a book called *Junius*, the writer of which was never discovered,'"—"why, that's a bull;" Mr. Cookson could not help chuckling as he made a dash and a correction,—"'and deaf Burke,'"—"'I never heard that he was deaf—oh, that was

another man, a prize-fighter, ho, ho, ho, ahem!'"—
"'and Burke were very much ashamed of themselves, and were hissed, and never alluded to the
subject, from which originated the phrase of
'burking the question;'"—"Pooh, pooh, never
make shots like that:"—"'and Sir Elijah Impey
was found Not Guilty, and all his property was
taken from him to pay the lawyers with.'" "Well,
well, it's not so bad," said Mr. Cookson, signing
his name at the bottom of the last page. "And
now, Edwards," he added, turning and looking the
boy straight in the eyes, "I have a good mind to
have you flogged."

"Me, sir!" exclaimed Edwards, turning pale;
"what for, sir?"

"Doctor Jolliffe does not flog for many things, but
there are certain offences he never fails to visit with
the utmost severity. Smoking is one of them."

"I assure you, sir, I have not—"

"Lying is another, so do not finish your sentence. I can smell the stale tobacco."

And indeed Edwards was wearing the jacket in
which he had indulged in that emetical luxury,
his first cigar, two evenings previously.

"But really, sir, it is no lie," he urged; "I have
not been smoking, and I cannot tell where the
smell comes from, unless it is my jacket, which I
wore in the holidays, when I sat in the room with

my father when he was having his cigar sometimes, and which has been in my box till the other
day. I am certain it cannot be my breath or
anything else."

"Come nearer; no, your breath and hair are free
from the taint. Well, it may be as you say, and
I am loth to suspect you of falsehood. But listen
to me, my boy; I am not assuming that you have
been smoking, mind, but only, as we are on the
subject, that you might do so. It may seem very
arbitrary that the rules against it are so very severe,
considering how general the practice is, but they
are wise for all that. However harmless it may
be for those who have come to their full growth,
smoking tobacco is certainly very injurious to lads
who are not matured. And indeed until the habit
is acquired it affects the digestion and the memory
of every one. Now, in these days of competitive
examinations, when every young fellow on entering life has to struggle to get his foot on the
first rung of the ladder, and all his future prospects
depend on his doing better than others, how
inexpressibly silly it is for him to handicap himself needlessly by taking a narcotic which confuses
his brain and impairs his memory, and which
affords him no pleasure whatever. I treat you as
a rational being, and appeal to your common sense,
and speak as your friend. Now, go."

Edwards was not such a ready liar as you may think him, though he certainly prevaricated He *had* worn that jacket in his father's smoking-room, and it *had* lain in his box during the early part of the term. He had not smoked again since the occasion commemorated, and that was two days previously, and he persuaded himself that his tutor's question applied to that day. But he knew in his heart that it didn't, and with the kind tones of his tutor's voice ringing in his ears he felt as if he ought to be kicked.

But when he went up to his room he found Saurin there, and any feelings of self-reproach he had had soon melted away.

"What's up, now?" asked his friend. "You look as if you had seen a ghost."

"I nearly got into an awful row, I can tell you!" replied Edwards. "My tutor smelt my jacket of smoke while he was correcting my theme."

"By Jove! And how did you get out of it?"

"I told him I had worn the jacket in my father's smoking-room."

"Ha, ha, ha! that was a good un. Well done, old fellow! I did not think you had so much presence of mind. You will make your way yet."

Edwards was on the point of protesting that what he said was the fact, but his guide, philosopher, and friend seemed so much pleased with the ingenuity of his plea that he could not bear to rob himself of the credit of it, and so he looked as knowing as he conveniently could, and chuckled, taking a pride in what five minutes before he was ashamed of.

"That's the worst of cigar-smoking, the smell clings so to the clothes and hair. Now, a pipe is much easier to get sweet again after, unless, of course, you carry it about in your pocket. Wore the jacket in your father's smoking-room about a month ago! and old Cookson was soft enough to swallow that. How old Slam would chuckle! I must tell him."

"Do you know, I am not quite certain that my tutor did altogether believe that I had not been smoking," said Edwards, his conscience stirring again a little bit now that he saw the man who had spoken so kindly to him incurring the terrible risk of forfeiting Saurin's esteem through a false imputation of too great credulity. "You see, he's a good-natured chap, and I think he wanted to believe if he could, and as my hair and breath did not smell, he gave me the benefit of the doubt."

"Thought it would bring discredit on his house if it were known to contain a monster who smoked tobacco," said Saurin, "and so was glad to pretend to believe the papa-smoking-room story. Well, it is possible; old Cookson may not be so great a fool as he looks. Anyhow, I am glad for your sake that he did not report you; old Jolliffe would not have been humbugged. He would have said, ' Your jacket stinks of tobacco, and jackets don't smoke of themselves.' And you would have got it hot, old fellow, for Jolliffe is mad against smoking."

CHAPTER IV.

AN OUTSIDE PROFESSOR.

AURIN'S master passion of vanity caused him to be fond of low company. This may sound odd to some, because many vain people are sycophants, who will do anything to be seen in the company of persons of title or high social position, and who cut the acquaintance of old friends, and even benefactors when they dare and can do without them, when they are of inferior grade. These are contented to shine with a reflected light; but Saurin's pride was of a different description, and he chafed at being a satellite, and always wanted to figure as a sun, the centre of his companions, who must revolve around him. How small a sun did not matter. And so, though really possessed of considerable abilities, he was happier when in the company of boors and clodhoppers, who owned his superiority and deferred to all he said, than he was with his equals, who presumed to question his opinions, differ in their tastes, and laugh at his failures.   This natural disposition had, unfortunately, been fostered by circumstances.   He was an only child, born in India, and had been sent over to England in his early infancy, and committed to the care of an uncle.   His parents died before they could come home, and he never knew them.   His uncle and guardian lost his wife very soon after the boy was sent to him.   He was older and had settled in life very much earlier than his brother, and his two children (girls) were married and living at a distance.   He resided nominally in the country, but after his wife's death lived a great deal in London.   So there was no one to look properly after the orphan, who associated with grooms and gamekeepers, and played with the village boys.   Unfortunately the best of these went to work, and it was only the idle good-for-nothings who were available as playmates. When his uncle had an inkling of what was going on he sent him to school, where he did not get on badly so far as learning was concerned, but unfortunately he did not *un*learn the lessons taught him by bumpkin ne'er-do-weels, and when he went home for the holidays he renewed his acquaintance with them with fresh zest.   He had a good voice, and would sing to the revellers at harvest homes and

other rural festivities as they sipped their ale, and
delighted in their applause and wonder at his
cleverness, and in the deference they paid him.
When he went to Weston his ambition took at
first a higher flight, and he dreamed of domin-
ating the school. With this idea he began to
study with some ardour, and his natural ability
enabled him to make good progress. At all the
games in which success brought consideration he
also tried to attain proficiency, and he endeavoured
in every way he could think of to court popularity.
But there were others as clever and cleverer than
himself, as good and better at football, running,
and cricket, and very many whose manners and
disposition were more attractive. He had not
got the patient persistency of Tom Buller, or with
his superior quickness he might have gone far
towards success. But he wanted to establish his
position at a jump, and every failure discouraged
and irritated him. And so his efforts became
more and more spasmodic, and he confined himself
to trying to become the head of a clique. But
his overbearing vanity and selfishness would show
itself too glaringly at times, and many who accepted him as a leader at first grew weary of him,
and Edwards was his only really faithful fol-
lower. Therefore he fell back upon Slam's, where
certain young farmers of the neighbourhood, for

whom he sometimes provided drink, applauded his songs and jokes, and fooled him to the top of his bent. But he none the less chafed at his want of appreciation in the school, and bitterly hated Crawley, who in a great measure filled the place which he coveted.

Since the cricket match in which he had figured so ignominiously, Saurin had become a confirmed loafer, and frequented the old reprobate's yard almost daily. And, indeed, a new attraction had been added to the establishment. Wobbler, the pedestrian, a candidate for the ten-miles championship of Somersetshire, was residing there during his training for that world-renowned contest. It cannot be correctly said that Wobbler was very good company, for indeed his conversational powers were limited, which was perhaps fortunate, seeing that his language was not very choice when he did speak. But he was a man of varied accomplishments; not only could he walk, but he could run, and swim, and box. Indeed he had only deserted the pugilistic for the pedestrian profession because the former was such a poor means of livelihood, closely watched as its members were by the police. Now, Saurin had long wished to learn to box, an art which was not included in the curriculum of the Weston gymnasium, and here was an opportunity. The professor's terms were half-a-crown a lesson, provided there was a class of at least four. The ordinary allowance of pocket money at Weston was eighteenpence a week, *plus* tips, *plus* what was brought back to school after the holidays. In the words of Mr. Slam, " it wouldn't run to it." There were seven occasional frequenters of the forbidden yard who were anxious to acquire the rudiments of the noble art of self-defence, but half-a-crown a lesson was a prohibitive tariff. Indeed it seemed contrary to principle to *pay* to learn anything. Saurin hit on a way out of the difficulty; he wrote this letter to his guardian:

" My dear Uncle,—I should like to learn gymnastics, fencing, boxing, and those things, but the regular man appointed to teach such things here is a duffer, and makes it a bore, keeping you at dumb-bells and clubs and such stupid work for ever, just to make the course last out, for the charges are monstrous. And so, hearing about this, Professor Wobbler, a first-rate instructor, I am told, has engaged a room in the neighbourhood, where he gives lessons at half-a-crown each, or a course of ten for one pound. It has to be kept secret, because the man appointed by the school would have the boys forbidden to go there if he knew. If you don't mind, will you please send the pound to me or to Professor Wobbler. I will send you his receipt if you pay him through me. Please do not mention the matter if it does not meet with your approval, as I should be very sorry to take the poor man's bread out of his mouth." This part of the epistle, a cunning combination of the *suppressio veri* and *suggestio falsi*, was given to all the others who were in the plot to copy. I am sorry to say that in several instances, including those of Saurin and Edwards, it was successful, and the class was formed.

The professor was not beautiful to look at. His forehead was low and projecting, his eyes small, his nose flat, his lower jaw square and massive. Neither were his words of instruction characterized by that elegance which public lecturers often affect, but they were practical and to the point, which after all is the chief thing to be looked at.

"You stands easy like," he said to Saurin, who was taking his first lesson in an unfurnished room of Slam's house, the fine weather having terminated in a thunderstorm, and a wet week to follow. "Don't plant your feet as if you meant to grow to the floor, and keep your knees straight—no, not stiff like that, I mean don't bend them. You wants to step forwards or to step backwards, quick as a wink, always moving the rear foot first, or else you'd stumble over it and get off your balance, and that would give t'other a chance. You must be wary, wary, ready to step up and hit, or step back out of reach. Keep your heyes on t'other's, and that will help you to judge the distance. Take 'em off for a bit of a second and you'll have his mawley well on your nose at once. Now, your left arm and fut in advance, not too much; keep your body square to the front. Your right arm across, guarding what we calls the mark, that's just above the belt, where the wind is. Let your left play up and down free, your foot and body moving with it graceful like. That's better. Now, try to hit me in the face as hard as you can; you won't do it, no fear; I should like to bet a pound to a shilling on that every time, and I won't hold my hands up neither. It's just to show yer what judging the distance is."

Saurin hesitated at first, and hit gently; but urged to try his best he at last struck out sharply, but could not reach the professor's visage. Sometimes he turned it slightly to the right, sometimes to the left, and the blow went past his ear. Sometimes he just drew his head back, and the pupil's fist came to within an inch of what he called his nose, but never touched it. This was a way the professor had of showing his credentials—it was his unwritten diploma proving his efficiency to instruct in the noble art. After this the boxing-gloves were put on, and the pupil was directed to walk round the professor in a springy manner, leading off at his face, the instructor throwing off the blows with an upward movement of the right arm. Next, after a pause for rest, they went on again, Saurin leading off, professor parrying and returning the blow, slowly at first, then quicker as the pupil gained skill and confidence in warding off the hit. Then the instructor led off, and the pupil parried and returned. Then one, two, three, four. And so the first lesson ended, and Stubbs, who was another of the class, was taken in hand. Now Stubbs had naturally let his beloved Topper loose as he passed through the yard, and the dog followed him into the room where the lesson was going on. So long as Stubbs led off at the professor Topper was quiet and happy; his master he thought was worrying someone, it was his human equivalent to killing a rat; but when the professor led off at *him*, the case was different, and Topper, without warning, went straight at the supposed assailant's throat. Fortunately the professor had a bird's-eye handkerchief round his neck, which protected it from the dog's teeth, for Topper sprang right up and fixed him. It was frightful to look at, but Stubbs had the presence of mind to seize his animal round the throat with both hands immediately and drag him away; his teeth were so firmly set in the handkerchief that that came too.

No one is a hero at all hours, and Wobbler came
as near being frightened as a soldier or a pugilist
can be supposed, without libel, to do. This made
him angry, and he used language towards the dog
and his anatomy, and his own anatomy, which is
not customary in polite society. Stubbs carried
the offender down to his kennel and chained him
up, and on his return offered a peace-offering of
beer, which was well meant but unkind, seeing
that the professor was in training and restricted
as to his potations. However, Topper's fangs had
not broken the skin, thanks to the handkerchief,
though certainly not to Topper. Mr. Wobbler recovered his equanimity, and affably condescended
to apologize for his remarks.

"I'm almost afeard as I swore, gents," he
observed, and his fear was certainly well founded.
"I was a trifled startled, you see, and expressed
myself as I felt, strong. Bull-terriers is nice
dogs, and I'm very partial to them, in their proper
place, but that's not a hanging on to my wind-
pipe; at least that's *my* opinion. But I'm sorry
if I spoke rough, which is not in my habits.
Nobody can say that Job Wobbler is uncivil to
his backers or his patrons."

A speech which was perhaps rather lacking in
dignity for a professor. The lesson then went
on, and was succeeded by others, sometimes in

the room, sometimes in the orchard, according to the weather. And when the pupils had attained a certain degree of proficiency they were paired off against one another, first for leads-off, at the head, parry and return at the body, stop and return at the head, and so forth. Finally, for loose sparring, the professor standing by and stopping them when they got wild, or began punching indiscriminately. Saurin made considerable progress, and was a long way the best of the class—so much so, indeed, that he had to play lightly with the others, or they would not all set to with him. Even such a critic as Slam expressed his approval, and this superiority was sugar and sack to Saurin, being indeed the first consolation he had received since the mortification of being turned out of the eleven. But, alas! sparring was not a recognized item of Weston athletics, and he could not gain the applause of the whole school by his proficiency, which was only known to a very few of the initiated. Unless, indeed,—and here a thought which had long lain dormant in his mind, for the first time assumed a distinct shape. Suppose he happened to come to an open outbreak with Crawley, and it ended in a fight, what an opportunity it would be to gratify his ambition and his hatred at the same time! He did not actually plan anything

of the kind, or say to himself that he would pick
a quarrel. The idea was merely a fancy, a day-
dream. Man or boy must be bold as well as bad
deliberately to form a scheme for bringing about
an encounter with a formidable enemy, and
Saurin was not particularly bold, certainly not
rashly so, and Crawley would be likely to prove
a very awkward customer. Instructors of any sort,
whether they are professors of mathematics, or
Hebrew, or of dancing, or boxing, have this in
common, that they are sure to take a special
interest in apt pupils; and so Mr. Wobbler paid
more attention to Saurin than to the others, and
showed him certain tricks, feints, and devices
which he did not favour everybody with. He
also gave him some hints in wrestling, and taught
him the throw called the cross-buttock. Saurin
used likewise to go to the highroad along which
the professor took his daily walks in preparation
for his match, and sometimes held the stop-watch
for him, and learned how to walk or run in a way
to attain the maximum of speed with a minimum
of exertion. The mere learning to box, and the
necessary association with a man like Wobbler,
would not have done the boys much harm of
itself. The deception practised in order to obtain
the money to pay him with, and the skulking and
dodging necessary for approaching and leaving

Slam's premises without being seen, were far more injurious to them, especially since the great freedom allowed to the boys at Weston was granted on the assumption that they would not take advantage of it to frequent places which were distinctly forbidden. And to do them justice, the great majority felt that they were on honour, and did not abuse the trust. But for Saurin, and for Edwards and a few others who followed Saurin's lead, the mischief did not end here. Mr. Wobbler sometimes unbended—Mr. Saurin was such a "haffable gent" there was no resisting him—and told anecdotes of his past experiences, which were the reverse of edifying. It was a curious fact that every action upon which he prided himself, or which he admired in his friends, was of a more or less fraudulent nature; and Mr. Slam, who was always present on these occasions, shared these sentiments, and contributed similar reminiscences of his own. It was true that the boys looked upon these two, and upon the young sporting farmers who sometimes dropped in, and boasted of poaching, and horse-cheating exploits in a spirit of emulation, as "cads," who had a different code from their own; but it is very difficult to associate with persons of any station in life who think it clever to defraud others, and consider impunity as the only test of right or wrong, and to laugh at their dishonourable tricks, without blunting our own moral sense. We cannot touch pitch without being defiled.

Another great evil was the beer-drinking, at any time, whether they were thirsty or not, which went on. Worse still, spirits were sometimes introduced. The frequenters of Slam's spent all their pocket-money at that place in one way or another; and the pity of it was, that most of them would much rather, certainly at starting, have laid it out in oyster-patties, strawberry messes, and ices, than in forming habits which they would very probably give their right arms to be rid of in after-life. The best hope for them, next to being found out, was that their course of boxing lessons would soon be over, and Mr. Wobbler would go away to walk his match and clear out of the neighbourhood, and that then they would give up frequenting this disreputable hole before the bad habits which they were so sedulously acquiring got a complete hold upon them. As it was at present, Topper was the only living being that had tried to do a good turn for them; if he had succeeded in worrying the professor, the whole clique would have broken up.

CHAPTER V.

HOSTILITIES COMMENCED.

MANY Weston boys who had nothing to do with Slam, who did not care for ratting, and saw no fun in being the proprietor of a dog that could only be seen occasionally and by stealth, took a perfectly legitimate interest in Wobbler as a competitor in the Somersetshire ten-miles championship, and when it became generally known that he was training in the neighbourhood (which was not for some time, nor until the number of boxing lessons subscribed for by the Saurin class had been pretty well exhausted), a good many repaired when time allowed to the nice bit of straight highroad some two miles off, where the pedestrian pounded along daily, with his body inclined somewhat forward, his arms held in front of his chest, a little stick in his right hand, fair heel and toe, at a rate of over seven miles in the hour. A group, of which Penryhn was one, were walking in that direction one afternoon, when Buller overtook them at a sharp run, pulling up alongside his friend.

"So you have come then after all?" said Penryhn.

"Yes," replied Buller, mopping his forehead. "I finished the task I set myself directly after you started, and thought I could catch you up. But it's hot!"

"Is it true that you have been elected into the house eleven?"

"Yes," replied Buller; "it seems rum, doesn't it?"

"I don't know why it should. I am sure I am very glad, old fellow, for I know that you wished it."

"Well, yes I did. I am uncommonly fond of cricket, don't you see, and have tried hard to improve."

"That you must have done, by Jove! But how was it?"

"Well, Robarts said something to Crawley, and Crawley came up to me the day before yesterday and said he had heard that I could bowl a bit; would I come and give him a few balls. So I went and bowled to him for an hour, and the result was that he called a house meeting, and I was put into the eleven."

"You will be in the school eleven next year, you see."

"I don't know," replied Buller; "it depends on how I get on, you know. I might make a regular mull of it."

"Bosh! not you; you have gone on improving too steadily for that," said Penryhn confidently. "This is one of the milestones the chap comes to; he will be here presently if we wait. What's the row over there?"

"Oh! one of those men with images, and some of our fellows, Saurin, Edwards, and that lot, chaffing him."

An Italian with a large tray of plaster of Paris figures on his head was tramping from one town to another, and seeing the groups of boys gathered in different parts of the road, thought he might do a stroke of business, so taking down the tray he solicited attention.

"I makes them all myself; I am poor man, but artist."

"Ah! and how do you sell them?" asked Saurin.

"Sheap, oh mosh too sheap; what you like to give."

"Will you take a shilling for the whole lot?"

"Oh! young gentleman, you make fun, you joke. Ha, ha! One shilling for the beautiful little statues! What joke!"

"Too much, is it? I thought so; not but what they would make capital cockshies."

A large pile of flints, hammered into a convenient size and form for missiles, lay handy, ready for repairing the road, and the coincidence caused Saurin's idea to become popular at once.

"Let's have one for a cockshy. Here's Bismark."

"He's a German, and I hate German; most abominable language I have had to tackle yet. Stick Bismark up on that gate, and we will shy from the other side of the road. Stick him up, I say, you jabbering idiot."

"Oh! sare, what pity to throw stone at the beautiful cast! Buy him and take him home, no break him."

In spite of his remonstrances the great chancellor was set up on the five-barred gate, and the boys began to pelt him from the heap of stones on the opposite side of the road.

"And who is to pay me for my beautiful images?" asked the Italian, in some trepidation for his money, it being difficult to say which of all these eccentric young savages was the actual purchaser.

"Oh! whoever does not hit it shall owe you for it."

"But I should like that you pay now, before you throw."

"Why, you idiot, how can we tell who hits and

who misses beforehand.   Stand out of the way can't you!"

"Good shot!" "That was near." "That has got him!" and down went the bust in fragments. Then a Cupid was exposed to missiles far more substantial than his own, and succumbed.   His mama was next sent up by these young Goths; fancy Venus herself being put in the pillory and stoned! What one thing after that could they be expected to respect? Not the infant Samuel, who, in spite of his supplicatory attitude, found no pity. Not Sir Garnet Wolseley, who was exposed to as hot a fire as he had ever been under before, with worse luck; not Mr. Gladstone, nor Minerva, nor Tennyson. The spirit of mischief, the thirst for destruction, grew wilder by gratification, and soon the whole stock of models was reduced to a heap of plaster fragments.

"Ah! well, I have sell them all quick to-day," said the Italian, putting a good face on the business, which yet looked to him rather doubtful, as it is very rare for people to indulge in mischief at their own expense. "It is twenty shilling, one pound you owe me, sare," he added to Saurin.

"*I* owe you!" cried Saurin. "I like that! Why, I hit more of them than anyone else, and it was those who missed the lot who were to be responsible.   Go to them, man."

"Oh! gentleman, kind gentleman, you are making fun of me. You speak to me first; you say, 'Put up the figures for shy.' I poor man, you gentleman. You laugh! Give me my money, you sare, or you, or you;" and the Italian grasped his long black hair with both hands, and danced about in a manner which amused his tormentors greatly, and their laughter put him a rage.

"You rob me," he cried, "I will go to the police; I will have you put in prison if you no pay me. Give me my money."

"We will make a cockshy of you if you don't look out," said one; and another actually threw a stone at him, an example which others were preparing to follow, when Crawley, with a group of boys who had seen nothing of the early part of the business, came up, and seemed inclined to take the Italian's part. The aggressors dropped their stones quietly and began to slip away.

"It's a beastly shame, and a disgrace to the school," said Crawley indignantly. Saurin heard him as he hurried off, and if he had had any money in his pocket he would have turned back, thrown it to the image man, and asked Crawley what he meant. But being without funds he was obliged to make off while he could, or the Italian would fix on him and follow him home. For to break away and show him a fair pair of heels across country would be impossible after an altercation with his school-fellow; it would be putting himself in too humiliating a position. So he walked on at a sharp pace, choking with suppressed passion.

"Where he live, that fellow; where he live?" cried the Italian. "Per Baccho, I will have the police to him! You know him, excellenza; tell me where he live?"

"I will not tell you that," said Crawley. "But here's half-a-crown for you."

A considerable number of boys had now collected, and as example, whether for good or evil, has an extraordinary effect on either boys or men, a collection was started. Some gave a shilling, some sixpence, and a sum of ten shillings was made up altogether, which was probably quite as much as the figures were worth. So the Italian calmed down and dried his eyes, for he had been crying like a child, and with a profusion of thanks took up his board and went his way. And it being time to go back to Weston, all the boys started off in that direction, leaving Mr. Wobbler to tramp backwards and forwards between his milestones in solitude. Of course some kind friend told all this to Saurin, and it exasperated him still more, if that was possible. One thing he was determined upon, Crawley must be repaid the money he had given to

the Italian figure-seller at once. After hunting in all
his waistcoat pockets and his drawers he could only
raise eighteenpence, so he went to Edwards' room.

"Look here, old fellow," he said; "lend me a
shilling till Monday, I want it particularly."

"I'm awfully sorry," replied Edwards, "I have
not got one."

"I'll pay you back on Monday, honour bright."

"I know you would; it isn't that. I assure you
I am not making excuses; you should have it
directly if it were possible; but I am as penniless
as a fellow can be, not so much as a postage-stamp
have I got."

"I must get a shilling somehow; whom to ask?"

"Ask Griffiths; he always has money," suggested Edwards.

"Hang the fellow, yes," said Saurin. "But he
will make such a favour of it if he lends it, and
he is just as likely as not to refuse. I have it,
though! He offered me half-a-crown for my cross-
bow last term, and I would not let him have it;
he shall now."

The cross-bow in question was an ingenious little
thing about six inches long, the bow of steel, the
string of catgut, the stock and barrel of wood, and
it projected marbles or spherical bullets with very
considerable force. It would raise a bump on the
head at twenty yards, and break a window at

thirty.　Griffiths also lived in Mr. Cookson's house, so that Saurin had only to go to his own room, get out, dust, and rub up the article, which had lain in a corner forgotten, and go up the other staircase.

"I say, Griffiths," he began; "in turning out some old things I have just come across this little steel bow which you wanted to buy of me, you know.　I am tired of it now, and so you can have it if you like.　Half-a-crown, I think, you said that you would give, was it not?"

Griffiths coveted the toy as much or more than ever he had done, but he was a born dealer; and when he saw that the other was anxious to sell he assumed indifference in order to lower the price.

"Why, you see," he said, "last term is not this term.　I was pretty flush just then, and had a fancy for the thing.　Now the money has gone, and I don't so much care."

"You won't have it then? oh! very well; all right."

"Stop, don't be in a hurry; I'll give you eighteenpence for it."

"Make it two shillings," urged Saurin.

"No; eighteenpence or nothing," Griffiths persisted.

"You old Jew!　Well, here it is then," said Saurin.

"Have you got a shilling?" asked Griffiths. "I have only got half-a-crown; but if you can give me change—"

Saurin took the coin, giving back a shilling without further remark. He was thinking that it would be more effective to offer Crawley the larger coin, instead of fumbling with small money, and the notion pleased him. Besides he was not particularly disappointed; so long as he got what he wanted at the moment, it was not his nature to look much further. But he did not sleep much that night. Again this Crawley had scored off him, by putting himself in the position of generous benefactor and chivalrous defender of the weak, with him (Saurin) for his foil. There was one comfort; he was not so much afraid of Crawley as he did not conceal from himself that he had once been. Hitherto he had feared that if it came to a quarrel, he would not get the best of it, and this had caused him to restrain himself on many occasions when he had longed to give vent to his feelings. But, now that he had skill and science on his side, the case was different, and the balance in his favour; and if this wonderful Crawley, whom everybody made such a fuss about, did not like what he had to say to him, he might do the other thing.

The boys were gathered about the quadrangle

in groups, waiting to go in for eight o'clock school, for the different class-rooms were not open till the master of each came with his key and unlocked the door, by which time all the class were expected to be outside, ready to go in with him. And so it was the custom to assemble rather early, and now, though it was ten minutes to the hour by the big clock, the majority had arrived. Directly Saurin came he looked for Crawley, and saw him standing chatting with some other fellows. He walked straight up to him.

"Oh, Crawley!" he said, "I hear that you paid that Italian blackguard half-a-crown for his broken crockery yesterday, and since he made his claim upon *me*, though I owed him nothing, I don't choose to let it look as if you had paid anything for me, so here is your money back;" and he tendered the half-crown, which the other did not put his hand out to receive. This exasperated Saurin still more. "Take it," he said; "only I'll thank you not to be so confoundedly officious again."

"I don't want your money," said Crawley quietly. "You are entirely mistaken; I paid nothing for you. If I knew the image man's address I would forward him your half-crown, but I do not. So you must hunt it up for yourself if you want to make restitution."

" But you paid him the money."

"That was an act of private charity. The man whom you call a blackguard—I don't know why, for *he* had not been destroying any defenceless person's property—had had a scoundrelly trick played him, and I and some other fellows got up a subscription for him, as anyone with a spark of gentlemanly feeling would be inclined to do. I am sorry that your contribution is tendered too late, but so it is."

" So you call me a blackguard and a scoundrel, do you?" hissed Saurin, who was quite beside himself with rage; and certainly Crawley's speech was the reverse of soothing. " You stuck-up, hypocritical, canting, conceited prig, I should like to break your nose for you."

" Break away, my hearty," said Crawley, putting his hands up; "but I am not a plaster of Paris image, mind you, and can hit back."

The sneer was another spur to Saurin's passion; his temples throbbed as if they would burst, and his look was as evil as a painter, wanting a model for Mephistopheles, could have desired, as he sprang at his enemy with an inarticulate cry, and struck at him with all his force. The boys closed round them, eager, expectant, those at a distance running up. But blows were hardly exchanged before someone cried, " Look out; here's the Doctor!" and the combatants were separated, and the crowd dispersed in an instant.

"We will meet again, I hope," said Saurin.

"Any time you like," replied Crawley.

"On Saturday afternoon in the dell, then."

"I shall be there, and I hope we shall not be interrupted." And they walked off in different directions, trying to look as if nothing was the matter, which was not so easy, Saurin being hardly able to restrain his excitement, and Crawley being flushed about the forehead, where the other's fist had struck him; otherwise he was no more discomposed than usual, and, being put on to construe soon after entering the school, acquitted himself very well and with the most perfect *sang froid*. Fortunately Saurin was not subjected to the same ordeal or he would have been considerably flustered, if not totally unable to fix his mind on the subject; and he might have excited suspicion as to something unusual going on, which again might have caused inquiry, and so spoiled sport. But he was not called up, the redness of Crawley's brow remained unnoticed, and all was satisfactory. This was Thursday, so there was a day's intermission before the fight, which was the general school topic. The weather, which had been very fine in the early part of the term, had broken up, the sodden grass was unfavourable for cricket and lawn-tennis, so that this little excitement came in just at the convenient time. I wonder why everything connected with fighting is so interesting ! Little children love playing at soldiers best of all games, and delight in destroying whole tin armies with pea-shooting artillery. With what silent eagerness the newspapers are devoured in war-time when the details of a battle appear ! If two cocks in a farm-yard get at one another the heaviest bumpkin from the plough-tail, who seems incapable of an emotion, grows animated. I suppose it is because of the animal nature of which we partake which frequently excites us to prey on other animals and quarrel with one another. Fights were very rare at Weston, but they took place occasionally, and there was even a traditional spot called the Fairies' Dell, or more commonly The Dell, where they were brought off. But for a boy of the standing and position of Crawley,—in the highest form, captain of the eleven, secretary and treasurer of the cricket and foot-ball clubs—to be engaged in such an affair was unprecedented, and the interest taken in it was so great as to set the whole school in a ferment. The dislike borne by Saurin to the other was well known, as also that he had attributed his expulsion from the eleven to him, though unjustly, since public opinion had

been well nigh unanimous on the point. As for
the chances of the combatants, only the small
clique who frequented Slam's, most of whom had
seen him sparring with the gloves, favoured that
of Saurin. The general idea was that the latter
was mad to try conclusions with one so superior
to him in every way, and that Crawley would lick
him into fits in about ten minutes. As for the
champions themselves, they awaited the ordeal in
very different frames of mind. To Crawley the
whole thing was an unmitigated bore. It would
get him into some trouble with the authorities
probably; it was inconsistent with his position in
the school, and was setting a bad example; then
he could hardly expect to avoid a black eye, and
it was only three weeks to the holidays, by which
time his bruises would hardly have time to disappear. His family were staying for the summer
at Scarborough, and his sisters wrote him enthusiastic accounts of the lawn-tennis parties there.
How could he present himself in decent society
with one of his eyes in mourning? But he saw
something comic in his own annoyance, and it
did not affect him sufficiently to interfere with
his studies or amusements. He neither feared
the contest nor desired it. He had no wish to
quarrel with Saurin, a fellow he did not care for,
it is true, but whom he did not think sufficiently

about to dislike. He thought rather better of him for having the pluck to attack him, and was a little ashamed of his own bitter words which had goaded the other into doing it. But really the fellow had addressed him in such an overbearing and insolent manner that he could not help replying as he did. After all, if he had to fight someone, he would rather it were Saurin than anyone else, since he appeared to hate him so much.

But if Crawley was cool about the matter, his antagonist was very much the reverse. When his passion expended itself he was not free from apprehension of the consequences of what he had done. Supposing he were ignominiously defeated, after having provoked the contest, what a humiliating position he would be placed in? In every way in which he had competed with Crawley he had hitherto been worsted, and he could not help fearing lest this superiority should still be maintained. However, the die was cast, he was in for it now, and must go through with it as best he could, and, after all, his recently acquired skill must stand him in good stead. Reason in this way as he might, however, he was nervous, and could not settle to anything for long. On Friday night, while Crawley was working in his room, there came a knock at the door, and when he called out, "Come in!" Tom Buller entered.

"I have got something I want to tell you, Crawley," he said. "I have just found out that Saurin has been taking lessons in boxing."

"Oh! of whom? Stubbs, Edwards, or someone equally formidable?"

"No; of Wobbler the pedestrian, who was once a pugilist, and who has been giving boxing lessons at Slam's."

"Oh! I see, that is what has screwed his courage up to the proper pitch. I understand it all now."

"Yes, but avoid wrestling with him; he is good at the cross-buttock, I hear. May I be your second?".

"Certainly you may, if you like; Robarts is the other, and thank you for wishing it, Buller."

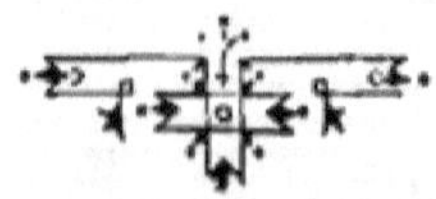

CHAPTER VI.

THE FIGHT.

BEYOND the fields where cricket was played there was a little wood, and in this wood a circular hollow, like a pond, only there was no water in it. It was a wonderful spot for wild flowers in the spring, and that was probably the reason why some romantic person had named it The Fairies' Dell. The boys, who were not romantic, as a rule, dropped the Fairies, and called it The Dell. As has been said, this spot was chosen as the arena for the few fistic encounters which the annals of Weston could enumerate, and a better place for the purpose there could hardly be. There was plenty of room for a ring at the bottom, and the gently sloping sides would accommodate a large number of spectators, all of whom had a good sight of what was going on, while the whole party were concealed from view.

At four o'clock on the Saturday afternoon this hollow was thickly studded with Westonians, and all the best places taken. The masters usually took advantage of the half-holiday to go out somewhere for the afternoon, but still ordinary precautions to avoid observation had not been neglected. The boys did not repair to the appointed spot in large noisy bodies, but in small groups, quietly and unostentatiously. Some of them took their bats and balls out, and began playing at cricket, and then stole off to the rendezvous, which was close to them. Saurin was first on the ground; he stood under the trees at the edge of the dell with Edwards and Stubbs, who acted as his seconds, trying to laugh and chat in an unconcerned manner, but he was pale, could hardly keep himself still in one position, and frequently glanced stealthily in the direction by which the other would come. Not to blink matters between the reader and myself, he was in a funk. Not exactly a *blue* funk, you know, but still he did not half like it, and wished he was well out of it.

Presently there was a murmur, and a movement, and Crawley, with Robarts and Tom Buller on each side of him, and a knot of others following, appeared. Without saying a word both boys went down the sides of the dell to the circular space which had been carefully left for them at the bottom, took off their jackets, waistcoats, and braces, and gave them to their seconds, who folded them up and laid them aside, tied pocket-handkerchiefs round their waists, turned up the bottoms of their trousers, and stepped into the middle of the arena.

" Won't you offer to shake hands?" said Stubbs to Saurin. " I believe it is usual on such occasions."

" Pooh!" replied Saurin, " that is in friendly encounters, to show there is no malice. There is plenty of malice here, I can promise you." He finished rolling up his shirt sleeves to the armpits as he spoke, and walked to the middle of the ring, where Crawley confronted him. All were wrapped in breathless attention as the two put up their hands, and every note of a thrush singing in a tree hard by could be distinctly heard.

The two boys were just about the same height and age, but Crawley had a slightly longer reach in the arms, and was decidedly more "fit" and muscular. But, on the other hand, it was evident directly they put their hands up, that Saurin was the greatest adept at the business. The carriage of his head and body, and the way he worked his arm and foot together, showed this. He moved round his adversary, advancing, retiring, feinting, watching for an opening. Crawley stood firm, with his eyes fixed on those of his antagonist, merely turning sufficiently to face him. At length Saurin, judging his distance, sent out his left hand sharply, and caught Crawley on the right cheek-bone. Crawley hit back in return, but beat the air; Saurin was away. Again Saurin came weaving in, and again he put a hit in without a return. The same thing happened a third, a fourth, and a fifth time, and then Crawley, stung by the blows, went at the other wildly, hitting right and left, but, overreaching himself, lost his balance and rolled over. The lookers on were astonished; they had expected Saurin to be beaten from the first, and though Crawley was so popular, murmurs of applause were heard, such is the effect of success. Buller knelt on his left knee so that Crawley might sit on his right. In the same manner Saurin sat on Edwards' knee. Saurin's face had not been touched, while that of Crawley was flushed and bleeding.

"You will not be able to touch his face just yet," said Buller. "Fight at his body and try to hit him in the wind. And never mind what I said yesterday about closing with him, we must risk his cross-buttock, and your superior strength may serve you."

"Time! time!" cried the boys, and the antagonists jumped up from their seconds' knees, and met again. Saurin had lost all his nervousness now; his superiority was evident, and he felt nothing but triumph and gratified malice. He did not stop to spar now, but directly he was within reach hit out with confidence. Crawley took the blow without flinching or attempting to parry it, and sent his right fist with all his strength into Saurin's ribs, just as Buller had directed him. Saurin recovered himself, and the round went on, Crawley being further mauled about the face, neck, and head, but getting a hit in now on the other's body, now a round right-hander on his side or the small of his back. In the end they grappled, wrestled, and rolled over together, and were then helped by their seconds to their respective corners. Saurin's face was still untouched, but he puffed and panted for breath, and seemed to feel the effect of the body blows.

"That is capital," said Buller to Crawley; "stick to that for the present, he will soon begin to tire."

"Why, Buller, you seem to be quite up to this sort of thing!" said Robarts in surprise.

"My elder brother went in for the Queensbury cups, and is always talking about boxing and fighting: that's how I know," replied Buller quietly.

"And that is why you wished to be my second?" asked Crawley, who, though his face was a pitiable object, was perfectly cool and self-possessed, and not a bit blown or tired.

"Yes," replied Buller; and "Time!" was again called.

The mass of the spectators looked upon the fight as won by Saurin already, and all the cheering was for him now. This opinion was further strengthened presently, for Crawley, seeing his antagonist panting, thought that at last he might get on equal terms with him, and rushed in to fight at close quarters, but he was met by a straight blow from Saurin's left fist right between the eyes, which knocked him fairly down on the broad of his back, where he lay quite dazed for a moment, till Robarts and Buller assisted him to his corner. The cheering and the cries of "Bravo, Saurin!" "Well hit, Saurin!" were loud and long; many thought that Crawley would not come up again. But though puffed about both eyes, and with a considerably swollen nose, Crawley was soon all right again, and as lively as when he began.

"If I only could mark him!" he said to his seconds. "It is so absurd to see him with his face untouched."

"Wait a bit," replied Buller. "Keep on pegging at his body and wrestling; I'll tell you when to go for his face. He is getting weaker for all that hit last round."

This was true, for Saurin's blows, though they got home, had no longer the force they had at first. In one round, after a severe struggle, he threw Crawley heavily, but the exertion told more upon himself than upon the one thrown. And he began to flinch from the body blows, and keep his hands down. Loafing, beer-drinking, and smoking began to tell their tale, in fact, and at last Buller said, "Now you may try to give him one or two in the face."

They had been at it nearly half an hour, and Crawley, who had been taking hard exercise daily and leading a healthy temperate life, was as strong as when he first took his jacket off. He could hardly see out of his right eye, and his face and neck were so bruised and tender that every fresh blow he received gave him exquisite pain. But his wits were quite clear, he had not lost his temper, and when down, in a few minutes he was ready to stand up again. He easily warded off a nerveless blow of his antagonist, returned it with one from his left hand on the body, and then sent his right fist for the first time straight into Saurin's face. Saurin got confused and turned half round; Crawley following up his advantage, followed him up step by step round the ring, and at last fairly fought him down amidst cheers from the boys, the tide of popularity turning in his favour again.

"You have marked him now, and no mistake," said Buller to Crawley as he sat on his knee. And there could be no doubt about that. The revulsion of feeling Saurin had gone through was great. After establishing his superiority, and feeling confident of an easy victory, to find his adversary refuse so persistently to know when he was beaten! To see him come up time after time to take more hammering without flinching was like a nightmare. And he felt his own strength going from the sheer exertion of hitting; and when he knocked Crawley down he hurt his left hand, which it was painful to strike with afterwards. Again, the body blows he received and thought little of at first began to make him feel queer, and now, when the other took a decided lead, he lost his head and got wild. For he was not thoroughly "game:" he had not got that stubborn, somewhat sullen spirit of endurance which used to be so great a characteristic of the English, and we will hope is not extinct yet, for it would be sad indeed to think that it had passed away. A brilliant act of daring with plenty of spectators and high hope of success is one thing; but to stand at bay when all chance seems gone, determined to die hard and never give in, is quite another. I like to see a fellow spurting when he is distanced; catching his horse, remounting, and going in pursuit after a bad fall; going back to his books and reading harder than ever for another try directly the list has come out without his name in it—never beaten, in short, until the last remotest chance is over. That is the spirit which won at Agincourt, at Waterloo, at Meeanee, at Dubba, at Lucknow, at Rorke's Drift. It was this that Saurin was deficient in, and that would have now stood him in such stead. Edwards was not the one to infuse any of it into him, for he was as much dismayed by the effects of the last round as his friend himself. Stubbs, indeed, tried to cheer him, inciting him to pull himself together, spar for wind, and look out for a chance with his sound right hand, but he was not a youth to carry influence with him.

In the next round Crawley closed with his adversary, who, when he at last struggled loose, rolled ignominiously over on the ground, and in point of beauty there was nothing to choose now between the visages of the two combatants.

"I—I can't fight any more," said Saurin, as he was held up on Edwards' knee, to which he had been dragged with some difficulty.

"Oh! have another go at him," urged Stubbs;

"he is as bad as you are, and you will be all right presently if you keep away a bit, and get down the first blow. Just get your wind, and science must tell."

"But I'm so giddy, I—I can't stand," said Saurin.

"Time!" was called, and Crawley sprang off his second's knee as strong as possible, but he stood in the middle of the ring alone.

"It's no good; he can't stand," cried Edwards. And then a tremendous cheering broke out, and everybody pressed forward to congratulate Crawley and pat him on the back. But he made his way over to Saurin, and offered to shake hands.

"It is all luck," he said. "You are better at this game than I am, and you would have licked me if you had not hurt your left hand. And look here, I had no right to speak as I did. And—and if you thought I wanted to get you out of the eleven you were mistaken."

Saurin was too dazed to feel spiteful just then; he had a vague idea that Crawley wanted to shake hands, and that it would be "bad form" to hold back, so he put his right hand out and murmured something indistinctly.

"Stand back, you fellows," said Crawley, "he is fainting. Give him a chance of a breath of air."

And indeed Saurin had to be carried up out of the dell, laid on his back under the trees, and have water dashed in his face, before he could put on his jacket and waistcoat and walk back to his tutor's house. And when he arrived there he was in such pain in the side that he had to go to bed. Crawley himself was a sorry sight for a victor. But his discomforts were purely local, and he did not feel ill at all; on the contrary, he was remarkably hungry. Buller was with him when he washed and changed his shirt, for he had been applying a cold key to the back of his neck to stop the nose-bleeding, and now remained, like a conscientious second, lest it should break out again."

"I say, Buller," said Crawley suddenly, "*you* never go to Slam's, I hope?"

"Not I."

"Then how do you know such a lot about prize-fighting?"

"I told Robarts; my elder brother is very fond of everything connected with sparring, and has got a lot of reports of matches, and I have read all the prize fights that ever were, I think. I used to take great interest in them, and thought I might remember something which would come in useful. There is a great sameness in these things, you know, and the principles are simple."

"I am sure I am much obliged to you for offering to be my second; I should have been licked but for you."

"I don't know that. I think you would have thought of fighting at his wind when you could not reach his face for yourself, and tired him out anyhow. But if I have been useful I am glad. You took pains to try my bowling when most fellows would have laughed at the idea; and there is the honour of the house too. What I feared was that you would not follow what I said, but persist in trying to bore in."

"Why," replied Crawley, laughing, "Saurin backed up your advice with such very forcible and painful examples of the common sense of it, that I should have been very pig-headed not to catch your meaning. But what rot it all is!" he added, looking in the glass. "A pretty figure I shall look at Scarborough, with my face all the colours of the prism, like a disreputable damaged rainbow!"

"There are three weeks yet to the holidays; you will be getting all right again by then," said Buller.

"I doubt it; it does not feel like it now, at all events," replied Crawley; and when supper-time came he was still more sceptical of a very speedy restoration to his ordinary comfortable condition. It was an absurd plight to be in; he felt very hungry, and there was the food; the difficulty was to eat it. It hurt his lips to put it in his mouth—salt was out of the question—and it hurt his jaws to masticate it, and it hurt his throat to swallow it. But he got it down somehow, and then came prayers, conducted as usual every evening by Dr. Jolliffe, who, when the boys filed out afterwards, told him to remain.

"By a process of elimination I, recognizing all the other boys in my house, have come to the conclusion that you are Crawley," said the doctor solemnly.

"Yes, sir," replied Crawley.

"Quantum mutatus ab illo! I should not have recognized you. Circumstantial evidence seems to establish the fact that you have engaged in a pugilistic encounter."

"Yes, sir."

"And with whom?"

"I beg your pardon, sir; I hope that you will not insist on my telling. It was my fault; we had a dispute, and I spoke very provokingly."

"Your mention of his name would not make much difference, if you were as busy with your fists as he seems to have been. But I am disappointed in you, Crawley; it vexes me that a boy of your age and standing in the school, and whose proficiency in athletic sports gives you a certain influence, should brawl and fight like this."

"It vexes me too, sir, I assure you."

"You should have thought of that before."

"So I did, sir, and also of the figure I should cut when I went home."

"Well, certainly," said the doctor, unable to help smiling, "I do not advise you to have your photograph taken just at present. But you know," he added, forcing himself to look grave again, "I cannot overlook fighting, which is a very serious offence. You must write a Greek theme of not less than two pages of foolscap, on the Blessings of Peace, and bring it me on Tuesday. And apply a piece of raw meat, which I will send up to your room, to your right eye."

Crawley ran upstairs rejoicing, for he had got off easier than he expected, and the application of raw meat gave him great relief, so that next day the swellings had very much subsided, though his eyes were blood-shot, and his whole face discoloured. But Saurin did not come round so soon: there were symptoms of inflammation which affected his breathing, and induced his tutor, Mr. Cookson, to send for the doctor, who kept his patient in bed for two days. He soon got all right again in body, but not in mind, for he felt thoroughly humiliated. This was unnecessary, for it was agreed on all sides that he had made a first-rate fight of it, and he decidedly rose in the estimation of his school-fellows. But Saurin's vanity was sensitive to a morbid degree, and he brooded over his defeat. A fight between two healthy-minded boys generally results in a close friendship, and Crawley made several overtures to his late antagonist; but as they were evidently not welcome, he soon desisted, for after all Saurin was not one of "his sort." And the term, as it is the fashion now to call a "half," came to an end, and though his wounds were healed, and his features restored to their original shape, Crawley had to go to Scarborough like one of Gibson's statues, tinted.

CHAPTER VII.

TREATING OF AN AIR-GUN AND A DOOR-KEY.

SAURIN met with a disappointment when he returned home. His uncle had intended to go abroad and take him with him, but this intention was frustrated by an attack of gout, which kept him to his country home, where his nephew had to spend the entire vacation, and he found it the reverse of lively. Sir Richard Saurin's house stood in the midst of a well-timbered park, and there were some spinnies belonging to the place also. At one time he had rented the shooting all round about, and preserved his own woods; but it was a hunting country, and the havoc made by foxes was found to be so great that he gave up preserving in disgust, and so, growing lazy, made that an excuse for dropping the other field shooting, which passed into different hands. So now there was no partridge-shooting, unless a stray covey chose to light in the park, and there were very few pheasants, though the rabbits were pretty numerous.

Sir Richard, being free from any paroxysm of his complaint when his nephew arrived, laughed at his black eye.

"Is that the result of your course of lessons in boxing?" he asked.

"Well, Uncle Richard, I should have come worse off if I had not had them," replied Saurin; "but one cannot fight without taking as well as giving."

"But why fight at all? That is not what you are sent to school for."

"I never did before, and it is not likely to happen again, only I was forced on this occasion to stand up for myself."

"Well, well," said Sir Richard, "I have something more serious to speak to you about."

Saurin felt his heart beat; he feared for a moment that his visits to Slam's, and the impositions he had practised, had been discovered; but this was not the case.

"It is not a very good report I have received of you this time," continued his guardian. "It seems that you have grown slack in attention to your studies, and have not made the progress which might fairly be expected from a boy of your age and abilities. Now, it is only right to warn you that the income left you by your father very little more than covers the expense of your education; and since a considerable portion of it consists of a pension, which will cease on your being twenty-one, it will not be sufficient for your support, so that you must make up your mind speedily what profession you will adopt, and must exert every effort to get into it. Our vicar here, a young man newly come, is a mathematician and a good German scholar, two subjects which gain good marks, I am told, in all these competitive examinations, and I have made arrangements for you to read with him every morning for a couple of hours."

This was not a very bright look-out for the summer holidays. "Since it was so very necessary for him to work, it was perhaps well that he should not have too much to distract him," he said sarcastically; but found some truth in the words, for he was forced into taking an interest in a German novel which the clergyman, with some tact, chose for him to translate. But the life *was* dull; when he sought out his former companions, the village scapegraces, he found that there had been a grand clear out of them; it was as if the parish had taken a moral purgative. Bill had enlisted; Tom, the worst of the lot, had (it was his mother who spoke) "got into bad company and gone to Lunnon;" Dick and Jim were in prison, and Harry had reformed and been taken into a gentleman's stables. Solitude!

His principal amusement was shooting rabbits. September was close at hand, and if he had sought the society of his equals, instead of making a bad name in the neighbourhood in former years, he would probably have had more than one invitation to better sport amongst the partridges; but he had such an evil reputation that the gentlemen of the county did not covet his society for their sons. Now, rabbit shooting in the winter, with dogs to hunt the bunnies through brush-wood, furze, or bracken, so that snap-shots are offered as they dart across open places, is very good fun; but the only way Saurin had of getting at them at this season was by lying in wait in the evening outside the woods and shooting them when they came louping cautiously out. He found excitement in this at first, but it was impossible to miss such pot shots for one thing, and he got very few chances for another. The report of the gun frightened them all into the wood, not to venture out again for some time, probably till it was too dark to distinguish them. The only chance was, when a rabbit had been got at one place, to go off at once to another wood at some distance and lie in ambush again there. In this way two, or at most three shots might be got in the short period of dusk. Fond as he was of carrying a gun, Saurin found this sport unsatisfactory after a week or so, though it was infinitely better than not shooting anything at all. But one day when he rode over to the county town, seven miles off, for cartridges, he saw a small air-gun of a new and improved pattern in the shop, which took his fancy very much indeed. It was beautifully finished, charged in the simplest way imaginable, and would carry either a bullet or a small charge of shot, killing easily, the man said, with the former at fifty yards, and with the latter at five-and-twenty. It would require some skill to hit a rabbit in the head with a bullet; and as there was no report to speak of, only a slight crack, killing or missing one would not scare the others. The price was not high, and as Sir Richard never objected to his having anything in reason that he wanted, and was, moreover, glad that the rabbits who committed sad havoc in the garden should be thinned down, he took it home with him and tried it that evening. Just about sunset he repaired to his favourite spot, a clump of three trees growing close together, behind which he could · easily conceal himself. A wood, full of thick undergrowth, well nigh impenetrable, ran in front and made an angle to the right, so that there were two sides from which the rabbits might come out. The air was perfectly still, not a leaf was stirring, and every note of a bird that was warbling his evening song, positively the very last before shutting up for the night, fell sharp and clear upon the ear, as Saurin knelt behind the trees, gun in hand, eagerly watching. Presently he saw something brown, rather far on his left, close to the wood. It came a little further out, and the long ears could be distinguished.

Saurin was rather doubtful about the distance, but, eager to try his new weapon, he took a steady aim and pulled. No smoke, no fire, nothing but a slight smack such as a whip would make. The rabbit raised its head, listened, and hopped quietly back into the wood. A palpable miss. But there on the right was another, not thirty yards off this one. Saurin slewed round, got the sight well on its head, and pulled again. This rabbit did *not* go back to the wood, but turned over, struggled a little, and then lay still. Saurin did not run out to pick it up, but kept quiet, and presently another came out, to see what was the matter with its friend apparently, for it louped up to the body; and he nailed that. And he missed two and killed two more, and then the rabbit community began to suspect there was something wrong, and kept in the wood. But, returning home, he stalked and shot another in the park, making a bag of five altogether, which pleased him immensely.

Next day he tried the shot cartridges on blackbirds and sparrows in the garden, and slaughtered not a few, to the gardener's great delight. It was not only the efficiency of so toy-like a weapon which pleased Saurin; the silence and secresy with which it dealt death had a charm for him. And so it happened that when the time came for him to return to Weston, he took the air-gun with him. It went into a very small compass, and was easily stowed in his portmanteau. He could smuggle it to Slam's and keep it there, and if he had no chance of using it, he could still show it off to Edwards and his other intimates, and also to the perhaps more appreciative eyes of Edwin Marriner and another, perhaps two other scamps of sporting tastes whom he met at Slam's on certain afternoons, when they guzzled beer, and smoked, and played sometimes at bagatelle, sometimes at cards, or tossed for coppers. And they won his money in a small way, and laughed at his jokes, and took interest in his bragging stories, and went into ecstacies over his songs, and really liked and admired him in their fashion. So the departure of Mr. Wobbler did not keep him away, and he went to the yard as much as ever. If he

had won the fight it would probably have made
a difference, and he might have tried once more
to compete for influence and popularity in the
school.   But now he had quite given up all ideas
of that kind.   He spoke to Crawley, and shook
his hand with apparent cordiality when they first
met after coming back, because he felt that it
would be ridiculous to show a resentment which
he had proved himself powerless to gratify; but
he hated him worse than ever, if possible.   If the
breaking up of the boxing-class did not diminish
Saurin's visits to Slam's, it had that effect on
the other members of it.   Stubbs was faithful to
his dog, and Perry to his hawk, and there were
other boys who had pets there, or who liked to
go on a wet day to see ratting, or the drawing of
the badger, an animal who lived in a tub, like
Diogenes, and was tugged out of it by a dog, not
without vigorous resistance, when anyone chose
to pay for the spectacle; the poor badger deriving
no benefit from the outlay.   But such visits were
fitful. Edwards, indeed, was faithful to his friend,
but even Edwards did not care for Slam's any
longer.   He had taken a violent passion for football, and often played, leaving Saurin to go to the
yard alone.   On Sundays, indeed, he could not
play football, but neither did he like playing
cards on that day.   Saurin laughed him out of

his scruples, but not all at once. But Saurin did not want companionship; he preferred that of Marriner & Co.

Edwin Marriner was a young farmer in the neighbourhood of Weston College, and he farmed his own land. Certainly it was as small an estate as can well be imagined, consisting of exactly two acres, pasture, arable, cottage, and pig-stye included, but undoubted freehold, without a flaw in the title. He was just twenty-one when his father died, a year before the time we are treating of, and then Lord Woodruff's agent made him an offer for his inheritance, which he stuck to like a very Naboth.

The price named was a good and tempting one, far more indeed than the land was worth; but when the money was spent he would have nothing for it but to become a mere labourer, or else to enlist, and he did not fancy either alternative, while he could manage to live, as his father did before him, on his patch, which spade-labour made remunerative. He worked for hire in harvest-time, and that brought something; the pig-stye yielded a profit, so did a cow, and there were a few pounds reaped annually from a row of bee-hives, for the deceased Marriner, though not very enlightened generally, had learned, and taught his son the "depriving" system, and repudiated the idiotic old plan of stifling the stock to get the honey. All these methods of making both ends meet at the end of the year were not only innocent but praiseworthy; but the Marriners had the reputation of making less honourable profits, and that was why Lord Woodruff was so anxious to get rid of them. The two acres lying indeed in the midst of his lordship's estates, was of itself a reason why he should be inclined to give a fancy price for them; but when the proprietor was suspected of taking advantage of his situation to levy considerable toll on the game of his big neighbour, who preserved largely, he became a real and an aggravated nuisance.

Marriner, as his father had done, openly carried a gun, for which he paid his license, and it was impossible, with reason, to blame him, for the rabbits alone would have eaten up every particle of his little stock if he took no measures against them. If he shot an occasional pheasant, or his dog caught a hare, or even two, in the course of the season on his own land, why, no one could wonder. But it was not necessary to sow buckwheat in order to attract the pheasants. And he had no right whatever to set snares in Lord Woodruff's covers, which, though they could not catch him, the gamekeepers were certain he did. One thing decidedly against him in the opinion of the gentry round about, was that he frequently visited Slam's, and Slam was regarded as a receiver of stolen goods, certainly so far as game was concerned, perhaps in other matters also. Edwin Marriner was a wiry-looking little man, with red hair and whiskers, quick bright eyes, and a look of cunning about his mouth. He had two propensities which interfered with one another: he was very fond of strong drink and very fond of money. The drink was delightful, but to spend the money necessary to procure it was a fearful pang. The best way out of the dilemma was to get someone to treat him, and this he did as often as he could. He had plenty of cunning and mother wit, and was skilled in woodcraft, but he was utterly innocent of anything which could fairly be called education. He had been taught to read, but never exercised the gift; he could do an addition sum, and write, with much labour, an ill-spelled letter, and that was all. And this was the individual selected by Saurin for a companion, and whose society he preferred to that of all his schoolfellows, Edwards not excepted. On half-holidays he would go to his little farm (which was half-an-hour's walk too far for ordinary occasions, now the days had grown short, and " All In," was directly after five-o'clock school), and talk to him while he was at work, for Marriner was industrious, though with a dishonest twist, and if he went to Slam's yard so often now it was because his gentleman friend brought some grist to his mill, besides often standing beer for him, and because he had business relations with Slam; though he liked the boy's company too, and admired his precocious preference for crooked ways, and hatred of lawful restraint. The fact was that they were drawn together by a strong propensity which was common to both, and which formed a never-failing topic of interesting conversation. This propensity was a love of sport, especially if indulged secretly, unlawfully, and at the expense of somebody else; in a word, they were arrant poachers, the man in fact, the boy at heart. Not but what Saurin had snared a hare too in his time.

For some time Marriner had been chary of confessing his depredations, for he was careful about committing himself, especially to a gentleman, who might naturally be supposed to side with the game-preservers. But when the ice was broken he talked freely enough, and from that time the intimacy commenced. Yet at times he had qualms, and feared that he had been rash to depart from his custom of close secrecy; and it often occurred to him that it would be well to draw Saurin into some act of complicity, and so seal his lips effectually and for ever. He felt and expressed great admiration for the air-gun, and suggested that they should try it some moonlight night upon the roosting pheasants. This was treated as a joke at first, a romantic idea which could not, of course, be carried into practice; but after it had been referred to and discussed again and again it did not look so utterly impossible. The principal difficulty was the getting out at night, but after many careful inspections of his tutor's premises Saurin saw how this might be managed. There was a small back-yard into which the boys had access at any time; this was surrounded by a high wall with a chevaux de frise at the top, which might be considered insurmountable unless one were Jack Sheppard or the Count of Monte Christo. But there was a door at the bottom, seldom used, hardly ever, indeed, except when coals came in. Outside there was a cart track, and then open field. It was the simplest thing, a mere question of obtaining a key to this door, and he could walk out whenever he liked. Yes, but how to get the key, which was taken by the servant to Mrs. Cookson when not in use? To watch when coals were next brought in for an opportunity of purloining it would be worse than useless, for a new lock would be put to the door, and suspicion aroused.

An idea occurred to him; he had read of impressions of keys being taken in wax, and duplicates being made from them. He asked Marriner if it were possible to get this done, and the reply was yes, that he knew a friendly blacksmith who would make a key to fit any lock of which he had the wards in wax, for a matter of say five shillings, which was leaving a handsome margin of profit for himself, we may remark in passing. Five shillings was a lot, Saurin thought, when he was not sure that he would use the key if he had it. Marriner did not know, perhaps it could be done for three; at any rate he might as well have the wax by him in case he got a chance. Curiously enough, he thought he had some in the house, though he sold all his honey in the comb as a rule. But a hive had been deserted, and he knew he had melted the wax down, and it must be somewhere. It was, and he found it, and he got a key and showed Saurin how to take an impression of it.

"Why, you have done it before then!" said Saurin.

"P'raps," replied Marriner, with a side glance of his cunning eyes. "A poor man has to turn his hand to a bit of everything in these hard times."

It was an early winter, and the weather turned

very cold, which caused a great consumption of fuel. And one morning, on coming in to his tutor's from early school, Saurin heard the small thunder of coals being poured into the cellar, and saw the yard door open, a wagon outside, and a man staggering from it under a sack. He ran up to his room, threw down his books, took the wax, and went back to the yard door, where he took a great interest in the unlading of the sacks. A fine sleet was falling, with a bitter north-east wind, to make it cut the face, so that there were none of the servants outside, and no one to see him but the two men who were busied in their work. Never was such an opportunity. He had the least possible difficulty in taking the key out of the lock, pressing it on the wax in the palm of his hand, in the way Marriner had shown him, and replacing it without attracting observation. Then he returned to his room, whistling care- lessly, and putting the wax, which had the wards of the key sharply defined upon it, in a seidlitz- powder box, to prevent the impression being in- jured, he locked it up in his bureau and went to breakfast.

Now that this had been accomplished so favour- ably, it seemed a pity not to have the key made. He might probably never want to use it; but still, there was a pleasant sense of superiority in the knowledge that he was independent of the "All In," and could get out at any hour of the night that he chose. So the next time he went to Marriner's cottage he took the box containing the wax with him, and Marriner paid him the high compliment that a professional burglar could not have done the job better. A week after he gave him the key, and one night, after everyone had gone to bed, Saurin stole down-stairs, out into the yard, and tried it. It turned in the lock easily, the door opened without noise, and he was free to go where he liked. Only there was no place so good as bed to go to, so he closed and locked the door again, and went back to his room, feeling very clever and a sort of hero. I am sure I do not know why. No one was taken into his confidence but Edwards, and he only because it was necessary to talk to somebody about his poaching schemes, and to excite wonder and admiration at his inventive skill and daring courage, and this Edwards was ready at all times to express. He was never taken to Marriner's, but he still occasionally accompanied his friend to the yard—on Sundays, usually, because of the card-playing, to which he had taken a great fancy. He still thought in his heart that it was very wrong, but Saurin laughed at such scruples as being so very childish and silly that he was thoroughly ashamed of them. Saurin, who was so clever and manly that he must know better than he did, saw no harm. Besides, he was very fond of playing at cards, and though he did not much like the very low company he met at Slam's yard now, he told himself that what was fit for Saurin was fit for him, and it was desirable, beneficial, and the correct thing to see life in all its phases. His hero's defeat by Crawley had not diminished his devotion one iota, for he attributed it entirely to Saurin having crippled his left hand when he knocked his adversary down. Even then he believed that Saurin would have won, only Crawley was in training, and the other was not. Crawley was all very well, but he lacked that bold and heroic defiance of authority which fascinated Edwards (himself the most subordinate soul by nature, by the way). The idea of Crawley's daring even to dream of going poaching, or breaking out at night, or having a false key made! No, he was a good commonplace fellow enough, but Saurin was something unusual,—which it is fervently to be hoped he was. Poor Edwards, with his weak character, which made it necessary for him to believe in someone and yield him homage; what a pity it was he had not fixed on a different sort of hero to worship!

CHAPTER VIII.

FROST, hard, sharp, crisp, and unmistakable; do you like it? It is very unpleasant when you get up of a morning; the water is so cold. And then going to school shivering, and being put on to construe when you have the hot ache in your fingers, is trying to the patience, especially if one is inclined to self-indulgence, and is aided and abetted when at home by one's mother.

But everything has its compensations. Without work play would become a bore; if there were no hunger and thirst there would be no pleasure in eating and drinking; even illness is followed by convalescence, with story-books to read instead of lessons, and license to lie in bed as long as you like, and so there is the delight, in very cold weather, of getting warm again; and there is also skating. Whether we like it or not we have to put up with it when it comes, and it came that year at an unusual time, before the end of November. We often indeed have just a touch at that period, three days about, and then sleet and rain; but this was a regular good one, thermometer at nineteen Fahrenheit, no wind, no snow, and the gravel-pits bearing. The gravel-pits were so called because there was no gravel there. There had been, but it was dug out, and carted away before the memory of the oldest inhabitant, and the cavities were filled with water. There were quite three acres of available surface altogether, and not farther than a mile from Weston; but "Ars longa, vita brevis est;" the art of cutting figures is long, and the period of practice short indeed. Considering the price spent in skates in England, and the few opportunities of putting them on, it seems barbarous of masters not to give whole holidays when the ice *does* bear. But then what would parents and guardians say? A boy cannot skate himself into the smallest public appointment, and the rule of three is of much more importance to his future prospects than the cutting of that figure. The Westonians made the most they could of their opportunity, however, and whenever they had an hour to spare the gravel-pits swarmed with them. Their natural tendency was to rapid running, racing, and hockey; but Leblanc, who was born in Canada, where his father held an appointment, and who had worn skates almost as soon as he had shoes, did such wonderful things as set a large number of them practising figure skating. Buller was bitten by the mania; he had never tried anything before but simple straightforward running on the flat of the skate with bent knees, so he had a great deal to learn; but with his usual persistency, when he once took anything in hand he did not regard the difficulties, and only dreaded lest he should not have sufficient opportunity of practising. He began, of course, by endeavouring to master the outside edge, which is the grammar of figure skating, and watched Leblanc, but could make nothing out of *that*, for Leblanc seemed to move by volition, as some birds appear to skim along without any motion of the wings. He could not give hints, or show how anything was done, because he could not understand where any difficulty lay. It was like simple walking to him; you get up and walk, you could not show any one exactly *how* to walk.

But there were two or three other fair skaters from whom more could be learned; Penryhn, for example, was a very decent performer of simple figures. He came from a northern county, where there was yearly opportunity of practice, and had been taught by his father, who was an excellent skater.

"The first great thing you must always bear in mind," said he, "is that the leg upon which you stand, while on the outside edge, must be kept straight and stiff, with the knee rigidly braced. You see some fellows there practising by crossing the legs; while they are on one leg they bring the other in front, and across it, before they put it down on the ice. This certainly forces you to get on to the outside edge, but it twists the body into a wrong position—one in which the all-important thing in skating, balance, cannot be acquired. Besides, it gets you into a way of bringing the foot off the ground to the front, whereas it ought always to be a little behind the one you are skating on, and it takes as long to get out of that habit as to learn the outside edge altogether pretty well. Why, here is Old Algebra positively with a pair of skates on!"

"Old Algebra," as a mathematical genius, whose real name was Smith, was called, skated very well too.

"Look here, Algebra," cried Penryhn, "I am trying to show Buller how to do the outside edge; can't you give him a scientific wrinkle?"

"The reason why you find an initial difficulty in the matter," said Algebra gravely, adjusting his spectacles, "is that you naturally suppose that if you bend so far out of the perpendicular, the laws of gravity must cause you to fall. But that is because you omit the centrifugal force from your consideration; remember what centrifugal force is, Buller, and it will give you confidence."

"Oh, I have confidence enough!" said Buller; "it's the power of getting on to the edge without overbalancing myself that I want, and all that rot about the laws of gravity won't help me."

"I fancied they wouldn't, but Penryhn asked for a scientific wrinkle. If you want a practical one, keep the head and body erect, never looking down at the ice; when you strike out with the right foot, look over the right shoulder; body and foot are sure to follow the eye, and clasp your hands behind you, or keep them at your sides; do anything but sway them about. That's it, you got on to the outside edge then; now boldly with the left foot, and look over the left shoulder. Never mind (Buller had come a cropper); you fell then because you did not let yourself go, but when your skate took the outside edge you tried to recover. You lacked confidence, in short, in the centrifugal force, and bothered yourself, instinctively, without knowing it, with the laws of gravity. Try again; you stick to that. Rigidity. Right foot—look over right shoulder, not too far, just a turn of the head. Left foot—look over left shoulder. There, you did not fall then. Trust to the centrifugal force, that's the thing," and he swept away with a long easy roll.

"A capital coach he would make," said Penryhn, admiringly. "He always tells you just what you want to know without bothering."

"Yes," said Buller, "I have asked him things in lessons once or twice, and he made it all as clear as possible, but I didn't know he was good for anything else. This is a grand idea for learning to skate, though; look here, this is all right, is it not?"

"Yes, you have got it now; lean outwards a little more, and don't bend forward. The weight should be on the centre of the foot."

There are few sensations more delightful than the first confident sweep on the outside edge, with the blade biting well into the clear smooth ice, and Buller felt as if he could never have enough of it, and he kept on, trying to make larger and larger segments of a circle, not heeding the falls he got for the next half hour, when it was time to be getting back, and he had reluctantly to take his skates off, and jog home at a trot. The next chance he had he was back to the ice and at it again.

Others who had got as far as he had began practising threes, or trying to skate backwards, but not so Buller. He must have that outside edge perfectly, and make complete circles on it, without hesitation or wobbling, much less falling, before he attempted anything else. Progress did not seem slow to him, he was used to that in everything, and he was surprised at improving as quickly as he did. All he dreaded was a heavy snow-fall, or a breaking up of the frost, and either calamity was to be expected from hour to hour. Before going to bed on the night of the third day of the ice bearing, he drew the curtain and looked out of window. The moon was nearly full, there was not a breath of wind stirring to shake the hoar-frost off the trees; all was hard, and bright, and clear. How splendid the pits would be now! How glorious to have the whole sheet of ice to one's self! why, with such a chance of solitary practice he might well expect to cut an eight, for he could already complete entire circles on each foot. If it were not for the bars to his window he would certainly go. The lane below had no building to overlook it; none of the windows of that part of the house where Dr. Jolliffe and his family, and the servants slept commanded the lane. He would have no other house to pass on the way to the gravel pits; really there would be no risk to speak of at all. The window was barely more than six feet, certainly not seven from the ground, and the brick wall old and full of inequalities where the mortar had fallen out, and the toe might rest; with a yard of rope dangling from the sill, to get in again would be the easiest thing possible. The more he thought about it the more simple the whole scheme seemed; if it were not for the bars. He examined them. The removal of one would be sufficient.

"You beast!" said Buller, seizing and shaking it. It seemed to give a little, and he shook it again: it certainly was not very tight, and he examined it further. It fitted into the wood-work of the window-frame at the top, and ter-minated at the bottom in a flat plate, perforated with three holes, by which it was secured by nails to the sill. Nails? no, by Jove, screws! Only the paint had filled in the little creases at the top of them, and it was simple enough to pick that off. His pocket-knife had a screw-driver at the top of it, he applied this and turned it; the screw came up like a lamb. So did the second; so did the third. The bar was free at the bottom, and when he pulled it towards him it came out in his hand! He replaced it, just to see if it would be all right. It was the simplest thing in the world, you could not tell that it had been touched. So he took it out again, laid it aside carefully, and considered.

He had no rope, but there was a leather belt, which he buckled round one of the other bars, dropping the end outside. Perhaps that would give rather a slight grip, so he also got out a woollen scarf, such as is sometimes called a " comforter," which he possessed, and fastened that to the bar also. With that there could be no difficulty in getting in again. Should he give Penryhn or any other fellow a chance of accompanying him? Well, on the whole, no. It was impossible that it should be discovered, but still, apparent impossibilities do happen sometimes. Suppose one of the masters had a fancy for a moonlight skate! He did not mind risking his own skin, when the risk was so slight, but to get another fellow into a row was an awful idea. Besides, two would make more noise getting out and in than one, and the other might laugh, or call out, or play the fool in some way or another. And as for being alone in the expedition, Buller rather liked that than otherwise. He was rather given to going his own way, and carrying out his own ideas unhampered by other people's suggestions.

So he quickly determined to keep his counsel and disturb no one. He had blown his candle out before first trying the bar, and had been working by the bright moonlight. Then he fastened his skates round his neck, so that they should neither impede his movements, nor clatter, and put one leg out of window, then the other, turned round, let himself down by the hands, and dropped into the lane. He looked up to see that the scarf was hanging all right; it was within easy reach of both hands; he gave it a pull to try it, and being satisfied, got over into the field, and started at a jog-trot for the gravel pits. It was glorious; utter stillness—the clear sheet of ice flooded with the moonbeams, a romantic sense of solitude, and a touch of triumphant feeling in having got the best of the world, and utilizing such a magnificent time, while others were wasting it in bed. He put his skates on and began. Whether the exhilaration of stealing a march upon everybody, or the impossibility of running up against anyone, or the confidence inspired by solitude, and the absolute freedom from being laughed at if he fell, were the cause, he had never gone like this before. Striking out firmly from the start, he went round the sheet of ice in splendid curves, the outside edge coming naturally to him now. A long sweep on the right foot, a

long sweep on the left, round and round, with
arms folded or clasped behind him. Not a trip,
not a stumble, not a momentary struggle to
retain the balance. It was splendid! Then at
last he began with the circles which he was so
anxious to perfect himself in. Round he went
on his right, in smaller compass than he had ever
accomplished one yet, with plenty of impetus to
bring him round at the end. Then round on the
left, quite easily, without an effort. Again with
the right, and so on, a capital eight. It was like
magic, as if he had acquired the art in an instant.
Or was he in bed and dreaming that he was
skating? It really seemed like it. If it were so,
he did not care how long it was before he was
roused. But no, he was wide awake, and the
phenomenon was simply the result of confidence,
following on good and persevering practice in the
right direction. Breaking away from his eight,
he swung round and round the pond again as
fast as he could go. Then he tried a three; the
first half on the outside edge, forwards was easy
enough, and he found no difficulty in turning on
the toe, but he could not complete the tail on the
inside edge backwards without staggering and
wobbling. He had a good two hours of it, and
then the moon disappeared behind a bank of
clouds and he prepared to go home. Skating in

the dark would be poor fun, and besides it was very late, so he made for the bank, took his skates off, and jogged back.

Mr. Rabbits, one of the masters, who was great at chemistry, and could tell you to a grain how much poison you swallowed in that water for which the Gradus sarcastically gives pura as a standing epithet, had been asked by the vicar of Penredding, a village five miles off, to give a lecture in his school-room to the parishioners, one of a series of simple entertainments which were got up to cheer the long evenings in the winter months. The vicar was an old college friend of Mr. Rabbits, who gladly consented, and like a wise man chose the subject which he was best up in, writing a very amusing and instructive but very elementary paper on Light, with plenty of illustrations and simple experiments, which kept his audience in a state of wonder and delight the whole evening, and sent them home with plenty to think and talk about afterwards. It was necessary to have a very early and hurried dinner, the lecture beginning at seven, so Mr. Rabbits went back to the vicarage after it was over to supper, after which there was a chat about the old college boat and so forth, and it was rather late when he started for home. He had refused the offer of a conveyance, considering that the

five miles walk on a bright still frosty night
would be a luxury, and so he found it, though for
the latter part of his journey the moon was
obscured.   It was not so dark, however, as to prevent his distinguishing objects, and as he passed
along the lane by which he entered Weston he
was sure he saw someone lurking under the wall
at the back of Dr. Jolliffe's house.   Suspecting
there was something wrong, he got into the shade
under the hedge and crept noiselessly along,
taking out of his pocket a piece of magnesium
wire which he had made use of in his lecture,
and a match-box.   Presently he saw the figure
raise itself from the ground towards a window,
and immediately struck a match and ignited the
wire, which he held over his head.   The whole
side of the house was at once as bright as day,
and a boy was distinctly seen getting in at the
window

"Buller!" exclaimed Mr. Rabbits, "what are
you doing there?"

"Please, sir, I am getting in," said poor Buller.

"So I perceive," said Mr. Rabbits; "but what
right have you there?"

"It's my own room, please, sir."

"Well, but what right then had you out of it at
this time of night?"

"None at all, sir, I am afraid."

"Then why did you do it?"

"I hoped not to be seen, sir."

"Hum!   What have you been doing?"

"Skating, sir."

"I shall report you in the morning."

Poor Tom Buller! How crest-fallen he felt as he conscientiously replaced the bar, and screwed it down again. How heavy his heart was as he took his clothes off and got into bed? What a fool he had been, he thought, and yet at the same time how awfully unlucky. Wrecked at the moment of entering the port! However, it was done now, and could not be helped; he must stand the racket. He supposed he should get off with a flogging. Surely they would not expel him for such a thing as that. Of course they would make an awful row about his breaking out at night, but he had not done any harm when he *was* out. And the doctor was a good-natured chap, he certainly would let him off with a rowing and a flogging. He had never been flogged; did it hurt very much, he wondered? at all events it would soon be over. He had thought for a moment while skating that perhaps it was a dream; how jolly it would be if it could only prove a dream, and he could wake up in the morning and find that the whole business was fancy. What a good job that he had not told Penryhn, and got him into a row as well. What a nuisance that old Rabbits was to come by just at the wrong moment; five minutes earlier or five minutes later it would have been all right. What thing was that he lighted? What a tremendous flare it made, to be sure. Well, it was no use bothering; happen what might he had a jolly good skate, and was firm on the outside edge for ever. Now the thaw might come if it liked, and Tom, who was a bit of a philosopher, went to sleep.

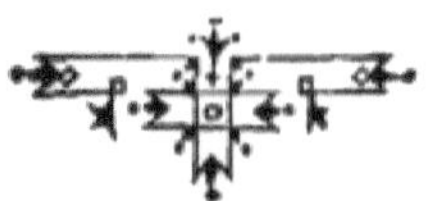

CHAPTER IX.

THE POACHERS.

BULLER was not the only Weston boy who broke out unlawfully that night. From Mr. Cookson's house as from Dr. Jolliffe's an adventurer stole forth. But Saurin's object was not so innocent as Buller's, neither was it so unpremeditated. For he nursed felonious designs against Lord Woodruff's pheasants, and the project had been deliberately planned, and, as we know, the key which was to open the yard door cunningly manufactured, a long time beforehand.

Edwards, as a result of talking about the expedition, and his friend's glowing anticipation of the fun of it, became quite anxious to join in. But Marriner did not think this advisable when Saurin put the matter to him. They only had one air-gun, and two were quite enough for a stealthy excursion of this kind. A third could

take no part in the proceedings, and would only
be an extra chance of attracting observation.   As
a matter of fact, Marriner would rather have been
quite alone, as his custom was on these predatory
occasions, and it was only his desire to make
Saurin an accomplice, and so seal his mouth,
which induced him to depart from his ordinary
custom now.   And to tell the truth, when the
time actually came, and Edwards saw his friend
steal along the yard, unlock and open the door at
the further end, and close it behind him, he was
glad in his heart that he was not going too.   Not
because it was wrong: he had got his ideas so
twisted that he thought it an heroic piece of
business altogether, and admired Saurin for his
lawless daring.   But he felt conscious of not
being cast in the heroic mould himself, and
actually shuddered at the thought of gliding
about the woods at dead of night, thinking that
someone was watching him behind every tree,
and might spring out upon him at any moment.
Especially when he curled himself up in bed, and
pulled the blankets snugly round him, did he feel
convinced that he was far more comfortable
where he was than he would have been in Lord
Woodruff's preserves.

Saurin had no compunctions of this sort; *he*
did not flinch when the time came; on the con-

trary, when he found himself out in the fields he felt a keen thrill of enjoyment. There was just enough sense of danger for excitement, not enough for unpleasant nervousness. To be engaged in what was forbidden was always a source of delight to him, and here he was braving the rules of his school and breaking the laws of his country all at once: it was like champagne to him. Yet it was the very height of absurdity to risk expulsion, imprisonment, perhaps penal servitude for *nothing*, literally for *nothing*.

He had no earthly use for the game when it was stolen, Marriner would have it and sell it, but the question of Saurin's sharing in the profits had not even been mooted. To do him justice he had not thought of such a thing, the sport was all that tempted him. The field of their operations was not to be near Marriner's house, but in a part of the estates a good bit nearer Weston, and on the other side of it. Marriner had learned that there was to be a poaching expedition on a large scale that night at the other extremity of the preserves, a good three miles off. He knew the men and their method. They used ordinary guns, killed off all they could in a short time, and got away before the keepers could assemble in force, or if they were surprised they showed fight. He never joined in such bold attacks, but when he knew of them took advantage, as he proposed to do on the present occasion, of the keepers being drawn away, to do a little quiet business on his own account in another direction. The place appointed for Saurin to meet Marriner was a wood-stack reached by a path across the fields, two miles from Weston. Closing the yard door behind him, but not locking it, he started off at a sharp walk, keeping in the shade whenever he could, though all was so still and noiseless that he seemed almost to be the only being in the world, when he had once got quite out of the sight of houses. But no, a night-hawk swept by him, so close as to make him start, and a stoat met him in the middle of a trodden path across a ploughed field; showing that there were other game depredators besides himself abroad. The way seemed longer than it was in the day-time, but at last he got to the wood-stack, where he saw no one, but presently a figure stole round the corner and joined him: Marriner with the air-gun and a sack.

"It's all right," he said, "I heard the guns nigh half-an-hour ago. There's never a watcher nor keeper within more nor a couple of miles off, and we have a clear field to ourselves."

Saurin took the gun, for it was an understood thing beforehand that he was to have all the

shooting, which indeed was but fair, and Marriner, carrying the sack, led the way to a coppice
hard by, indeed the wood forming the stack had
been cut out of it.   He crept on hands and knees
through the hedge and glided into the brushwood,
Saurin following, for some little distance.   Suddenly he stopped, laid his hand on his companion's
arm, and pointed upwards.   Perched on the branch
of a tree, and quite clear against the moonlit sky,
was a round ball.

" Pheasant?" asked Saurin.

"Yes," was the reply.   "And there's another
roosting there, and another yonder, and another—"

" I see them," replied Saurin in the same whispered tones.   And raising his air-gun he got the
roosting bird in a line with the sights, which was
as easy to do pretty nearly as in broad day, and
pressed the trigger.   The black ball came tumbling down with a thump on the ground, and Marriner, pouncing upon it, put it in his sack.   A
second, a third were bagged without stirring from
the spot.   A few steps farther on another, who had
been disturbed by the whip-cracks of the air-gun,
had withdrawn his head from under his wing.   But
he did not take to flight at once, being comfortable
where he was and the sounds not very alarming,
and while he hesitated he received a violent shock

in the middle of his breast, which knocked him off his perch powerless and dying. A little further on another, and then yet another were bagged: it was a well-stocked coppice, and had not been shot yet. Lord Woodruff was reserving that part for some friends who were coming at Christmas, and with the prospects of whose sport I fear that Saurin somewhat interfered that night. The sack indeed was pretty heavy by the time they had gone through the wood, and then Marriner thought that it would be more prudent to decamp, and they retraced their steps by a path which traversed the coppice. Once back at the wood-stack they were to separate, so before they left the coppice Marriner put down his now heavy sack, and Saurin handed him the air-gun, which he stowed away in his capacious pocket. Then they went on, and just as they were on the edge of the wood came suddenly upon a man.

"Hulloa! young gentleman," exclaimed he to Saurin, who was leading, "what are you up to? What has the other got in that sack?"

Marriner slipped behind the trees.

"I have got *you*, at anyrate," said the man, seizing Saurin by the collar.

The latter would not speak lest his voice should be recognized afterwards, but he struggled all he knew. The man soon overpowered him; but

Marriner came to the rescue. Throwing down the sack of pheasants, he had taken from his pocket an implement of whalebone with a heavy knob of lead at the end, and coming behind the man, both whose hands were holding on to Saurin, he struck him with it on the head as hard as he could. The keeper's grasp relaxed, he fell heavily to the ground, and Saurin was free. The man lay on his back with his head on the path, and the moonbeams fell on his face.

"Simon Bradley," muttered Marriner. "To be sure he lives this way, and was going home after the alarm on t'other side."

Saurin was seized with a violent shivering from head to foot.

"He isn't, I mean to say you have not—eh?" he said.

"Dunno, and don't much care, curse him!" replied Marriner. "It would be laid to t'other chaps if he is."

"But we ought to do something; get him some help," urged Saurin, who had not become sufficiently hardened to like such devil's work as this. "If he is living he will be frozen to death lying out such a night as this."

"Oh, he will be all right!" said Marriner. "He's only stunned a bit. He will come to in ten minutes and get up and walk home."

"But can't we leave word at his house, and then be off?"

"That would be a fool's trick, that would. Why, it would bring suspicion on us, and if he is a gone coon—it's impossible, you know, almost—but *if* he is, we should get scragged for it. Come, I didn't think you was so chicken-hearted, or I wouldn't have brought you out. Let's get away home at once while we can, and don't go a putting your neck in a halter for nowt."

Fear overcame compunction, and Saurin turned and fled. How he got home he did not know, but he seemed to be at the back door of the yard immediately almost. Then he steadied himself, went in, locked the door, and stole up to his room and to bed. *He* did not sleep that night. The face of the gamekeeper lying there in the moonlight haunted him. He wished, like Buller, but oh, much more fervently, that the whole business might turn out to have been a nightmare. But the morning dawned cold and gray, and he got up and dressed himself and went in to school, and it was all real. He could not fix his attention; his mind would wander to that coppice. Had the gamekeeper come to, tried to struggle up, fainted, fallen back, perished for want of a little assistance? Or had he got up, not much the worse, and had he seen his face clearly, and, recognizing that it was a Weston boy, would he come to the school and ask to go round and pick him out?

"Saurin!"

It was only the voice of the master calling on him to go on with the construing, but he had so entirely forgotten where he was that he started and dropped his book, which caused a titter, for Saurin was not habitually either of a meditative or a nervous turn. He felt that he really must pull himself together or he would excite suspicion. "I beg your pardon, sir," he said; "my hands are numb, and I dropped the book. Where's the place?" he added *sotto voce* to his neighbour.

"I think your attention was numb," said the master.

Saurin had the chorus in the play of Euripides, which was undergoing mutilation at his fingers' ends, so he went on translating till he heard, "That will do. Maxwell!" and then he relapsed into his private meditations. After all, he had not struck the blow, Marriner's trying to drag him into a share of the responsibility was all nonsense. They might say he ought to have given the alarm, or gone for a doctor, but nothing more. And yet he fancied he had heard somewhere that to be one of a party engaged in an unlawful act which resulted in anyone being killed was complicity or something, which included all in the crime. One thing was clear, he must keep his counsel, and not let Edwards or any-one know anything about it, because they might be questioned; and he must guard against show-ing that he was at all anxious. And why should he be? A man did not die for one knock on the head; he was probably all right again. And he could not have seen his face so as to recognize him; it was quite in the shade where they had been struggling. It was all nonsense his worrying himself; and yet he could not help listening, expecting a messenger to come with some alarm-ing intelligence, he could not define what. After school Edwards came up to him and drew him aside confidentially, full of eagerness and curio-sity.

"Well," he said, "was it good fun? How did it all go off?"

"It was a regular sell," replied Saurin, smother-ing his impatience at being questioned, and forcing himself to take the tone he was accustomed to assume towards his chum in confidential com-munications.

"How! did you not meet Marriner?"

"Oh, yes! I met him all right; but it was no good. There were other poachers out last night, and we heard their guns, so of course we could not attempt anything, because the gamekeepers would all have been on the look-out. You were well out of it, not coming, for it was precious cold work waiting about, and no fun after all."

"What a bore! But you will have better luck next time, perhaps."

"I hope so, if I go; but the fact is, I have lost confidence in Marriner rather. He ought to have found out that those other fellows were going out last night, don't you see? At least he always brags that he knows their movements. And it will be some time before the moon serves again; and then the Christmas holidays will be coming on; and by next term the pheasants will all have been shot off. The chance has been missed."

"Well, at all events, you have got back all right and not been discovered. Do you know, when one comes to think about it, it was an awful risk," said Edwards.

"Of course it was," replied Saurin; "that made all the fun of it. Rather idiotic, though, too, since one hopes to preserve game one's self some day. It would be a better lark to go out to catch poachers than to go out poaching."

"A great deal, I should say. Not but what that is risky work too. Those fellows do not flinch from murder when they are interrupted."

"What makes you say that?" cried Saurin

quickly, turning and catching him sharply by the arm.

"I don't know!" replied Edwards, astonished at the effect of his words. "I have read about fights between gamekeepers and poachers in books, and heard of them, and that; haven't you? How queer you look! Is there anything the matter?"

"Not a bit of it," said Saurin, regretting his imprudence; "only, I was frozen hanging about last night, and when I got back I could not sleep for cold feet, so I am a bit tired. And I think I have caught cold too. And you know," he added, laughing, "having enlisted in the ranks of the poachers last night, at least in intention, I feel bound to resist any attacks on their humanity. But, as a matter of fact, I believe that they do show fight for their spoil and their liberty when they find themselves surprised. Shots are exchanged and mischief happens sometimes. But my poor little air-gun would not be a very formidable weapon in a row, I expect. Its peppercorn bullets are good for a rabbit or pheasant, but would hardly disable a man. The gamekeeper with his double-barrel would have a good deal the best of it. But, I say, my cold has not taken away my appetite. Let us get in to breakfast, and hang poaching."

CHAPTER X.

THE FATES ARE DOWN UPON BULLER.

OM BULLER had finished his breakfast, and was ruefully preparing his lesson in his room, when he heard his name being called up the staircase. "Buller! I say, Buller!"

"Well, what's the row?" he asked, opening his door with a sinking heart. The voice of the caller sounded singularly harsh and discordant, he thought.

"Oh, Buller! the doctor wants to see you in his study."

"All right!" replied Buller; "I will come at once."

But though his mouth said "All right," his mind meant "All wrong." He had entertained the absurd hope, though he hardly admitted the fact to himself, that Mr. Rabbits, with whom he was rather a favourite, would not report him, forgetting, or not realizing, the great responsibility which Mr. Rabbits would incur by failing to do so. Well, he would know the worst soon now at anyrate, that was one consolation, for there is nothing so bad as suspense, as the man said who was going to be hanged.

Dr. Jolliffe's study was in a retired part of the house, not often visited by the boys. Here the uproar of their voices, and their noisy tread as they rushed up and down the uncarpeted staircases, could not be heard. Here thick curtains hung before the doors, which were of some beautifully grained wood (or painted to look like it), and gilded round the panels. Thick carpets lined the passages, rich paper covered the walls; all the surroundings were in violent contrast to the outer house given up to the pupils, and gained an exaggerated appearance of luxury in consequence.

Buller, with his heart somewhere about his boots, tapped at the awful door.

"Come in!" was uttered in the dreamy tones of one whose mind was absorbed in some occupation, and who answered instinctively, without disturbance of his thoughts.

Buller entered and closed the door behind him. The doctor, who was writing, and referring every now and then to certain long slips of printed paper which were lying on the table at his side, did not speak or look up, but merely raised his hand to intimate that he must not be disturbed for a moment.   So Buller looked round the room; and noted things as one does so vividly whenever one is in a funk in a strange place; in a dentist's waiting-room, say.   The apartment was wonderfully comfortable.   The book-cases which surrounded it were handsome, solid, with nice little fringes of stamped leather to every shelf.   The books were neatly arranged, and splendidly bound, many of them in Russia leather, as the odour of the room testified.   Between the book-cases, the wall-paper was dark crimson, and there were a few really good oil-paintings.   The fireplace was of white marble, handsomely carved, with Bacchantes, and Silenus on his donkey—not very appropriate guardians of a sea-coal fire.   On the mantel-piece was a massive bronze clock, with a figure of Prometheus chained to a rock on the top, and the vulture digging into his ribs.   And Buller, as he noticed this, remembered, with the clearness afforded by funk spoken of above, that an uncle of his, who was an ardent homeopathist, had an explanation of his own of the old Promethean myth.   He maintained that Prometheus typified the universal allopathic patient, and that the vulture for ever gnawing his liver was Calomel.   The clock was flanked on each side by a

grotesque figure, also in bronze. Two medieval
bullies had drawn their swords, and were preparing for a duel, which it was apparent that neither
half liked. A very beautiful marble group, half
life-size, stood in one corner, and gave an air of
brightness to the whole room. And on a bracket,
under a glass case, there was a common pewter
quart pot, which the doctor would not have exchanged for a vase of gold. For it was a trophy
of his prowess on the river in old college days,
and bore the names of good friends, now dead,
side by side with his own. The table at which
the doctor sat was large, with drawers on each
side for papers, and a space in the middle for his
legs, and was covered with documents collected
under paper-weights. It took Tom Buller just
two minutes to note all these objects, and then
the doctor looked up with an expression of
vacancy which vanished when he saw who stood
before him. He tossed his quill-pen down, took
off his spectacles, and said:

"Well, Buller, what have you got to say for
yourself?"

Tom hung his head, fiddled with a button of
his jacket, and murmured something to the effect
that he did not know.

"It is a very serious offence of yours that has
been reported to me, nothing less than breaking

out of the house, out of *my* house, in the dead of night. A most enormous and unparalleled proceeding. Why, in the whole course of my experience I never knew of a boy having the audacity —at least it is extremely rare," said the doctor, somewhat abruptly breaking the thread of his sentence. For he suddenly remembered, conscientious man, that when an Eton boy himself he had committed a similar offence for the purpose of visiting the Windsor theatre. "Suppose that in consequence of your example the custom spread, and the boys of Weston took to escaping from their rooms at night and careering about the country like—" He was going to say like rabbits, but the name of the master who had detected the offender occurred to him, and dreading the suspicion of making a joke he changed it to—"jackals, howling jackals." "Have you been in the habit of these evasions?"

"Oh, no, sir!" cried Tom, encouraged by something in the doctor's tones to speak out. "I never thought of such a thing till last night, just as I was going to bed. But the moon was so bright, and the bar was so loose, and the ice bears such a short time, and I take so much longer than others to learn anything, and I was so anxious to get perfect on the outside edge, that I gave way to the temptation. It was very wrong, and I am very sorry, and will take care nothing of the sort ever happens again."

"So will I," said the doctor drily. "These bars shall be looked to. And who went with you?"

"No one, sir, no one else knew of it. I just took my skates and went. I did not see how wrong it was, sir, then, as I do now. I am slow, sir, and can only think of one thing at a time."

"And the outside edge engrossed all your faculties, I suppose."

"Yes, sir."

Dr. Jolliffe would have given something to let him off, but felt that he could not; to do so would be such a severe blow to discipline. So he set his features into the sternest expression he could assume, and said, "Come into my class-room after eleven-o'clock school."

"Yes, sir," replied Buller, retiring with a feeling of relief; he was to get off with a flogging after all, and he did not imagine that castigation at the hands of the doctor would be particularly severe. For the head-master's class-room contained a cupboard, rarely opened, and in that cupboard there were rods, never used at Weston for educational purposes. For if a boy did not prepare his lessons properly it was assumed that they were too difficult for him, and he was sent down into a lower form. If he still failed to meet the school requirements, his parents were requested to remove him, and he left, without a stain on his character, as the magistrates say, but he was written down an ass. Such a termination to the Weston career was dreaded infinitely more than any amount of corporal punishment or impositions, and the prospect of being degraded from his class caused the idlest boy to set to work, so that such disgraces were not common. The birch, then, was had recourse to simply for the maintenance of discipline, all forms of imprisonment being considered injurious to the health. And an invitation to the doctor's class-room after school meant a short period, quite long enough, however, of acute physical sensation, which was not of a pleasurable character.

But everything is comparative in this world, and Tom Buller, who had feared that expulsion might be the penalty exacted for his offence, or at anyrate that his friends at home would be written to, and a great fuss made, was quite in high spirits at the thought of getting the business over so quickly and easily. He found a group of friends waiting for him to come out of the doctor's study, curious to know what he had been wanted for, Tom not being the sort of fellow, they thought, to get into a serious scrape; and when he told them that he had got out of his window the night before to go skating, that Mr. Rabbits had caught him as he was getting in again by lighting up some chemical dodge which illuminated the whole place, and that he was to be flogged after eleven-o'clock school, they were filled with admiration and astonishment. What a brilliant idea! What courage and coolness in the execution! What awfully bad luck that old Rabbits had come by just at the wrong moment! They took his impending punishment even more cheerfully than he did himself, as our friends generally do, and promised to go in a body and see the operation. One, indeed, Simmonds, lamented over his sad fate, and sang by way of a dirge—

> " 'Here a sheer hulk lies poor Tom Bowling,
>   The darling of our crew,' "

in a fine tenor voice for which he was celebrated. And this being taken as an allusion to the branch of cricket in which Buller had learned to become a proficient, was considered a joke, and from that time forth the object of it was known as Tom Bowling.

Eleven o'clock came, and they all went into school, and Buller did his best to fix his attention on what he was about instead of thinking of what was coming afterwards. Dr. Jolliffe's class was select, consisting of a dozen of the most proficient scholars, Crawley and Smith being the only two of those mentioned in this story who belonged to it. He had hardly taken his chair ten minutes before a servant came in with a card and a note, stating that a gentleman was waiting outside, and that his business was very pressing. The doctor glanced at the card, which was Lord Woodruff's, and then tore open the note, which ran thus:

"Dear Dr. Jolliffe, can I speak to you a moment. I would not, you may be sure, disturb you during school hours if there were not urgent reason for the interruption."

"Where is Lord Woodruff?" he asked, rising from his seat.

"Waiting in the cloister at the foot of the stair, sir."

And there indeed he found him, an excitable little man, walking up and down in a fume.

"Dr. Jolliffe," he cried, directly he saw him, "were any of your boys out last night? Tut, tut, how should you know! Look here. There were poachers in my woods last night, and the keepers, hearing the firing, of course went to stop, and if possible arrest them. The rascals decamped, however, before they could reach the place, and the keepers dispersed to go to their several homes. One of them, Simon Bradley, had some distance to walk, his cottage being two miles and more from the place. As he passed through a coppice on his way he came upon a boy and a figure following with a sack, whether man or boy he could not say, as it was in deep shadow. He collared the boy, who was big and strong, and while he was struggling with him he was struck from behind with a life-preserver or some such instrument, which felled him to the ground, bleeding and senseless. After some time he came to, and managed to crawl home, and his wife sent off to tell me, and I despatched a man on horseback to fetch a surgeon. And Bradley is doing pretty well; there is no immediate fear for his life. Of course he has recovered his wits, or I could not give you these details, and he is certain that the fellow he was struggling with was a Weston boy."

"Well, you see, Lord Woodruff," said the doctor, "unless the poor fellow knew the boy, he could hardly be sure upon that point, could he?"

"Pretty nearly, I think, Dr. Jolliffe. Your boys wear a distinctive cap of dark flannel?"

"Yes; but when they get shabby they are thrown aside, and many of the village youths round about get hold of them and wear them."

"Aye," said Lord Woodruff, "but Bradley is confident that this was a young gentleman; he wore a round jacket, with a white collar, and stiff white cuffs with studs in them, for he felt them when he tried to grasp his wrists. No young rustic would be dressed in that fashion, and, taken together with the cap, I fear that it must have been one of your boys."

"It looks suspicious, certainly," said the doctor, somewhat perplexed.

"I am very sorry indeed to give you trouble, and to risk bringing any discredit on the school," said Lord Woodruff. "But you see one of my men has been seriously injured, and that in my service, and if we could find this boy, his evidence would enable us to trace the cowardly ruffian who struck the blow."

"Then you would want to—to prosecute him, in short."

"In confidence, doctor, I should be glad not to do so if I could help it, and if he would give his evidence freely it might be avoided. But it may be necessary to frighten him, if we can find him, that is. And, doctor, allow me to say that if this were merely a boyish escapade, a raid upon my pheasants, I should be content to leave the matter in your hands, considering that a sound flogging would meet the case. But my man being dangerously hurt alters the whole business. I owe it to him, and to all others in my employ, not to leave a stone unturned to discover the perpetrator of the outrage, and I call upon you, Dr. Jolliffe, to assist me."

The doctor bowed. "Can your lordship suggest anything you would like done towards the elucidation of this mystery?" he said. "In spite of the jacket and cuffs, I find it difficult to suppose that any Weston boy is in league with poachers. But you may rely on my doing all in my power to aid you in any investigation you may think desirable."

"I expected as much, and thank you," replied Lord Woodruff. "It occurred to me, then, that it might be well, as a preliminary measure, to collect the boys together in one room and lay the case before them, promising impunity to the offender, if present, on condition of his turning queen's evidence."

"It shall be done at once," said the doctor. "Will you speak to them, or shall I?"

"It does not much matter," replied Lord Woodruff. "Perhaps the pledge would come better from me, the natural prosecutor."

"Very good."

The doctor returned to his class-room, not too soon. One of the young scamps had taken his chair, and was delivering a burlesque lecture, near enough to the head-master's style to excite irreverent laughter. They listened for his step upon the stair, however, and when he entered the room they might have been taken for a synod discussing a Revised Edition by the extreme gravity of their demeanour.

"We must interrupt our studies for a short time, I am sorry to say," observed Dr. Jolliffe. "I wish you to assemble at once, but without noise, in the schools. And, Probyn, run round to the other class-rooms, and tell the masters, with my compliments, that I wish their classes also to go there at once, and arrange themselves in their proper places, as on Examination Days."

The "Schools" was a large room which held all Weston; but the college was liberal in the matter of accommodation, and only three classes were habitually held in it, that so the hubbub of voices might not be inconvenient. For some persons are so constituted that when you seek to instruct them in Greek, they take an intense interest in mathematics, if treated upon within their hearing, and *vice versâ*. But every class had its appointed place in the schools, all the same, and in a few minutes after the summons had gone forth, the boys, not quite broken-hearted at having to shut up their books, were reassembled in the large room, wondering what on earth had happened to cause such an unparalleled infraction of the daily routine. One sanguine youth suggested that they were to have an extra half-holiday in consequence of the fine condition of the ice, and he had many converts to his opinion; but there were many other theories. Saurin alone formed a correct guess at the real matter in hand, conscience prompting him.

No sooner were all settled in their places than the head-master came in accompanied by Lord Woodruff, who was known to most present by sight, and curiosity became almost painful.

"It is he who has begged us the half-holiday," whispered the prophet of good to his neighbour. "Shall we give him a cheer?"

"Better wait to make certain first," replied his more prudent auditor.

Next the roll was called, and when all had answered to their names Dr. Jolliffe announced that their visitor had something serious to say to them; and then Lord Woodruff got up.

"No doubt some of your fathers are preservers of game for sporting purposes," he said, "and you all know what it means. I preserve game in this neighbourhood; and last night one of my keepers was going home through a wood where there are a good many pheasants, for it has not been disturbed this year, when he met two persons. They may not have been poachers, but poaching was certainly going on last night, for the guns were heard, and the man naturally concluded that they were trespassing in pursuit of game, for why else should they be there at that hour of the night. And so, as was clearly his duty, he endeavoured to secure one of them. But just as he had succeeded in doing so, he was struck down from behind with some weapon which has inflicted serious injuries upon him. He has recovered his senses, and laid an information that the person he seized was a Weston boy."

There was a murmur and a movement throughout the assembly at this sensational announcement. Saurin, who felt that he was very pale, muttered "Absurd!" and strove to assume a look of incredulous amusement.

"Now, boys, listen to me. I take a great interest in Weston College, and should be sorry to see any disgrace brought upon it. And indeed it would be very painful to me that any one of you should have his future prospects blighted on first entering into life for what I am willing to look upon as a thoughtless freak. But when the matter is once put into the hands of the police I shall have no further power to shield anyone, and if they trace the boy who was in that wood last night, which, mind you, they will probably do, safe as he may think himself, he will have to stand his trial in a court of justice. But now, I will give him a fair chance. If he will stand forward and confess that he was present on the occasion I allude to, and will say who the ruffian was that struck the blow, for of complicity in such an act I do not for a moment suspect him, I promise that he shall not be himself proceeded against in any way."

There was a pause of a full minute, during which there was dead silence; no one moved.

"What!" continued Lord Woodruff; "were you all in your beds at eleven o'clock last night? Was there no one out of college unbeknown to the authorities?"

He looked slowly round as he spoke, and it seemed to Buller that his eyes rested upon him. Though he knew nothing of this poaching business, he was certainly out, and perhaps Dr. Jolliffe had told Lord Woodruff so, and this was a trap to see if he would own to it, and if he did not, they might suspect him of the other thing. He half rose, and sat down again, hesitating.

"Ah!" said Lord Woodruff, catching sight of the movement; "what is it, my lad? speak up, don't be afraid."

"I was certainly out of the college last night," said Buller, getting on to his feet, "but I was not near any wood, and I did not meet any man, or see or hear any struggling or fighting."

"It has nothing to do with this case, my lord," interposed the doctor. "This boy went late to the gravel pits to skate, and was seen by one of the masters. It was a breach of the regulations, for which he will be punished, but nothing more serious."

"Oh! if he was seen skating by one of the masters that is enough. Might I speak to the gentleman?"

"Certainly."

And Mr. Rabbits was called forward and introduced.

"Oh! Mr. Rabbits, you actually saw this boy skating last night, did you?"

"No, not exactly. He was getting in again at his window when I surprised him?"

"May I ask at what time?"

"About half-past twelve."

"And how, if you did not see him, do you know that he was out skating?"

"He said so," replied Mr. Rabbits innocently.

"And his word is the only evidence you have that he was not elsewhere?"

Mr. Rabbits was obliged to confess that it was.

"Buller! come here," cried the doctor. "Now, did anyone see you at the gravel pits, or going there, or coming back?"

"No, sir."

"Think well, because you may be suspected of having gone in an exactly opposite direction. If any friend was with you I am certain that he would be glad to give himself up to get you out of a really serious scrape. Shall I put it to the boys, my lord?"

"It is of no use, sir," said Buller. "I was quite alone, just as I told you, and no one knew I was out. I did not think of it myself till a few minutes before, when I found the bar loose. And I did not open my door even. And I saw no one, going or returning, till Mr. Rabbits lit his chemical as I was getting in at the window."

"It is very painful to—ah—to seem to doubt your word, in short," said Lord Woodruff with hesitation, for he was a gentleman, and Tom's manner struck him as remarkably open and straightforward. "But you know it is impossible to accept anyone's unsupported evidence in his own favour, and I really wish that you could produce some one to corroborate your rather unlikely story. Assuming for a moment that you were in the company of poachers for a bit of fun last night, and that you saw something of this affray, and being caught as you got home, were frightened into accounting for your being out at so late an hour by this story of going skating in the moonlight; I say, assuming all this, I appeal to you to save yourself from serious consequences, and to forward the ends of justice by telling anything you know which may put us on the traces of the fellow who has injured my poor gamekeeper. A fellow who would come behind and strike a cowardly blow like that, trying to murder or maim a man who was simply doing his duty, does not deserve that you should shield him. Come, will you not denounce him?"

"But how can I tell about things of which I have no knowledge whatever?" cried Buller, who was getting vexed as well as bewildered. "What I have said is the exact truth, and if it does not suit you I cannot help it. Believe me or not as you like, there is no good in my going on repeating my words."

"I cannot accept the responsibility of taking your bare word in such a matter," said Lord Woodruff, more stiffly, for Tom's tone had offended him; "a magistrate may do so. Of course I shall not adjudicate in my own case," he added, turning to Dr. Jolliffe. "Mr. Elliot is the next nearest magistrate, and I shall apply for a warrant against this youth to him."

Tom Buller experienced a rather sudden change of sensation in a short period. A quarter of an hour ago he felt like a culprit, now his heart swelled with the indignation of a hero and a martyr. To be accused of poaching. and asked to betray a supposed accomplice in what might prove a murder, just because he happened to be out after ten one night, was rather too strong, and Tom's back was up.

"You had better go to your room, Buller, and wait there till you hear further," said Dr. Jolliffe, not unkindly.

To tell the truth the doctor was a good deal ruffled by this accusation, brought, as it seemed to him, on very insufficient grounds, against some member of the school. But he was determined to be as cool and quiet about it as possible, and not to give any one a chance of saying that he had obstructed the ends of justice. For if he took the highly indignant line, and it were proved after all that one of his boys was involved in the scrape, how foolish he would look!

"And you really mean to have this boy up before Mr. Elliot on a charge of poaching?" he asked.

"What else can I do?" said Lord Woodruff. "His own obstinacy in refusing to tell what he knows is to blame."

"But supposing that he really knows nothing, how can he tell it? I know the boy well, and he is remarkably truthful and straightforward. Intensely interested, too, in the studies and sports of his school, and the very last to seek low company or get into a scrape of this kind."

Lord Woodruff smiled and shook his head.

CHAPTER XI.

CIRCUMSTANTIAL EVIDENCE.

HAVE you ever stood near a bee-hive when something unusual was going on inside? When a swarm was meditated, or you had cut off the communication with a super which you meant to take? Just such a buzz and murmur as then arises might have been heard in Weston court-yard when the boys poured out from the schools, only increased so much in volume as the human vocal organs are more powerful than the apiarian. And surely not without cause, for the scene which had just been enacted, without any rehearsal, for their benefit was simply astounding.

"Fancy Tom Buller the chief of a gang of poachers!" cried Saurin. "By Jove, I did not think it was in him, and fairly confess that I have not done him justice. He is a dark horse and no mistake."

"Why, you don't for a moment suppose that

there is anything in it, do you?" asked Robarts.
who heard him.

"I don't know, I'm sure," replied Saurin; "perhaps not. Awful liars those keeper chaps, no
doubt. We shall know all about it in time, I
suppose."

"It would not be bad fun if one got a fair price
for the game one took," said Griffiths. "But the
risk and difficulty of selling it would be so great
that one would be certain to be robbed."

"What an ass Tom Bowling was to give himself up; it would have been all right if he had sat
still."

"I don't know that. He had already been
caught breaking out of college, don't you see, and
they would have been certain to put this and that
together."

"Who would?"

"Old Jolliffe."

"Not a bit of it. I twigged his face when
Buller stood up, and he looked as vexed as possible. *He'd* never have told."

"I am not sure of that, and I think Buller was
right not to risk it."

"Fussy old chap, Lord Woodruff!"

"Not a bad sort altogether, I believe, if you rub
him the right way."

"No more am I; give me everything I want,

and never thwart me, and I am the easiest fellow to live with in the world."

That is a sample of the way the matter was discussed and commented upon. But the most astonished of the whole school, and the only one who could not trust himself to make any remark at all in public, was Edwards. For the second time that day he had to watch his opportunity for a private conference with Saurin, and when he found it he opened on him eagerly.

"What a chap you are! And so you had a regular fight with keepers, and nearly did for one; and all you said this morning was that the whole thing was a failure and a sell. And even when we talked about gamekeepers catching poachers, and the poachers resisting, you kept it all dark."

"Why, it was a serious thing to talk about, you see," said Saurin.

"Well, I think you might have trusted me at all events," replied Edwards somewhat reproachfully.

"Trust you! My dear fellow I would trust you with my life," said Saurin. "But I thought it better to keep Marriner's attack on this keeper secret for your sake. There was sure to be a row, and in case of the inquiry coming in this direction, and your being questioned, it would be so much jollier for you to be able to say that you knew nothing about it. Whereas, if I had entered into all the details, it would have bothered you. For, to tell the truth, I feared the man was killed; now he is not hurt much, I don't care."

"They would not have got anything out of me," said Edwards.

"Perhaps not," replied Saurin. "But those lawyers are awful fellows when they get you into the witness-box, and make you say pretty nearly what they like. I had much rather have nothing to tell them myself if I were to be put in such a position, and I thought you would feel the same."

"You are right, so I do," said Edwards. "What a fellow you are, Saurin, you think of everything!"

"It is different, now that they have got hold of that ass, Buller; what a joke it all is, isn't it?"

"Yes," replied Edwards, in a tone of hesitation, however, as if he did not quite see the humour of it. "Rather rough upon Buller, though, don't you think?"

"Not a bit of it; he has got off his flogging."

"But suppose he comes in for something worse?"

"How should he? They cannot prove that he was in the coppice when he was about three miles in the opposite direction, you know. Now, if I were once suspected, they would find out that

I constantly went to Slam's, who finds agents to sell the game for all the poachers round, and some of the keepers too, if the truth were known, and that I had been seen in Marriner's company; who is considered to make a regular income out of Lord Woodruff's pheasants, and they would have some grounds to go upon. But Buller is all right."

But though he spoke like this to quiet Edwards, Saurin did not care whether Buller got into serious trouble or not. He was a friend of Crawley's, had seconded him in the fight, and given him advice which contributed as much as anything else to Saurin's defeat. If he were expelled and sent to prison it would not break his (Saurin's) heart. The only fear was that if Edwards blabbed—and he was so weak that he could not be absolutely trusted—fellows would think it horribly mean to let Buller be punished unjustly for what he himself had done. And on this account, and this account only, he hoped that Buller would get off.

Mr. Elliot, the magistrate, lived at Penredding, the village where Mr. Rabbits had gone to lecture, and thither Tom Buller was driven in a close fly, the doctor accompanying him. Lord Woodruff, who had come to Weston on horseback, rode over separately. Mr. Elliot was a man of good common sense, though his opinions were not quite so weighty as his person, which declined to rise in one scale when fifteen stone was in the other. He was a just man also, though perhaps he was less dilatory in attending to the wishes of a member of one of the great county families than he might be in the case of a mere nobody. If a rich man and a poor one had a dispute, he considered that the presumption was in favour of the former, but he did not allow this prejudice to influence him one iota in the teeth of direct evidence.

Just after the fly had left Weston some snow-flakes began to fall. "Ah!" thought Tom, "it may snow as hard as it pleases now. I have had a good turn at any rate. I was not able to do the outside edge when the frost set in, and now I can cut an eight. I wish, though, I could keep my balance in the second curl of those threes. I must practise going backwards, and stick to that next time I have a chance."

Dr. Jolliffe, who saw that he was absorbed in reflection, thought that he was dwelling upon the serious nature of the position in which he found himself, and would have been amused if he could have read the real subject of his meditations. But he could not do that, so he read the proof-sheets of his new treatise on the digamma. The snow fell thicker, and by the time they reached

Penredding the country was covered with a white sheet.

Mr. Elliot, who had been warned of their coming, was ready to receive them, and Lord Woodruff came forward with an inspector of rural police, and told his story, which was written down by a clerk and read over. Then the whole party set out on their travels again and drove to the cottage of the wounded gamekeeper, where they were received by a young woman, who had been crying her eyes red, and to the folds of whose dress two little children clung, hiding their faces therein, but stealing shy glances now and then at the quality, and the awful representative of the law, who had come to visit them.

"The doctor has told us that it would do your husband no harm to say before me what he has already told Lord Woodruff," said Mr. Elliot to her. "I was rejoiced to hear that he is doing so well. It was a most shameful, brutal, and cowardly attack, and we are most anxious that the offender should be brought to justice."

"Yes, sir," said the woman. "Doctor thinks it may quiet him like to have his dispositions took, and then he may go to sleep."

"Exactly. Will you be so kind as to tell him that we are here?"

She pushed the children into an inner room,

ran upstairs, and presently reappeared, asking them to walk up. Bradley was in bed, propped with pillows. A handkerchief was tied round his head, and his face was pale from loss of blood. Either from that cause, or on account of the shock to the nervous system, he was also very weak.

"How do you feel now, Bradley?" asked Lord Woodruff gently, going to the bed head.

"Rayther queer as yet, my lord," was the reply.

"No doubt. But you have a good hard head, and there is nothing serious the matter, the doctor says. But it may be some days before it will be prudent for you to go out, so, as we want to get on the traces of the fellow who struck you at once, Mr. Elliot has kindly come over to take your deposition here, instead of waiting till you were fit to go to Penredding."

When Tom Buller saw the woman and children, and then afterwards their strong bread-earner reduced to such a condition, he indeed felt heartily glad that there was no truth in the accusation against him. To have had any part in bringing about such a scene of family distress would have been too much for him.

The wounded man told his story clearly enough, and then Tom Buller was told to stand in the light where he could see him clearly.

"Noa," said the wounded man, "I could not

say who it wor. There was a bright moon, but the boy was in the shadow, and I got no clear look at his face; but he wor one of the Weston young gentlemen, I am sartin of that. A bit bigger than him, I should say, but I couldn't say for sure. He wor a strong un, I know that."

When all this was written down, back they went to Penredding again, slower now, for the snow was getting deep, and assembled once more in Mr. Elliot's study, where Buller was warned against criminating himself, and then allowed to speak. He had been out that night, but in a contrary direction, skating; no one had seen him, and he had no witnesses.

"There is hardly any case," said Mr. Elliot. "The boy owns that he was out the night of the assault, and the gamekeeper swears he was struggling with a boy, whom he thinks was rather bigger. But there are no marks of any struggle having taken place upon the lad. There may be reason for suspicion, but nothing more."

"Exactly; and I do not ask for a committal, but only for a remand, to give the police an opportunity of collecting further evidence," said Lord Woodruff.

"And I do not oppose the remand," said Dr. Jolliffe. "I am perfectly convinced of the boy's complete innocence; but in his interest I should like the matter to be gone into further, now the accusation has once been made."

"Very good; this day week, then. And I will take your bail for his appearance, Dr. Jolliffe."

And it being so arranged, everybody went home through the snow; and the police took up a wrong scent altogether, that, namely, of the gang that had been taking game in another part of the preserves earlier in the night, and to which it was somewhat naturally supposed the other two belonged. And one of them was traced, and a reward, together with impunity, was offered to him if he would turn queen's evidence, and say who had struck down the keeper. But the man, of course, could tell nothing about it.

As for Tom Buller, he went back to his lessons as usual, and was a hero. It was something novel to have a fellow out of prison on bail at Weston, and the boys racked their brains for some evidence in his favour. His flogging was put off *sine die*, for the doctor felt it unjust to deal with his case scholastically while the question of his punishment by the laws of the country was still pending. The only boy who thought of anything practical was Smith, "Old Algebra," as they called him. He went up privately to Mr. Rabbits one day and said, "I beg your pardon, sir, but might I speak to you for a moment?"

"Certainly, Smith," said Mr. Rabbits; "what is it?"

"When you saw Buller getting in at the window by the light of your magnesium wire, did you notice his skates?"

"Bless me!" cried Mr. Rabbits; "now you mention it, I think—nay, I am sure I did. They were hanging round his neck. To be sure; why, that tends to corroborate his assertion that he went skating."

"Will it not be enough to clear him, sir?"

"Well, not quite, I fear. You see, they may say that he might have started to go skating, and met with this poacher, and gone off with him out of curiosity. But still it is worth something, and I shall make a point of appearing before the magistrate and giving evidence on the point. It was a very good idea of yours—very."

When the snow ceased, the boys took brooms with them to the gravel pits and cleared a space, which grew larger every time they went to skate on it, some of the hangers-on of the school helping forward the work for what coppers and sixpences they could pick up. But they were lazy, loafing dogs, and the boys did most of it for themselves. Buller did not go to the ice any more, however; though not expressly forbidden, he thought the doctor would not like it; it would

look as if he did not take his position seriously
enough. It was for the sake of skating that he
had broken out at night and got into this scrape,
and so now he would deny himself.

The week passed, and Buller again went over
with Dr. Jolliffe to Mr. Elliot's house at Penredding, Mr. Rabbits this time accompanying him.
The frost still held, and the boys went skating.

I have said that there was no recognized system
of fagging at Weston; yet, when a fellow in the
head-master's class told a boy in the lowest form
to do anything, why, it so happened that he
generally did it. So, when Crawley observed:
" There's a beautiful bit of smooth ice under here.
I say, you two, Penryhn and Simmonds, suppose you take those brooms and clear a bit
of it."

Penryhn and Simmonds acted on the suggestion.
After clearing some twenty square yards of beautiful black ice, Simmonds turned up something
hard, which he picked up and invoked Jupiter.

" What is it?" asked Penryhn.

" Findings, keepings," responded Simmonds.

" Let's look," said Penryhn. " Why, that is
Buller's knife!"

"Ah, ah! how do you know that?"

" Why, it has a punch in it; he lent it me to

punch a hole in my strap when we got home from skating one day. It has his name engraved upon it somewhere; there it is, look, on that plate— 'T. Buller.'"

"Like my luck!" sighed Simmonds; "I never found anything yet but what it belonged to some other fellow."

"What was that you said, Penryhn, about Buller lending you his knife?" asked Crawley, who was cutting threes on the new bit of ice. "What day was it?"

"The day before the snow; yesterday week, that was."

"What time?"

"In the evening, just before supper, when I was cleaning up my skates for next day. By Jove! I see what you are driving at. Buller has not been any day since, so he must have dropped it when he came that night."

"Of course. Now, you and Simmonds run back to school, find Cookson, who is senior master now the doctor's out, ask leave to go over to Penredding, and cut there as hard as you can split."

The pair were off before he could finish his sentence.

The party assembled in Mr. Elliot's library was the same as on the week previously, with the addition of a detective, who had detected nothing, and Mr. Rabbits, who now testified that he saw skates hanging round Buller's neck when he was getting in at the window. The question was concerning a further remand, for the magistrate firmly refused to commit the boy for trial on the evidence before them. "I grant that it is suspicious; he was out late at night when he had no business to be, and that same night a Weston boy was, almost to a certainty, seized by Bradley in the coppice. But if one boy could get out another might, and now it is proved that this one had his skates with him at the time. No jury would convict on such evidence." He did not even like granting a remand, but neither did he like to stand out too strongly against the wishes of Lord Woodruff.

At this juncture voices were heard outside, and presently a constable opened the door and said that two young gentlemen from Weston had something to say.

"Found the real culprit, perhaps," muttered Lord Woodruff.

"Bring them in," said the magistrate, and Simmonds and Penryhn entered, hot, excited, and still panting for breath.

"Please, sir, we have leave from Mr. Cookson, and I have found Tom Bowling—I mean Buller's knife," said the former, addressing Dr. Jolliffe, who waved his hand towards Mr. Elliot in silence, and frowned.

"Wait a bit, my lad, do not be flurried," said the magistrate; "stand there. Let him be sworn," he added to the clerk. And Simmonds took his first legitimate oath.

Then he told the simple story which we know. And when he had done Penryhn kissed the book in his turn and completed the chain of evidence. It was really quite sufficiently clear, that unless yet another boy had got out, and gone skating on the gravel pits that night, taking Buller's knife with him and losing it, that he himself had been there as he said; and therefore that he was not in the coppice, two miles on the other side of Weston. Lord Woodruff himself was convinced, and Buller was at once discharged, everybody shaking hands with him.

"And, Buller," said Dr. Jolliffe as they left the house, "as I hope that the anxiety you have been subjected to by your own unlawful action will prove sufficient punishment, I shall not take any further notice of your breaking out that night. Let it be a lesson to you, that you cannot engage in what is unlawful without assuming something which is common to *all* criminals, and running the risk of being mixed up with them." Which was a beautifully mild preachee to take the place of floggee.

Tom Bowling received quite an ovation next day, and did not know what to do with his popularity. He was ready enough to skate now, but a thaw came, and there was no other chance afforded that term.

CHAPTER XII.

A HOLIDAY INVITATION.

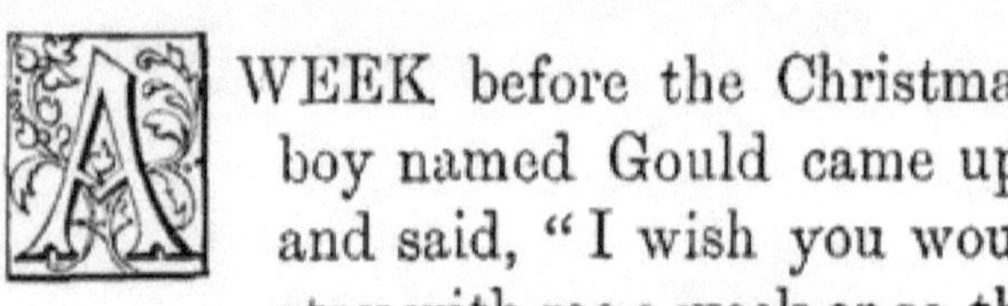

WEEK before the Christmas holidays a boy named Gould came up to Crawley and said, "I wish you would come and stay with me a week or so this Christmas at my father's place in Suffolk, Nugget Towers. The best of the shooting is over, the partridges being very wild by now, and it is not a pheasant country, as there are no woods to speak of. But there are a good many snipe down towards the river, so you had better bring your gun. Besides we will have a day's partridge driving, for there are plenty, if you could only get at them. And there is a pack of fox-hounds that meets about ten miles off once a week at least, and some harriers close by. I generally go out with the harriers. We can give you a mount; you do not ride above twelve stone I should say, do you?"

"No, I should think not, but I have not been

weighed lately," replied Crawley. "You are very kind, I am sure, but does your father know? Perhaps he has made arrangements to fill his house."

"Oh no! it is all right. My father does not bother his head about such things; he is perpetually going to London, and thinking of business. But my mother and sisters want you to come, and have told me to ask you."

"I am much obliged to them, they are very good. And I should like it very much," said Crawley, somewhat more hesitatingly than it was his wont to speak.

For this invitation was rather a hot coal on his head. Gould had courted his acquaintance and he had rather snubbed him, not liking him particularly. He was rich, which mattered to nobody, but he gave himself airs on the strength of it, and that did. There are few things more irritating than to hear anyone perpetually bragging of his money, and if you happen to be poor yourself I do not think that it helps you to sit and listen more patiently. And then Gould was an injudicious flatterer; he made the flattered fellow uncomfortable. It is a nice thing, flattery, and causes one to feel good all over, if it is delicately applied with a camel's-hair brush, as it were. But Gould laid it on with a trowel. He only

courted success; if anyone were down he would
be the first to spurn him.

Now, Crawley was undoubtedly the boy held
in greatest estimation in the school: captain and
treasurer of the cricket and football clubs, good-
looking, pleasant in manners, open, generous,
clever at lessons, he was a special favourite with
masters and boys, and therefore Gould burnt his
incense before him. For to be Crawley's chum
was to gain a certain amount of consideration in
the school, and Gould did not mind shining with
a reflected light. He was not like Saurin in that
respect, whose egotism saved him at least from
being a toad-eater. Gould was vain enough, but
his vanity was of a different kind. But hitherto
all his efforts had been in vain, and Crawley had
rather snubbed him. This had not prevented
Gould from talking about him, exaggerating his
merits, and bragging about his intimacy with him
at home. It was always "my friend Crawley
and I" did this, that, and the other. So that
Mrs. Gould wrote to him one day asking whether
he would not like his inseparable to come and
stay with him during the holidays; and Clarissa
Gould added a postscript to the effect that as he
was so clever he would be of great use to them
in their private theatricals.

Crawley was one boy amongst a rather large

family of girls; the father was dead, and the
mother, though able to live in ordinary comfort,
was far from rich. She could not indulge in
carriages and horses, or men-servants, for example,
and she lived near London for the sake of her
daughters' education. So that Crawley had never
had an opportunity of gaining proficiency in those
sports which cannot be indulged in without a
good deal of expenditure, and he looked upon
hunting and shooting as sublime delights far out
of his reach at present, though perhaps he might
attain to them by working very hard, some day.
His ambition was to enter the army, not that he
thought drill any particular fun, or desired the
destruction of his fellow-creatures, or ever indulged in dreams of medals, bars, triumphal
arches, and the thanks of parliament, but simply
because he might get to India, stick pigs, and
shoot tigers. Shooting! hunting! Gould's words
made his nerves tingle from head to foot with
excitement. And he had thought the fellow who
now offered him a taste of such pleasures a muff,
a bore, a sycophant, and done his best to avoid
him! How wrong it is to have prejudices!

"Well, then, when will you come?" asked
Gould.

"As soon as it is convenient to have me after
Christmas," replied Crawley. "I must spend the

Christmas week at home, you know; but then I am free. I should tell you, though, that I cannot shoot or ride a little bit. I have never had any practice, and you will find me an awful duffer."

"All right; fellows always say that."

"Yes, I know they do sometimes, in mock modesty. But in my case it's a fact, and I warn you, that I may not spoil your fun."

"My dear fellow," said Gould, "you could not do that unless your want of skill were catching. I should be glad if I could put you up to a wrinkle or two."

"On those terms, then, I shall be very glad to come."

"That is all right."

What a happy stroke for Gould! he had come to call Crawley "my dear fellow" already.

The idea of his new friend putting him up to a "wrinkle or two" rather tickled Crawley. Gould was so poor a performer at cricket, fives, lawn-tennis, football — everything which required a ready hand, a quick eye, and firm nerves—that Crawley could not imagine his beating him even with the advantage of previous knowledge. Yet he had not exaggerated his own deficiencies. Bring his gun, indeed! The only gun he had to bring was a single-barrelled muzzle-loader which had belonged to his father. With this he had

shot water-rats, sparrows, and, on one occasion
when they were very numerous, fieldfares; but
not flying—he had never attempted that. No; he
had stalked his small bird till he got within thirty
yards of the bough where it was perched, and taken
a steady pot-shot. As for riding, when a very
little boy during his father's lifetime he had had a
pony; and two or three times since, when staying
at watering-places in the summer, he had mounted
a hired hack. So that his ideas of sport were
gathered entirely from books and pictures, to
which, when they treated of that subject, he was
devotedly attached. What happy hours he had
spent poring over *Jorrock's Hunts, Mr. Sponge's
Sporting Tour*, and the works of the *Old She-
karry!* When he went to a picture-gallery he was
listless until he came upon some representation of
moving adventure by flood or field, and then the
rest of the party could hardly drag him away.
He had a little collection of coloured prints in his
room at home, gathered at various times, and
highly esteemed by him, which conveyed a somewhat exaggerated idea of equine powers. For in
one a horse was clearing a stream about the width
of the Thames at Reading, and in another an
animal of probably the same breed was flying a
solid stone wall quite ten feet high. Now he was
to have a little taste of these often-dreamed-of

joys, and the idea absorbed his thoughts and made him restless at night.

To do him justice, he did not think about it on first meeting his mother and sisters when he went home; but on the second day of his return the invitation and all it promised came back to him, and he broached the matter to Mrs. Crawley at breakfast-time. "Please, Mother, I have had an invitation to spend a week with a school-fellow after Christmas."

"Oh, and who is he?" asked Mrs. Crawley.

"A chap named Gould; they are awfully rich people—just the sort I ought to know, you know. They live in Suffolk at a place called Nugget Towers."

"And what sort of boy is he? Because, of course, Vincent, we must ask him here in the summer in return."

"Well, he is always very civil to me, and I don't know any harm of him; but he is not good at games and that, and not much fun to talk to— so I have never been quite so thick with him as he wished. That makes it all the more civil of him. He must have talked about me at home, for his mother sent the invitation."

"Well, Vincent, I am glad you spoke of it at once, for we must make haste to look over your linen, which generally comes home in a terrible state. You had better go to-day to the tailor and get measured for your dress clothes; but you were to have had them for Christmas any way, so that will be nothing extra."

For Crawley, it must be mentioned, had arrived at an age and height when a tail-coat was a necessary garment if he went anywhere of an evening.

"No, Mother," he said, "except a pair of porpoise-hide boots and some leggings; and could I have a gun, do you think? There will be some shooting, you know."

"A gun, Vincent! Will not the one you have already do?"

"Oh, no, Mother—it is so old and out of date, I should be laughed at. I might just as well take an arquebus or a cross-bow."

"Is not a gun a very expensive thing?"

"Why, you may make it so, of course; but I don't want that. I have been studying the *Field*, and I can get a good central-fire breech-loader for £10."

"Ten pounds is a good deal," said Mrs. Crawley thoughtfully; "but I suppose you must have a gun if you want one. Only remember, Vincent, that I am not rich, and your education and other expenses are very heavy. And there are your sisters to be thought of—what with their dresses and their music, drawing and dancing, I have to be very careful."

"Oh, of course, Mother," said Crawley, going round and kissing her; "what a dear you are!"

And his heart smote him as he thought of certain "ticks" he owed at school, and had not yet had the courage to confess to. For Vincent Crawley, though he had many good qualities, was by no means perfect. He was rather spoiled by indulgence at home and popularity at school, and thought a good deal too much of himself for one thing, and for another he was inclined to be thoughtless and extravagant in money matters. It is excellent to be generous with money which is absolutely our own; but to seek to get the credit for generosity at other people's expense is quite another, and not at all an admirable thing. Crawley knew this in theory, but practically, if he wanted anything and could get it, he had it; and if a friend had a longing for ices, strawberry mess, oyster-patties, or any other school luxury, he would treat him, running up a score if he had not the cash in his pocket to pay with. And if there was generosity in this impulse, I fear that there was ostentation too. It added to his popularity, and popularity had become as the air he breathed. *For the only real test of generosity is self-denial.* If you go without something you really want in order to oblige someone else, that is genuine, admirable, and somewhat rare. But if you have everything you want and forego nothing whatever by conferring a favour, you may show good nature, careless indifference to the value of money, or a pleasant sense of patronage, but not necessarily true generosity. That *may* be the spirit which dictates your conduct, but the act does not prove it.

Now, in Crawley's case, his mother was the only one who had to exercise self-denial. But he never thought of that. He prided himself on being a very generous fellow, and so he was by nature, but not so much so as he took credit for, and he was growing more selfish than otherwise, which was a pity. He went up to London, and was measured for his dress clothes, and got his boots and gaiters, and then sought out and found the gun-shop, mentioned in the *Field,* and instead of pretending to be knowing about firearms, wisely told the shopman why he came to him, and that he trusted him entirely, being quite unable to judge for himself, which made the man take particular pains to select him a good one, and show him how to judge if the stock suited him; namely, by fixing his eyes on an object, and bringing the gun sharply up to his shoulder. Then closing the left eye, and looking along the barrel with the right, to see whether the sight was on the object. If he had to raise or lower the muzzle to obtain that result, it was obvious that it did not come up right for him. At length he got one which suited him exactly, and he was shown the mechanism by which the breeches were opened and closed, and learned how to take it to pieces, put it together again, clean it, and oil it.

Finally he bought it, together with a hundred cartridges, fifty being loaded with snipe-shot, and fifty with number five; all on the gunmaker's recommendation, to whom he explained the kind of shooting he expected to have. He would not let it be sent home for him, but took it off himself.

"You only hold it straight, sir, and I'll guarantee the gun will kill well enough," said the maker as he left.

What a charm there is in a new bat, a new gun, a new fly-rod, a new racket; how one longs for an opportunity to try it! Really it is often a consolation to me to think that very rich people lose all that. When everything is so easily obtained, nothing is of any value. Crawley at any-rate was delighted with his new possession. He took it to pieces and put it together again for the benefit of every member of the family, besides a good many times for his own private delectation, and practised aiming drill and position drill by the hour together, without knowing that there were any such military exercises.

The frost set in again, however, a week before Christmas, and when the ice bore, he had to leave his new toy alone, for besides practising himself, his sisters required tuition in the art of skating. And you must not think that he found the time hang heavy to the day of his departure; he was too fresh home, and of too genial a disposition for that, besides which it was Christmas time. But he did look forward with pleasurable excitement to his visit, for all that.

The day came at length, and he started for Barnsbury, snugly ensconsed in a first-class carriage, with wraps, and comic papers, and a story by Manville Fenn with a thrilling picture on the cover, and his beloved gun in the rack over his head. His mother had suggested travelling second-class, but he durst not, for fear someone should meet him at the station. He was right in that expectation, for when the train stopped at Barnsbury he saw Gould and a man in livery waiting for him on the platform.

"All right! how are you, old fellow?" said Gould, shaking him by the hand. "How good of you to come! No hunting in such a frost as this, so I thought I would drive over myself."

Crawley said something civil, and the groom touched his hat and asked what luggage he had, taking his gun-case from him as he spoke.

"It will be brought after us in the tax-cart," said Gould, "which has come over too. I hate a lot of luggage in the trap I am driving, don't you? Leave it to William and come along; it will be all right;" and he led the way out of the station, where there was a dog-cart with another liveried servant on the seat, and a handsome nag in the shafts, waiting at the door.

The man jumped down and touched his hat; Crawley got in; Gould gathered up the reins, sat beside him, and started, the man springing up behind as they moved off, and balancing himself, with folded arms, as smart and natty as you please.

Crawley wondered more and more that he had never perceived any superiority in Gould; surely he must be very blind.

"It is only half-an-hour's drive, behind an animal like this," said his new friend. "The frost is giving, so we may have a run with the harriers in a few days. In the meantime there are a good many snipe. We will have a crack at them to-morrow morning, if you like."

"I should like very much," replied Crawley.

The country they were driving through was not very picturesque, as it wanted wood, a strange

want for Suffolk; but they soon came to a lodge
with a gate, opened for them by a curtseying
woman, and admitting them to a park where
there were trees, and fine ones, though standing
about by themselves, not grouped together.
They spun along through this up to a large white
house with a colonnade in front, and a terrace,
with urns for flowers and statues all along it,
looking bare and cheerless enough at this time of
year. But the hall made amends when they
entered it, for it was warm, luxurious, and bright
enough for a sitting-room. Two footmen in
plush and with slightly powdered hair inhabited
it, and one of them helped Crawley to get rid of
his wraps, and then Gould led the way to the
drawing-room, where Mrs. Gould and three
daughters were drinking tea and eating muffins
and things, for fear they should have too good
appetites for dinner, I suppose, and introduced
him.

Crawley shook several hands and accepted a
cup of tea, and sat down on a very low and very
soft seat, which he could have passed the night
in luxuriously if beds had run short, and felt as
awkward as you please. He always was shy in
ladies' society. Not in that of his sisters, of
course; he patronized them and made them fag
for him. It was certainly their own fault if they

did not like it, for they had taught him. But they did like it, he being one of his sort, and not often at home, and in return he waltzed with them, which was a bore, and gave them easy service at lawn tennis, which made him slow, and was generally an amiable young Turk.

But the Misses Gould did not look like being fagged, rather the reverse. They were all grown up, at least to look at, though one was not yet "out." Clarissa, the next, a girl of eighteen, came and sat down by him and talked to him, for which he felt very grateful, for he was beginning to wish the floor to open and let him through. At first, indeed, she talked of things he knew nothing about: balls, and levees, and the four-in-hand club, and the Orleans. But finding the service was too severe, and he could not send the ball back, she asked if he was fond of the theatre, and as he was, very, and had been to one a few nights before, he became more like himself, and showed some animation in his description of the piece he had seen, and the performers.

At this juncture a quiet-looking man out of livery came softly into the room, and asked him deferentially for his keys, as his luggage had arrived. Seizing the idea that he proposed to unpack for him, an operation he disliked, he gladly gave them up, wondering whether these rich people ever did anything for themselves at all.

"I see that you are great upon acting," said Miss Clarissa when the valet was gone, "and I am so glad! For we are getting up some private theatricals; you will take a part?"

"Why," said Crawley in some dismay, "I never yet tried to act myself; I am afraid I should spoil everything."

"Oh no! we have heard all about you from my brother, you know; you have a good memory, have you not?"

"I believe so; I have never found much difficulty in learning by heart."

"That is one good thing to begin with; we will soon see if you can act at all. Some of our friends are coming over to-morrow for rehearsal. We have agreed to try *St. Cupid, or Dorothy's Fortune*, and we want a 'Bellefleur.' You will take the part, will you not? I am to be 'Dorothy Budd.' You will not have so very much to do. Do you know the play?"

"No, unfortunately, and I—" Crawley began, meaning to back out; but Miss Clarissa cut him short.

"No matter," she said, "I will fetch you a copy," and she got up and returned presently with a little book. "You had better read it all through, and mark your parts with the tags. The tags, you know, are the last sentences of the speaker before you, to which you have to reply. You can learn some while you are dressing for dinner; that is a capital time. And I will give you a hint or two this evening in the billiard-room. You don't mind?"

What could Crawley say? He *did* mind, not bargaining for learning lessons in the holidays; but he could not show himself so uncivil a boor as to refuse. So he promised to do his best, and when the gong sounded, took his little book up into the bed-room with him.

CHAPTER XIII.

CRAWLEY IS TAKEN DOWN THREE PEGS.

"GOOD gracious!" A large fire was burning in the grate; an easy-chair was drawn up on one side of it; over the back of an ordinary one opposite a clean shirt was warming itself, with the studs inserted in the front and the wristbands. On the bed the dress clothes were neatly laid out; the patent-leather boots stood at attention on the hearth-rug; hot water steamed from a japanned jug on the wash-hand stand; two wax candles lit up the dressing-table; two more stood on another near the fire, which had also writing materials on it. The room could not have been prepared for a duchess, because a duchess would not wear a black coat and trousers; and besides, they were certainly *his* clothes.

Dressing took Crawley about ten minutes, and he had an hour for the operation. So he looked

hurriedly through the play, and marked the parts
allotted to Ensign Bellefleur. It did not seem
very much, so he felt a little encouraged, and
taking Miss Clarissa's advice, set the book open
on the table and began learning what he would
have to say while going on with his toilet. He
had a really surprisingly retentive memory, and
picked up a good bit even in that little time.

He found Mr. Gould in the drawing-room when
he went down, and the old gentleman asked him
after his progress in study, and what profession
he intended to adopt, in a pompous and conde-
scending way; but it was only a few sentences,
for there were other gentlemen there, who came
up and button-holed him seriously, and with
whom he seemed to hold portentous conversation,
politics, perhaps, or shares, or something of that
kind. Then the ladies assembled, and the second
gong boomed, and the people paired off. Crawley
timidly offered his arm to Miss Clarissa, rather
fearing he was doing wrong, and ought to go to
someone else. But she took it all right; and he
quoted from the play he had been studying:

"'Here we escape then. Come, cousin! nay,
your lips were set for pearls and diamonds, and
I'll not lose the promised treasure.'"

"'Well, good counsel is a gem,'" the young
lady responded smartly. "'But, George, I fear

me you'll never carry the jewel in your ears.'
The quotation is not apt, though, for you evidently have carried my good counsel in your ears, and been learning your part already. How good of you!"

Here was a chance for Crawley to say something pretty; but he could not think of what it should be till afterwards.

If the ladies' society was a little thrown away upon him he appreciated the dinner, which was ·by far the most luxurious meal he had ever seen in his life. A table-d'hote at Scarborough had hitherto been his beau ideal of a feed, but that was not in the race with the Gould banquet. And the champagne; on the few occasions when he had had a chance of tasting that wine, he had got all he could and wanted more. But now his only care was not to take too much of it, lest it should get into his head.

"Are you studying your part?" asked his neighbour, for he had been silent for some time.

"No," he replied; "I was thinking that if your brother lives like this every day, he must find the fare rather unpalatable when he goes back to Weston."

"I believe he does," said Miss Clarissa laughing. "At least he writes home grumbling letters enough, and we have to send him hampers of good things

—Perigord pies and that. Don't stop longer than you like," she added as the ladies rose. "Papa will go on talking about stupid things all night."

And shortly afterwards young Gould, who had taken his sister's place when she went, proposed that they should go to the billiard-room and knock the balls about. So they went and made a four-handed game with two of the girls. And then Miss Clarissa read over the scenes in which Crawley had to take part with her, and made him repeat what he had learned, with appropriate action. And he got partially over his shyness, and spent rather a pleasant evening, thanks, a little bit, I fancy, to a little vanity. His friend came to have a chat with him after they had gone up to their rooms, and when he left Crawley could not help thinking what a pity it was that his sister Clarissa had not been the boy and he the girl. She was such a much better sort of fellow for a friend; had more go, and was heartier. Before he finally turned in he read the part of Ensign Belle-fleur over again, for he felt too much excited by the novelty of everything to sleep, if he went to bed. At last, however, reading the same words over repeatedly quieted his nerves, and he slept soundly till morning.

"You are still inclined to have a try for the snipe?" asked Gould at breakfast. "It is still thawing, and the ground will be very sloshy; I hope you have got thick boots."

"Yes, and if I hadn't I do not mind a little wet," replied Crawley. "But I can't find my gun anywhere."

"Oh, that is all right in the gun-room."

This was another new idea to Crawley, who previously thought that it was only ships in Her Majesty's navy, and not houses, that had gun-rooms. They visited it presently, and Crawley found his property taken out of its case, put together, and standing side by side with others in a glass cupboard. He took it down and left the house with his companion. On the terrace they found a keeper with the dogs, and started off for the marshy ground by the river.

"Put a few cartridges loose in your pocket," said Gould. "William will carry the rest."

The low-lying lands were intersected by deep trenches, which divided them into fields just as hedges would. These were now frozen over, but the ice was melting fast, and water stood on the top. Along them walked the two gunners, William the keeper following with Scamp, the retriever, in a leash; for Scamp would hunt about and put everything up far out of range.

"Look out, Crawley!" cried Gould, as a snipe flushed in front of him.

He would not have known it was a snipe unless Gould had told him, as it was the first he had ever seen alive. He tried to take aim at it, shutting the left eye as if he were shooting at a target with a rifle, which caused him to twiddle his gun about as if he were letting off a squib, for the bird darted about as though on purpose to dodge him. So he pulled one trigger, and then, quite by accident, for he did not know how to find it in his flurry, the other, and I don't suppose went within two yards of the snipe with either barrel. With a steadier flight, having now got well on the wing, it sailed within reach of Gould, who knocked it over.

"Wiped your eye, old fellow!" he cried triumphantly as Scamp came back with the bird in his mouth.

"Yes; I told you I was a duffer," replied Crawley, who took note that the best way was to wait for the bird to have done his zigzagging. So he steadied himself, and the next chance he had he did wait. But not a bit could he cover the bird with that little knob of a sight, and when the smoke cleared away he saw it careering like a kite with too light a tail in the distance. Gould also missed twice, and then shot one the moment it was off the ground, before the erratic course commenced.

"That looks the easiest dodge," thought Crawley, and the next shot he had he tried it with the first barrel, missed, waited till the snipe was flying more steadily and gave it the second barrel, missed again. He got quite hot, and felt sure the keeper was laughing at him, but that official only said: "I'd put in a cartridge with bigger shot now; there's some duck, I think, in yon bit of rushes by the river."

They did as he advised, and they walked down to the spot. In went the spaniels, and out came a fine mallard, ten yards in front of Crawley, and sailing away from him as steady as a ship. He could cover this large evenly-flying mark as easily as if it were on a perch nearly, and when he pulled trigger the duck stopped in his flight, and fell with a heavy splash in the river, into which Scamp plunged as if it were midsummer, and presently brought the duck to land. Crawley felt the elation which always accompanies the first successful shot at a bird on the wing; at any-rate he had killed something, and might do well yet when the strangeness wore off.

He had another chance at a duck a little while afterwards, but this time the bird flew across and not straight away from him, and as he held his gun still at the moment he got the sight on the duck and fired, of course, since the duck had not the politeness to stop too, the charge went about two yards behind it.

"I beg your pardon, sir," said William, "but if you takes aim like that you will never hit 'em; 'tain't possible. You must forget all about your gun, and only look at the bird, and pull the trigger the moment you gets a full sight of him. The gun will follow your eye of itself, natural."

"I know I ought to keep both eyes open," said Crawley, "but I forget."

"Well, that is best, to my thinking, though I have known some good shots too who always shut the left eye. But whether or no the chiefest thing is not to see that sight on your gun when you shoot, but only to look at the bird."

They went on to another snipe patch, and soon Crawley missed again.

"Never mind, sir," said William, "it's a knack, snipe shooting is, and no one can catch it without practice. I've seen good partridge, aye, and rabbit shots, miss 'em time after time, and I've knowed good snipe shots poor at anything else too."

At last, by trying to follow the keeper's directions, Crawley did hit a snipe as it was flushed, but it was his only one. They were much more plentiful than usual in that part, and lay like stones, so that they had plenty of shooting, and William groaned in spirit over the opportunity of sport that had been wasted on two boys. What a tip Sir Harry would have given him in his delight if he had come out with him on such a day!

Thirty-five cartridges had Crawley burned when they turned homewards in the afternoon, and the result was one duck, one snipe; if he had possessed a tail, how closely it would have been tucked between his legs! He hardly dared look the animals who had those appendages in the face; how they must have despised him! Gould, who was a bad shot, had bagged five couple, and patronized him insufferably. When they got home he found a warm foot-bath ready in his room, which was a most refreshing luxury, and having made himself presentable he went down to the drawing-room, where the neighbours who were going to act in the forthcoming play were assembled at afternoon tea preparatory to the rehearsal. And presently they adjourned to the library and went through the play, a certain Mr. Foljambe, to whom everybody paid implicit obedience, directing and instructing them.

Crawley knew his part, and paid attention to what he was told, and the great man considered that he would do, if he could only get over a certain shy awkwardness. And indeed it was a provoking thing to Clarissa Gould, that when they went through their scenes alone together he acted in a manner that really showed great promise, but if a third person were present he was not so good, and with every additional spectator the merit of his performance diminished. There was only one scene in which he managed completely to forget himself and become the person he represented, and that was where he crosses swords with the hero, and is disarmed. He could fence a little, and did not quite like playing at getting the worst of it when it was not certain that he ought to have done so; but still, the violent action, and the clash of steel helped him to get rid of that feeling that he was making a tomfool of himself which confused him when he had to make a lot of spoony speeches to the girl.

Mr. Foljambe encouraged him with the assurance that being dressed for the part would give him confidence; in a strange dress, a false moustache, and a painted face, he would not know himself in the glass, and would feel that the spectators did not entirely recognize him either. It was necessary to make the best of him, for there was no other Ensign Bellefleur available.

The men of the day before had taken their departure, and were succeeded by a more lively lot, for there was to be a partridge drive and a big lunch on the morrow, and most of those who were to take part in it slept at Nugget Towers that night. So, instead of shares and companies, Mr. Gould the father held forth upon agricultural prospects, the amount of game, and the immediate renewal of hunting, in consequence of the complete change in the weather.

"You ought to have had a good many snipe by the way, Gould," said one of the guests. "They are always found in those water meadows of yours at the end of a frost."

"My son and his young friend can tell you best about them," replied Mr. Gould. "I believe they have been out after them to-day."

"Ah! and what sport had you?" asked the inquirer, turning to young Gould.

"Oh, I got five couple."

"And your friend?"

"I only shot one," said Crawley with an uneasy laugh.

"Come, I say, Lionel," said Clarissa Gould to her brother, "I am not going to have my cousin Bellefleur treated in this manner. You are a nice sort of host to leave your guest the worst of the shooting."

"He had as many shots as I had," said young Gould, whose desire of self-glorification smothered any soupçon of good taste which he might have acquired, "only he missed them all."

"Indeed, yes," said Crawley, concealing his

sense of humiliation in the very best way; "why I fired two barrels at one snipe before Gould killed it for me. I am a perfect novice at all field sports."

"Ah!" observed the first inquirer, "I know I fired away a pound of lead before I touched a snipe when I first began. But what a lot of them there must have been if you killed five couple, Lionel."

"I do not think I should care for shooting if I were a man," said Clarissa to Crawley. "But hunting, now, I should be wild about. I hunt sometimes, but only with the harriers. Mama will not let me go out with the fox-hounds, and they meet so far off that I cannot fall in with them by accident, for there is no cover near here. But the harriers are to go out the day after to-morrow, if the frost does not return, and I am looking forwards to a good gallop. Are you fond of hunting?"

"I know that I should be," replied Crawley, "but I do not own a horse, and never have a chance of it."

"Oh, well, we will mount you; I think Daisy will be quite up to your weight, Sir Robert certainly would, but Daisy is the nicest to ride."

After dinner there was music, and Crawley was asked if he could sing. There was no backing out, for young Gould had bragged about his friend's voice, which was indeed a good one though untrained. But he only sang Tubal Cain, Simon the Cellarer, and one or two others of that sort, of which the music was not forthcoming. At last, however, Julia Gould, who was the pianist, found John Peel, which he knew, and he found himself standing by that young lady, confused and shame-faced, trying to make his voice master a great lump there seemed to be in his throat. To make it worse the hubbub of voices ceased at the first notes, though it had swelled the louder during previous performances. All the men began marking the time with heads and hands, and when the chorus came first one and then another joined in, and it ended in a full burst of sound, just as when Crawley sung it at school. This gave him confidence, and he sang the second and remaining verses with spirit, the choruses swelling louder and louder, and when he finished there was much hand-clapping. So at last he had a gleam of success, and Lionel Gould, who had been growing a little supercilious, returned partially to his old conciliatory manner.

Next day a large party sallied forth with their guns, and Crawley was placed under a high, thick hedge, and told to look out for partridges as they came over his head. Young Gould was some little distance on his left; and at about the same interval on his right Sir Harry Sykes, a neighbouring squire famous for his skill with the gun, had his station. Beaters had gone round a long way off to drive the birds towards them, and soon shots were heard to right and left; and then Crawley saw some dark specks coming towards his hedge, and prepared to raise his gun. But it was like a flash of lightning; they were over and away before he could bring his gun up. Gould had fired, indeed, though ineffectually, but Sir Harry had a brace. Three more appeared; this time Crawley fired his first barrel at them before they were within shot, and then turning round, gave them the second after they had got far out of it. More came; Gould got one, Sir Harry another; a brace, flying close together passed not directly over Crawley, but a little to his right; and Sir Harry having just fired and being unloaded, Crawley let fly at them, and by a lucky fluke they both came rushing to the ground, stone-dead.

"Good shot, boy!" cried Sir Harry. He had hardly spoken before more birds came directly towards him; Crawley watched; he shot one as it came on, and immediately, without turning round, raised his gun, head, and arms, till it seemed as if he would go over backwards, and fired again with equally deadly effect.

This second feat Crawley did not attempt to imitate, but a steady shot as they came on he did keep trying, and not entirely without success, for every now and then a partridge came tumbling nearly into his face. But Gould shot two to his one, and he did second worst of the party. However, it was such quick and wholesale work that individual prowess was taken little notice of. And then there was a long, hot luncheon, which some of the ladies came out to, and another drive a few miles off in the afternoon.

It was all very exciting, and Crawley found the day a great deal too short; but still he would have preferred the snipe-shooting, if he could only be alone with no one to see his misses. There seemed more sport in finding your game than in having it driven up to you.

When he went up to dress for dinner he found a hamper of game there, with a blank label attached, for him to put any address he liked. So he wrote his mother's; and when it arrived she gave him most unmerited credit for skill, forethought, and trouble-taking. The Goulds certainly did things in a princely way.

It rained softly all that night, clearing up about nine in the morning, when those who were going out with the harriers had been half-an-hour at breakfast—Miss Clarissa, who was one of them, taking that meal in her habit. Crawley could hardly eat for excitement. The moment the water for his tub had been brought he had jumped up, and, directly he was dressed, hurried to the stables to see the horse he was to ride.

"And which is it to be?" asked Miss Clarissa.

"Well, I meant to take your advice and Daisy; but the groom said she had a delicate mouth and required a light hand, which I cannot have, you know, for want of practice. And he said Sir Robert was the stronger animal and would stay better, though not so fast. So I fixed on Sir Robert."

"And he will carry you very well if you can hold him; Lionel can't."

"What can't I do?" asked young Gould across the table, with his mouth full of game-pie.

"Hold Sir Robert."

"Why, his mouth is a bit hard, but I can sit him anyhow."

"Oh, yes, he goes easy enough."

The horses were soon brought round, and they all—a party of five—went out. Miss Clarissa, the only lady, put her foot into Mr. Foljambe's proffered hand and vaulted lightly into the saddle. Crawley could mount without awkwardness; he had learned enough for that, and he knew what length of stirrup suited him, and could trot along

the road or canter over the grass without attracting attention; so all went well till they reached
Marley Farm, where the meet was. But directly
Sir Robert saw the hounds he got excited and
wanted a gallop—a thing the frost had debarred
him of for weeks. So he kicked up his heels and
shook his head, and capered about in a manner very
grateful to his own feelings, but most discompos-
ing to his rider, who was first on the pommel,
then on the crupper, then heeling over on the
near side, then on the off—though both sides
threatened to be off sides if these vagaries took a
more violent form.

When the hounds were turned into a field and
working, Sir Robert evidently thought: "Come!
I can't be standing still all day while those dawd-
ling dogs are bothering about after a hare; a
gallop I must have!" And he began to fight for
his head; and it took all Crawley's strength—
and he was a very muscular youngster—to hold
him. Sir Robert did get away half across the
field once and nearly demolished a hound, with
twenty voices halloing to Crawley to come back,
and the master using language which his god-
fathers and godmother never taught him, I am
certain. I can only quote the mildest of his
reproofs which was: "Go home to your nursery
and finish your pap, you young idiot, and don't

come endangering the lives of animals a thousand times more valuable than yourself!"

Poor Crawley, wild with shame and rage, managed to haul his horse round and get back to the others, when it did not improve his temper to see the broad grin on young Gould's face.

"Don't fight with your horse, youngster," said an old gentleman kindly. "The more you pull, the more he will pull too."

And Crawley loved that old gentleman, and would have adopted him for a father, or at least an uncle, on the spot, especially when he found his advice serviceable; for, loosing his reins when Sir Robert did stand still, and only checking him lightly when he tried to dart forward, kept him much quieter.

But would they never find that hare? Yes, at last there was a whimper, and another, and then a full burst, and away went the hounds, and the field after them, and, with one final kick up of his heels, Sir Robert got into his stride. Crawley forgot anger, vexation—everything but the rapture of the moment. The life of the scene, the contagious excitement of dogs, horses, and men, the rapid motion, it was even beyond what he had imagined. So across a field to a little broken hedge, which Sir Robert took in his stride without his rider feeling it. Then sharp to the right towards a bigger fence, with a ditch beyond; nothing for a girl to crane at, but having to be jumped. Crawley, straining his eyes after the hounds, and not sitting very tight, was thrown forward when the horse rose, and, when he alighted, lost his stirrup, reeled, and came over on to mother earth; and when he rose to his feet he had the mortification to see Sir Robert careering away in great delight, and he proceeded to plod through the heavy ground after him.

"Whatever made you tumble off? Sir Robert never swerved or stumbled!" cried Miss Clarissa as she swept by him. But his wounded vanity was hardly felt in the greater annoyance of being out of the hunt.

But the best of harriers is that you hardly ever *are* out of the hunt. The hare came round again; some good-natured man caught the horse and brought him back to the grateful Crawley, who remounted and soon fell in with the hounds at a check.

"I say, you know," said Mr. Foljambe, "if you get another fall I shall exert my authority as theatrical manager and send you home. I cannot have my Ensign Bellefleur break his neck when the part is not doubled."

"No!" said Miss Clarissa, "not before Wednesday."

Whimper, whimper; they hit it off and away again. Another fence with hurdles in it, and a knot of rustics looking on in delight. More cautious now, Crawley stuck his knees in and leaned back, and, when Sir Robert alighted, was still on, with both feet in the stirrups, but very much on the pommel, and not in an elegant attitude at all.

"Oh, look at he!" cried a boy with a turnip-chopper in one hand and a fork for dragging that root out in the other. "He be tailor."

"It's agwine to rai-ain, Mister Lunnoner!" added another smockfrock; "won't yer get inside and pull the winders up?"

Even the clodhoppers jeered him; and that confounded friend of his, Gould, was close beside and laughed, and would be sure to repeat what he heard. Never mind, it was glorious fun. He came off again later in the afternoon, but that was at a good big obstacle, which most of the field avoided, going round by a gate, and Sir Robert stumbled a bit on landing, which made an excuse. But this time the horse, who was not so fresh now, waited for him to get up again. He felt very stiff and sore when it was all over and they were riding home again; especially it seemed as if his lower garments were stuffed with nettles. As for his tumbles, the ground was very soft,

and he had not been kicked or trodden on, so
that when he had had a warm bath he was as
right as ninepence, only a little stiff.

Gould came to see after his welfare while he
was dressing, and hoped he was not hurt, and
expressed an opinion that he would learn to ride
in time, and was glad they had only gone out
with the jelly dogs instead of the foxhounds, or
his friend and guest would not have seen anything of the run. All which was trying, coming
from a fellow who had looked upon him as an
oracle, and to whom he had condescended. At
dinner, too, he was chaffed a little; but the hardest
rider in the county, who had condescended to go
out with the harriers to try a new horse, the fox-
hounds not meeting that day, and who was dining
with Mr. Gould afterwards, came to his rescue.
" Never mind them, lad," he said; " you went as
straight as a die. I saw you taking everything
as it came, never looking for a gap or a gate, and
it is not many of them can say the same."

This was Saturday, and Crawley was glad of a
day of rest when he got up next morning, he was
so stiff. On Monday preparations for the private
theatricals began in earnest. Dresses came down
from London, and were tried on and altered; the
large drawing-room was given up to the hands of
workmen, who fitted up a small stage at one end

of it, with sloping seats in front, that all the guests might see. Those who were to act were always going into corners and getting some one to hear them their parts, and there were rehearsals. It was all a great bore to Crawley, who would fain have spent the time in shooting or riding, of which he got but little, so exacting was Miss Clarissa; and he was to go home on the Thursday, the day after the entertainment.

As the time approached, too, he felt more and more uncomfortable; he had found out from young Gould that the whole thing had been got up by his sister Clarissa, who thought herself a very good actress, and wished to show off; and he could easily see that he would not have been asked to the house at all if it had not been for his school-fellow's talk about what a clever individual he was—able to do everything. Now, next to Sir Valentine May, no character in the comedy is so important for the display of Dorothy Budd's (Clarissa's) performance as Ensign Bellefleur; and the more clearly Crawley saw this, the more fervently did he wish that he was out of it. It was too late now, however, and as he got on very fairly in the rehearsals, he began to hope he should pull through somehow.

On Tuesday the house was filled with company, and he was asked to give up his room and go to

the top of the house, which, however, was no
trouble to him. His clothes of seventeen hundred
and fifteen were though, when the eventful evening came, and his wig, and the man who fitted it
and daubed his face. And yet, when all the
fidgeting was over, he wished that it had to
begin again, that he might have a further respite.

The play began, and during the first scene he
stood at the side envying the cool self-possession
of Captain Wingfield, who had the part of
"Valentine," and every one of whose speeches
was followed by laughter from the unseen audience. When the second scene opened Miss
Clarissa joined him, looking charming in her
old-world dress; they were to go on in company,
and he made a strenuous effort to pull himself
together. But when he found himself in the full
glare of the foot-lights, and looking before him
saw the mass of expectant faces which rose, rank
behind rank, half-way to the ceiling, his head
went round, his brain became confused, and his
first sentence was inaudible "Speak up!" said
Miss Clarissa in a loud whisper, and he uttered
"And have you no ambition?" in a louder key
indeed, but in trembling accents, and standing
more like a boy saying a lesson.

The audience cannot hiss in private theatricals,
but they could not help a suppressed titter, which

confused Crawley still more.   He forgot what he had to say, and looked appealingly to the prompter, who prompted rather too loudly.   Altogether the scene was spoilt, and Clarissa furious.

He did a little better in the second act, but not one quarter so well as he had in rehearsals, and was ready to punch his own head with vexation when the whole thing was over, and he had got rid of his costume and the messes on his face.

He went to bed instead of to supper, and next morning at breakfast no one alluded to the performance before him.   Soon afterwards he took his leave of all but Miss Clarissa, who kept out of his way, and Lionel Gould drove him to the station very sulkily, for his sister had vented her displeasure upon *him*.   And so they said an uncomfortable good-bye, and Crawley felt much relieved when he found himself alone in the train, with the humiliations of his visit behind him. They did not do him any harm, quite the contrary; he was made of better stuff than that. Of course he felt sore at his failures, when he was used to play first fiddle.   When the devil of conceit is cast out of us the throes are severe.   But by the time he got home Crawley was able to laugh at his own mishaps.   Perhaps Gould got the worst of it after all.   "*That* friend of yours an Admirable Crichton!" said his sister.   "A fine set you must be!"

CHAPTER XIV.

THE DESCENT OF AVERNUS.

A WORSE resident than Mr. Wobbler the pedestrian took up his abode at Slam's, and this was no other than his son, Josiah Slam, who had gone to London as the only field wide enough for his talents ten years before, and had only been occasionally heard of since. Now, however, he thought fit to pay his parents a visit, and did not appear to be in prosperous circumstances, though it is probable that he had money, or money's worth, or the prospect of it, for Slam was not the man to kill the fatted calf for a prodigal son, unless he saw the way to making a good profit out of the veal, the hoofs, and the skin.

Josiah was a young man of varied accomplishments, all of which were practised for the purpose of transferring other people's cash from their pockets to his own. He called himself a sportsman, and no doubt the operation alluded to was sport, to him. Arriving about Christmas time, when holiday making was general, he gleaned a little at the game of skittles, at which many of the agriculturists round about thought they were somewhat proficient; but cunning as he was he could not go on disguising his game for ever, and so directly he saw that the yokels were growing shy of playing with him, he gave it up. The Sunday pitch-and-toss and card assemblages were also a source of profit to him. Marriner thought he could cheat, and had indeed stolen money in that way from his companions, and there was nothing Josiah Slam liked better than dealing with a weaker member of his own fraternity. He allowed Marriner to cheat him a little, and pretended not to discover it; played at being vexed; drew him on, and fleeced him of his ill-gotten gains.

But it was apparent that he played too well at these amusements also, so then he showed them a game at which everybody might win, except himself. Where it was all chance, and skill could not interfere. Roulette, in short. The room in which Professor Wobbler had given his boxing lessons had a table fitted up in it, and on this table the wheel-of-fortune, with its black and red compartments, and its little ivory ball to rattle round and finally fall into one of them, was placed, with a cloth marked in compartments answering to those in the wheel for the gamblers to stake their money upon. This game proved very fascinating to the dissipated amongst the farmers' sons round about, and to some of the farmers too, and money which ought to have gone to buy stock, or for the rent, was lost at that table. Of course some of them won occasionally, and considerable sums, for them, too; that formed the fascination of it.

But the agricultural interest was depressed, and ready money not forthcoming to the extent Josiah Slam desired; so upper servants of the neighbouring gentry were admitted, under strong vows of secrecy, and more than one gamekeeper's and huntsman's family was short of coals and meat that winter, because the money to provide such necessaries was left on that satanic, innocent-looking table. Every night this gambling went on, and Josiah made a good deal of money by it, being prepared, however, to clear out of the neighbourhood at the first symptom of the police having caught scent of the affair.

Ready money was waning and business growing slack when the Weston boys came back from the Christmas holidays, and Josiah, who knew that some of them frequented his father's yard, saw a fine opportunity of augmenting his gains by setting his little ball rolling in the daytime for their especial benefit. The scheme was nearly stifled by its own success; on the very first occasion a boy won four pounds, and could not conceal the triumphant fact from two or three intimate friends, who each whispered it to two or three others, and the consequence was that on the next Saturday afternoon no fewer than thirty Westonians came to Slam's yard seeking admittance. This alarmed old Slam, who saw a speedy prospect of discovery, and of that hold upon him which the authorities had long been seeking, being afforded them, to the consequent break up of his establishment. Better small safe profits which should last, he thought, than a haul, which after all must be limited to the amount of the school-boys' pocket-money, and be shared with his son, and the stoppage of all his little sources of profit. Not to mention the prospect of legal punishment. So the thirty had to go away again grumbling, with their money in their pockets. *O fortunati, si sua bona norint!*

But small parties of the initiated were still admitted, amongst them, of course, Saurin and his shadow, Edwards. The latter, who, as was said in a former chapter, had a peculiar fondness for games of chance, was positively infatuated with this device of young Slam's. It interfered with his studies by day, and he dreamed of it by night, so much did it engross his thoughts. He was never easy unless staking his shillings on that table, and watching eagerly whether the little ball would drop into a red hole or a black one. Saurin did not take half the interest in it at first, the principal attraction for him lying in the illegality, and the tampering with what he had heard and read of as having been the ruin of so many thousands. And he thought what fools they must be. There were many ways in which he could well imagine anyone spending his last penny, but not over a toy like this. But one day he came away a winner of a couple of sovereigns, and there was something in seeing the shillings and half-crowns gathering into a pile before him which caused him to catch the sordid fever with which his friend was infected. Hitherto he had made his stakes carelessly, but now he took a deeper interest in the thing. Sometimes he had won a few shillings and Edwards had lost, and at other times it went the other way, but the winner's gains were never so great as the loser's losses, and it was evident that the difference must remain with the conductor of the game, Josiah Slam.

"Why, we have been practically playing against

each other for that rogue's benefit!" exclaimed Saurin, when he made this discovery. "In future we must always stake our money the same way." And this they did.

Then Saurin had another bright idea. It was an even chance each time whether red or black won, just the same as heads or tails in tossing, so it could not go on very long being one or the other in succession. Then, supposing they staked on red, and it turned up black several times, they had only to persevere with red and increase the stake and they must win their losses back, while if it was red several times they would have a clear gain.

This appeared to Edwards as a stroke of genius, and he was in a state of fever till they had an opportunity of putting it in practice. And it answered at first; but presently one colour, the wrong one, won so many times running that all their united capital went into Josiah's bank. They looked at one another in blank dismay; there was an end to their speculations for the rest of that term, and by the next Mr. Slam junior would have decamped from the paternal abode, for when the racing season commenced he flew at far higher game than the purses of rustics and school-boys.

"Can't come no more, can't yer?" said Josiah. "I'm sorry for that, though I expect I should be a loser, for you play well and knows a thing or two, you do. But it's the sport I care for more than the money, and I should have liked yer to have another chance. I know what I did once when I were in that fix; I just took and pawned my watch, and with the money I got on it I won back all I'd lost and more on the back of it, in a brace of shakes, and then took the ticker out again all comfortable."

"But there is no pawnbroker near here."

"No, in course not, and such a thing might not suit gents like you neither. Not but lords and markisses does it often; and if ever you really did want a pound or two very bad, for a short time, there's my father, as goes over to Cornchester perpetually, would pop anything light and small for yer, and bring yer back the money and ticket safe enough."

The hint took; old Slam was intrusted with Edwards' watch that evening, and shortly afterwards with Saurin's; and later on with all the pins and rings they possessed, though these were not worth much.

This may all sound accountable in Edwards, who was so weak and soft; but Saurin, though vicious, was no fool, and such excessively absurd conduct may appear to you inconsistent with his character. But that is because you do not know the rapidly enervating and at the same time fascinating mastery which gambling has on the mind of one who gives way to it. It is a sort of demoniacal possession; the kind-hearted, amiable man becomes hard and selfish, the generous man mean and grasping, the strong-minded superstitious under its influence. It may seem strange to enact laws to prevent people from risking their own money if they choose, but every civilized government has found it absolutely necessary to do so. For the losing gamester always thinks that with a little more money to risk he would certainly win all back again, and the thought maddens him so that he will not even shrink from crime to obtain it.

One day when the pair were penniless, and had no more means of raising money, young Slam generously offered them a loan, only requiring them to sign a paper acknowledging the transaction. To prevent their feeling themselves placed under an obligation he delicately allowed them to sign for more than they had received, a proposition which Saurin acceded to with alacrity. Edwards, though he also signed, did so with hesitation, and expressed fears about the safety of the transaction afterwards.

"Pooh!" said Saurin, "the I O U is mere waste paper; we are both under age, and can snap our fingers at him if he demands payment. Besides, we will pay him back the first time we win enough."

"But supposing we don't win enough? we have been very unlucky lately," objected Edwards.

" All the more reason why luck should change," replied Saurin. " But suppose it does not, all the money will have gone into the fellow's pocket, so we shall have repaid him in reality, don't you see?"

Edwards didn't quite. If you borrow a shilling of any one to gamble with, and lose the stake and pay him with the shilling you have borrowed from him, he does not exactly get what is due to him. However, Edwards made no reply; no doubt Saurin knew best.

Crawley lost a little of the estimation in which he had been held that term. It was extremely mean of Gould to gossip about his guest's discomfitures at Nugget Towers, but the temptation to glorify himself at the other's expense was too strong. He had plenty of pocket-money always, and rich men or rich boys are sure to have some one to listen to them with a certain amount of deference, and if Gould was not popular exactly, his hampers were.

"I had Crawley to stay with me at Christmas, you know," he said. " He's a good fellow; pity he's so awfully poor. He had never been in a decent house before, and was awfully astonished. He had what they call 'the keeper's gun,' a ten-pound thing; our head-keeper twigged it. Good gun enough, I daresay, but not what a gentleman has for himself. But he could not use it; worst shot I ever met, by Jove! I showed him a thing or two, and he began to improve by my hints. He is not above taking hints, I will say that for him; and his riding! Why, I thought from those prints in his room that he was ever such a swell; but I don't believe he was ever outside a horse before. Even the ploughmen laughed at him. 'Get inside and pull up the windows!' they called out."

And so he went on, somewhat exaggerating all Crawley's failures, not so much out of any ill-will as for self-glorification. You may know the pas-time of boring a hole through a chestnut, threading it on a string, and fighting it against other chest-nuts: if you hit on a very tough chestnut, and with it broke another one, it is, or used to be the rule that your chestnut counted all the victories of the one it split in addition to its own, of which a care-ful account was kept. So that if a chestnut was a fiver, and it beat a tenner, it became at one leap a fifteener. In something the same way Gould had an idea he might score by Crawley, who was thought so much of for his proficiency in many things. If he himself was so much richer, such a better rider and shot, it ought to be assumed that if he took the trouble he could also beat him at cricket, football, mathematics, German, and free-hand drawing. It was not very logical, and indeed he did not put the matter to himself so nakedly as that, but that was the sort of idea which influenced him nevertheless.

At the same time I fear that there may have been a little spite in his feelings too; he had been a good deal snubbed by his sister Clarissa for introducing a friend who had gone far to spoil her triumph in the play she had got up with such pains and forethought, and he much regretted having ever asked him. Gould's bragging would not have been much believed, only Crawley confirmed it. "Yes," he said, "I went to stay with Gould's people; very kind of them to ask me. They live in grand style; I thought I had got to Windsor Castle by mistake at first. I should have enjoyed it immensely if they had not made me act in private theatricals, which I hate, and I am afraid I came to utter grief over it. Took me out snipe-shooting; did you ever shoot at a snipe? bad bird to hit; Gould got some. I suppose one would pick up the knack of it in time. And, yes, we went out with the harriers; I had never sat a horse when he jumped anything before, and I came a couple of croppers. But it was great fun, and I did not hurt myself. Gould did not get a fall, oh no; he is used to it."

A good many were rather disgusted with Gould when he talked in the way he did, and Buller let him see it. "It's awfully bad form to ask a fellow to your house, and then boast that he can't do things that he never tried before, so well as you can," he blurted out.

"Oh, of course, we all know that Crawley is perfect in *your* eyes," sneered Gould.

"That's rot," said Buller elegantly; "but I do know this, that you might have practised anything you know, shooting, riding, anything, all your life, and if Crawley had a week's practice he would beat your head off at it; come, then, I'll bet you what you like."

"That is impossible to prove."

"No matter, it does not need proof; every fellow with eyes in his head must see it. But that's nothing. If you were ever so much better it would be just as mean to brag about it."

Crawley had no idea that Gould bore him any grudge, and being grateful to him for his invitation, sought to give him those opportunities of intimacy which he had evidently coveted before. But it was Gould now who drew back, somewhat

to the other's relief, for he could not bring himself
to care much about him.

Well, all this foolish talk of Gould's did have a
certain effect: a good many boys lost some faith
in their idol, and began to suspect that its feet
might be of clay. And then Crawley took to
reading very hard that term, for his time for trying to get into Woolwich was approaching, and
he was very anxious not to fail; and this made
him less sociable, which affected his popularity.
It did not interfere with his sports; he was as
energetic at football as ever, and took his usual
pains to make the boys pay up their subscriptions,
for he was secretary and treasurer. But that was
not exactly a genial duty, though everybody was
glad that somebody else would take the trouble.
And for the rest, he was now always working hard
or playing hard.

"Hulloa, Edwards!" he said one day about the
middle of term, "you have been very lazy about
your football lately; you promised to be good at
it, you know. It's a pity to give it up."

"But I have not," said Edwards. "I am going
in for it again now." And he meant it; for the
last penny of the loan had vanished, and he felt
the need of excitement and action of some
kind.

"That's right, old fellow," said Crawley. "Of

course you play for your house against ours in the match."

" I believe so."

"Come and have a game this afternoon," said Crawley, turning back after they had parted; for the pallid and careworn face of the other struck him, and he thought very likely a little exercise and bustle was just what he wanted, but that he felt listless, as one does sometimes, when one is glad afterwards if some one else will save us the trouble of making up our minds, and start us.

"No, thanks," replied Edwards, "I can't come to-day, I have something else I must do. But I shall practise regularly after to-day." And he went on his way to meet Saurin, and go with him to Slam's yard.

For a crisis had arrived in their affairs which assumed a most serious aspect. It was no longer a question of obtaining the means of continuing their gambling; they had awakened from that dream, and saw what dupes they had been. And indeed the Slams, father and son, found that their little game was being talked about in the neighbourhood too freely for safety, and had abruptly discontinued it. Josiah, indeed, was about to take his departure altogether, and in announcing that intention to Saurin and Edwards, demanded immediate payment of the money he had advanced them, in consideration of which they had jointly signed an acknowledgment for five pounds. They had, indeed, kept away from the yard when their money was all gone, but Josiah Slam was not to be balked in that manner. He went over to Weston, and accosted Saurin in the street.

"I cannot pay you just now; don't speak to me here, we shall be seen," said Saurin.

"What do I care for that?" replied Josiah. "If you don't come to me I'll come to you."

"I will come to the yard to-morrow afternoon, only do go away now," urged Saurin.

"You had better," said the man significantly. And so Saurin and Edwards were now on their way to the yard.

"Well, gents, have you got the money?" asked Josiah Slam, who admitted them. "I hope so, for I wants to be off, and I'm only a-waiting for that."

"No," replied Saurin, "we have not got it; it is not likely. We did not sign that paper until we had lost everything to you, and we shall not have any more till after Easter. Perhaps we may pay you then, though I don't consider we owe you anything really. You have won it all back, and a lot more besides."

"What's that to do with it?" cried young Slam.

"You had as good a chance of winning of me, hadn't yer?"

"No, of course not," replied Saurin. "I am not certain that we had any chance at all."

"What d'yer mean? yer——"

"Oh, don't bluster and try to bully," said Saurin. "I'm not afraid of you."

"Oh, you're not, ain't yer, my game chicken? but I have got your I O U."

"Much good may it do you! Why, we are under age, and it's of no value at all."

"And you call yerself a gentleman! Yah! But I'm not so green as yer think, my boy. Of course I knowed it warn't a legal dokiment. But it's proof enough for me. If you don't pay I shall take it to yer master, and see if he won't pay it for yer."

"Don't be a fool; you know very well he would not."

"No, I don't; at any rate I shall try it on."

"It would do you no good, I tell you."

"If not, it would do you two chaps harm, I know; why, you would get it pretty hot if yer master knowed yer had come here at all; and if he found you'd been playing cards on a Sunday, and roulette, and pawning yer watches and things, I'll bet a hundred it wouldn't make it better. Gents like you can allus get money somehow;

write to yer friends; it's only two pun ten apiece, and they won't stick at that to get you out of such a shindy as this will be.   This here's Thursday and I'm bound to go on Monday. If you don't bring them five pounds by then, I'll go to your master with that ere I O U in my hand on Monday morning as sure as I stand here. So now you know."

And with this ultimatum the rascal dismissed them. They walked slowly along the lane leading to Weston with hearts as heavy as could be, for indeed they were at their wits' end. If this fellow fulfilled his threat, and they had no doubt he would, it most certainly would result in expulsion for them both. To write home for more money was out of the question, for each had exhausted every conceivable excuse for doing so already, and any further application would only bring a letter to Dr. Jolliffe asking the reason for all this extravagance, instead of cash, and so precipitate the calamity rather than ward it off. A less shameful peccadillo might have been confessed, but this low-lived gambling, this association with a fellow like Josiah Slam, how could it be spoken of? Impossible! Well, but what was to be done? Anything, anything to stave off the immediate peril; but what? That thought haunted each of them all day and during a sleepless night, and when they met on the following morning each looked at the other to see if he could detect any gleam of hope in his face.

"Look here," said Saurin, "there is just a chance, not a good one, but still a chance. That fellow Gould always has heaps of money, and from all these stories of Crawley's visit to him at Christmas his people must be very rich. Now he is not a generous fellow, but he likes to show off. And if we went to him and told him all about it, and that we were dead certain to be expelled if we could not raise five pounds, do you not think he might lend it us till after Easter?"

"I am afraid he won't," replied Edwards, "but it is worth trying."

"You see, it would be something for him to brag about afterwards," continued Saurin. "It would make him look important and influential that he had got two fellows out of such a row, and was the only one in the school who could do it."

"It is worth trying at any rate," said Edwards. "Ask him this afternoon."

CHAPTER XV.

A CRIME.

ONCE every term the cricket and football committees assembled to transact business. They learned what funds were in hand, what subscriptions had been paid and what were in arrear, also the expenditure for balls, nets, goals, stumps, rolling the ground, and all other items. After which, rules were discussed, and arrangements for future matches made. It was part of the principle of the school that the boys should manage all these things for themselves, as it was considered that to learn practically how to set such matters going and keep them in order was quite as educational as to acquire the right use of the subjunctive. All that the authorities had to do with the arrangement was that when the day and hour for a committee meeting was fixed, the master in whose house the secretary was gave leave for his pupil-room to be used for the occasion; and it was also customary to ask one of them to audit the accounts. These assemblages were of a twofold character: during the first part, when the accounts were read out, and what had been done gone over, any boy who liked might attend and ask questions. But when arrangements for the future were discussed, the room was cleared of all but the committee. Experience had brought that about; for when outsiders had been allowed to remain, the number and variety of absurd and futile suggestions which were made, prevented any conclusion being come to at all.

Since Crawley was the secretary and treasurer of both the cricket and football clubs there was only one general meeting, at which the accounts of both were taken together, instead of two in the term, as when those offices were vested in different individuals. Crawley had found these burdens rather onerous this term; with that stiff examination looming nearer and nearer every month he began to feel serious, for he had set his heart upon getting into the artillery if he could, and he was going at his subjects in downright earnest, with no shirking or trifling when the humour was not on him. So that the time it took him to prepare these accounts, and still worse, to collect the subscriptions, he did rather grudge. But he never dreamed of resigning on that account; he had undertaken these duties, and would go on with them without grumbling. Perhaps he had the feeling which energetic folk who are accustomed to other people leaning on them are naturally apt to acquire, that things would get into a muddle without him. However he had got in the subscriptions, docketed his papers, and prepared everything for the meeting that evening, and the last finishing stroke being put, he locked all up in the japanned box which he kept in his room, with "Weston Cricket Club" neatly painted on it in white letters, changed his clothes for flannels, and ran out to the football field.

He had not been gone a quarter of an hour before Saurin and Edwards approached the house on their visit to Gould, who was also an inmate of Dr. Jolliffe's. They had chosen that time in order to find him alone, for he had had a slight sprain of the ankle—not enough to lay him up altogether, but sufficient to prevent his playing at football; and as he was rather glad than otherwise of an excuse to sit in with a novel, the chances were that he was now so occupied. It was a fine March day, with a bright sun and a cold east wind—not high enough to be unpleasant though, unless you dawdled about. When they came to the side-door which led to the boys' part of the house, which was a separate block of buildings from the doctor's residence, though joined to and communicating with it, Saurin stopped and said: "I think perhaps you had better wait here for me; I shall get on better with him alone."

"All right!" replied Edwards with a feeling of relief, for he dreaded the interview with Gould beyond measure. It is nervous work to ask anyone to lend you money, unless you are quite hardened. Saurin felt that too; it was a bitter pill for his pride to swallow, with the prospect on one side of a refusal and on the other of being subjected to insolent airs of superiority, for Gould was not the fellow to grant a favour graciously. But he had a stronger will than Edwards, and the situation made extreme measures necessary.

He entered the passage alone, then, and mounted the staircase, not meeting anyone. Dead stillness pervaded the house except for the trills of a canary at the far end of the second landing. Crawley's door was open as he passed, and he saw his clothes strewn about over a couple of chairs and the japanned box standing in a corner by his bureau. Saurin passed on, the song of the canary growing louder as he advanced, and knocked at Gould's door; there was no response. "Gould!" he cried, "Gould! are you in?" As there was still no answer he turned the handle and looked in; there was the canary hanging in the window, through which the sun poured, and his shrill notes went through his head; but no Gould. "Plague take it!" muttered Saurin; "it is all to do now another time, and I cannot get this suspense over. I wonder where the fellow has gone to!"

He closed the door again and retraced his steps slowly. When he repassed Crawley's room he stopped and listened. Not a sound except the bird's song. His heart beat so quickly that it was like to choke him, and he grew quite giddy. "Crawley!" he said in an unsteady voice, for though he saw the room was empty he had an insane fancy that he might be there, invisible, or that this mist before his eyes might prevent his seeing him. Then he mastered his apprehensions with an effort, and stepped into the room. Going to a chair, he felt the coat which hung over the back; there were keys in the pocket. Then he listened again; not a sound, for the singing of the canary had stopped. Ten minutes later Saurin went downstairs quietly, stealthily. He found Edwards waiting for him outside, took him by the arm, and led him away.

"Have you seen anyone?" he asked eagerly, but in a voice which he could not keep from trembling.

"Not a soul," replied Edwards.

"Then, come along to my tutor's—quick! get

your flannels on; and we will go into the football field. We are late, but can get in on one side or another."

"But, have you succeeded? Will Gould lend the money?"

"No, he won't; and I would not have fellows know I asked him for worlds; so I am glad no one saw us."

Saurin was as white as a sheet, he trembled all over, and there was a look in his eyes as of a hunted animal. That one in whose courage, presence of mind, and resources he trusted so entirely should be affected to such a degree as this, appalled poor Edwards; what a black gulf, indeed, must yawn before them!

"Is there no chance at all, then?" he asked in piteous accents.

"Yes, it will be all right; I—I have thought of something else," stammered Saurin. "Don't mind me—I'm knocked over by asking a favour and being refused; that's all. I shall be all right directly. Only swear you will never say a word to anyone about it. I tell you I have thought of a way to silence that villain Slam, and I will go and see him the first chance. It will be all right if you only hold your tongue. And now look sharp and let us change and go and play football; there's lots of time."

They had reached their own rooms by this, and Edwards did what Saurin told him, wondering, but partly reassured; and in a few minutes they were on their way to the football field, where they were hailed by their own house and paired off on different sides.

Saurin had sulkily retired from all the school sports for some time, and the boys wondered at the energy with which he now rushed into the game. The fact was he felt the necessity for violent exertion to escape reflection and drown thought in fatigue. He could not do it, but he succeeded in regaining the mastery over his nerves, his looks, his speech. As for Edwards, he played more listlessly than usual; and the thought occurred to several that afternoon that if Saurin would only take up regular practice again he would be a greater source of strength to the house team than Edwards. And they wanted to be as strong as possible, for the match with the doctor's house was approaching, and they feared that they were a little overmatched.

That evening a good many boys were assembled in Dr. Jolliffe's pupil-room to hear the reports concerning the cricket and football clubs, which were really one, as the same subscribers belonged to both, and it was only for clearness and to avoid confusion of accounts that they were treated separately; besides that, one boy could not always be found to undertake, like Crawley, the management of both. There were the committees, and besides them a sprinkling of the curious, who did not care to listen to the debit and credit accounts, but had the Anglo-Saxon instinct for attending public meetings of any kind, so that the room, though not half full, contained a respectable audience, when Crawley with his japanned box in his hand entered, and went to the place reserved for him at the head of the table.

"I have not a long story to tell you," he said, producing his keys and inserting one in the lock of the box. "Fellows have paid up pretty well, and we are rather in funds. The principal expense has been a new roller which we were obliged to have, the old one being quite worn out, and besides, as many of you have often observed, not heavy enough. Indeed the committee have been blamed rather severely by enthusiastic cricketers on this score, as if they had taken weight out of the roller, or could put extra weight into it; and I have sometimes thought that if the critics would have sat on the roller instead of on us, it would have been more effective." Laughter; for a little joke goes a long way on these solemn occasions. "Mr. Rabbits has kindly audited our accounts, which are satisfactory, I believe; here they are, if any one likes to look at them. We do not owe anything, and there are two pounds in hand for the football, and seven pounds twelve shillings for the cricket accounts, which I have here. Hulloa! what is this?" and Crawley changed countenance as he opened a portmonnaie which he took out of the box, and drew from it a five-pound note. "I have been robbed!" he cried. "There were four half-sovereigns, two sovereigns, and twelve shillings in silver, besides this bank-note in the purse this morning, and now there is only the five-pound note here!"

The consternation caused by this announcement was so great that for quite a quarter of a minute there was a dead silence, and then ejaculations, suggestions, questions, began to pour.

"Perhaps it is loose in the box," said some one, and the papers were immediately all taken out, and the box turned upside down to prove the futility of *that* perhaps.

"Well, never mind; of course I am responsible," said Crawley presently, recovering himself. "I was taken by surprise, or I should not have made all this fuss. The money will not be wanted till the cricketing season begins next term, and I can make it good by then."

Outsiders then took their departure, leaving the committee to any deliberations that might remain, and carrying the news of the robbery far and wide, so that it became the principal topic of conversation throughout the school that evening. Of course it lost nothing in the telling, and some received the information that Crawley's room had been regularly cleared out that day, all his books, clothes, and pictures taken, besides five pounds of his own and twenty of the public money.

The committee had not much business to transact. The day for the match at football between Dr. Jolliffe's and Mr. Cookson's houses was settled, a suggestion that some new turf should be laid down on a part of the cricket-field where the grass had been worn past recovery was agreed to, and the members who did not board at Dr. Jolliffe's were back at their own houses before "All-In."

But the excitement about the loss of this money was naturally greater in the house where it had taken place than anywhere else, and as the boys talked about it at supper the servants heard of it. It was evident that though no accusation might be made, suspicion would be very likely to fall upon them, and as they were anxious to have the matter sifted, the butler was deputed to report the whole affair to the doctor. So when prayers were over Dr. Jolliffe told all present to remain where they were, and then calling up Crawley, he asked him whether the account he had heard was correct.

"I did not mean to report it, sir," said Crawley, "but it is true that four pounds in gold and twelve shillings in silver were taken from the tin box belonging to the cricket and football club this afternoon."

"When did you last see this money?"

"At about a quarter to three, sir. As it was a half-holiday I thought I would get all my papers ready against the cricket and football meeting this evening. I set to work at that at a little after two; it did not take me very long, as they were all ready before, and only wanted arranging, and a little memorandum written out of what I wanted to say, for fear I should forget anything. When I had done I counted out the money in hand, and put it in a purse which I have always used for the subscriptions; there was the sum I have mentioned and a five-pound note. I put the purse back in the box, locked it, placed the keys in my coat-pocket, changed my clothes, and went out to play at football. I heard the clock strike three just after I had begun to play."

"And when did you miss the money?"

"At the meeting, when I opened the box."

"You had not done so again till then after locking it up, when you went out?"

"No, sir."

"You are sure?"

"Positive, sir."

"And the five-pound note was not taken?"

"No, sir; that was left."

"Was it in the same compartment of the purse as the gold and silver?"

"No, sir; but it could be seen if the purse was opened, and why it was not taken too I cannot imagine."

"That is not so difficult of explanation. But now I must ask you a painful question; but it is your bounden duty to answer it without reserve. Have you any suspicions as to who may have taken it?"

"None whatever, sir. I am almost certain that there was not a boy in the house. I was the last to remain in. Indeed I found all but three in the football field, and I know where they were, for I saw them playing at fives as I passed the court. At least two were playing, and the third, who had hurt his foot, was looking on."

"Do you mean to say, for it is necessary to be accurate, that you recognized every boy in the house except these three in the football field yourself?"

."Not exactly, sir; but we have been talking the matter over, and those whom I did see can answer for all the rest."

"And who were the three boys in the Fives Court?"

" I was the looker-on, sir," said Gould, stepping forward.

"And when did you leave?"

"When the others left off play, sir. We all returned together at tea-time."

" That is right, sir," said Smith and Simmonds. "We were the two playing at fives, and Gould went and returned with us." (Of course it is not meant that they said all this together, in chorus, as people do in a play; but they both stood forward, and Smith was the spokesman.)

"And now, Crawley," resumed the doctor, "are you sure that the money was not taken *after* your return. You left your room again, perhaps, before the meeting?"

" Yes, I did for a short time, sir; but then I had the keys in my pocket; and the box was fairly unlocked. There are no marks of violence; and it's a Brahma, so, whoever did it, must have had the right key."

" I am very glad that all the boys in my house seem able to prove so clear an *alibi*," said the doctor. " That will do."

When they had all dispersed Dr. Jolliffe made inquiries amongst the servants. The fat cook indignantly demanded that her boxes should be searched;

but one coin of the realm is so like another that there did not appear to be much object in that, beyond the pleasure of inspecting a very smart bonnet in reserve for Easter, and other articles of apparel. The maids who waited on the boys were very much cut up about it. They never went near the rooms after they had once cleaned them up in the morning till supper-time, when they turned down the beds (which were set on end and shut up to look like cupboards during the day), and filled the jugs and cans with fresh water, &c. But it was impossible for them to prove their absence during those two hours—from three to five—so clearly as the boys could, though they could testify to one another's not having been away for many minutes at a time. It was extremely unpleasant for them, and for the butler and another man-servant in a less degree also, for, though they had no business to go into the boys' part of the house, it was possible that they might have gone there without having any business.

But there was no reason to conclude that any-one residing in the house at all was the guilty party; any person could walk in from the street at any hour. Itinerants often passed through the place with mice, squirrels, and other things, which they tried to sell to the boys, and one of these might have slipped up-stairs. But, no; a man

like that would not have known that there was
likely to be money in that particular box; it certainly looked more like the action of someone who
had good information.

Such were the speculations and reasonings
which were rife in Weston for the next few days;
and then the topic began to grow stale, for no one
had been seen hanging about the house that afternoon, and there was no satisfactory peg upon
which to hang conjecture. One hard fact remained;
poor Crawley was answerable for four pounds
twelve shillings which had been stolen from him,
and this came at a time when he was particularly
anxious to spend as little money as possible. He
did not make much fuss about it, and only to
Buller, his friendship with whom grew stronger
the more they knew of one another, did he speak
his mind.

"My poor mother!" he said during a Sunday
walk the day after the robbery; "I shall have to
ask her for the money, and it is precious hard
upon her. I have been abominably extravagant,
and she is not rich, and there are a lot of us. I
owe a good bit to Tiffin, and to my London tailor
too, but he will wait any time. Tiffin duns me,
hang him! though why he should be devoted to
capital punishment for asking for his due I don't
know either. I should not have had such a lot of

patties, fruit, ices, and stuff. He will have to be paid at latest when I leave; and at that time, if I get into Woolwich, there will be my outfit. And then I must needs buy a gun and a license for just three days' shooting with Gould last Christmas; and tipping the groom and keeper was a heavy item besides. One of my sisters is delicate, and can't walk far; and they could keep a pony-carriage if it wasn't for me. And now, here is another fiver I must rob my mother of just because I left my keys in my coat when I changed my dress—sheer carelessness!"

"Never mind; you will get into Woolwich next examination, and then you will soon get a commission, and draw pay, and not want so much from your mother."

"Yes, I think of that, and it is some consolation; but still it is in the future, don't you see, and I must ask her for this stolen money at once. By Jove! I wish I had come back unexpectedly for something, and caught the fellow taking it! I wonder who on earth it can be!"

"I have no idea. Not Polly the maid, I'll take my Davey; I have so often left money and things about, and never lost a halfpenny."

That same Sunday Saurin and Edwards were standing with two or three others in the quadrangle, when Gould limped by.

"How is your ankle getting on, Gould?" one of the group called out.

"Better, thanks," he replied, joining them. "I say, if it had kept me in yesterday afternoon Crawley might have thought I took the money! What a joke, eh? Fancy my wanting a paltry four pounds odd."

"You were not in?" cried Edwards; and he could have bitten his tongue out immediately afterwards.

But the surprise was too great for his prudence. He and Saurin had gone to their own tutor's house before repairing to the football field, you may remember, and that route did not pass the Fives Court. So that it was the first intimation Edwards had that Saurin lied when he said he had asked Gould for a loan, and been refused.

"No," said Gould, looking at him in surprise; "what made you think I was?"

"Only your sprain," said Edwards, recovering himself. "Some fellows were saying that if you were in, the thief must have trod very lightly for you not to have heard him, as your room is so near. But as you were out, and all the other fellows too, he had the coast clear, you know."

"What is your idea about the whole thing, Saurin?" asked Gould; "you are a sharp chap."

"Oh, I don't know," said Saurin. "I should not

be very much surprised if the money turned up, and there proved to have been no robbery at all."

"What on earth do you mean?"

"The chances are I am wrong, no doubt, but it is possible. Crawley is a very careless fellow, you know, about money matters."

"But how could he have made a mistake, when he counted out the money such a short time before?" asked one of the group. "I was present at the meeting, and you should have seen his surprise when he took up the purse."

"Oh, I dare say it is all as you think," said Saurin. "I only know that if I had charge of money I should always be in a muddle. I never know anything about my own, and it is little enough to calculate; if I had to keep it separate from that of other people I should always be bothered between the two. But no doubt Crawley is better at business than I am."

"I say; he is awfully poor, Crawley is, and tries to make a show as if he were rich," said Gould. "I know he has been dunned by old Tiffin lately, and it is quite possible he may have paid him out of the club money and got confused, eh? Of course, what I say is strictly between ourselves."

CHAPTER XVI.

AN ACCIDENT.

"IT is no business of mine," said Saurin, turning on his heel. "But if any fellow likes to get up a subscription to make good Crawley's loss, real or imaginary, I'll subscribe." And he sauntered off, whistling carelessly.

Edwards had already detached himself from the group, feeling that he must be alone to think upon the tremendous and horrible revelation which had just dawned upon his mind. As Saurin passed him he hissed in his ear the one word "Fool!" And there was such an evil look of mingled rage and fear on his face as the human countenance is seldom deformed by.

But Edwards met it without quailing, and there was nothing but aversion in the glance he gave him back. The scales had fallen from his eyes, and his infatuation was dissipated. Never again was he to listen greedily to Saurin's words, and think them wiser than any others. Never more would he admire and applaud him; build castles in the air, forming wild projects for the future in his company, or associate willingly with him. They exchanged no other word, and Saurin went his way, strolling in a leisurely manner till he was out of sight; and then quickening his pace he took the direction of Slam's yard. At the rate he was walking he soon got there, and going round to the well-known back-door, he knocked. It was not long before he saw an eye reconnoitring him through a crack.

"Come, do not keep me waiting here all day while you are squinting through that hole!" he cried with a savage oath. "Let me in."

Josiah Slam said apologetically that he wanted to make sure who it was, and admitted him.

"Have you got the money, master?" he asked.

"I have got four pounds, and that is all we can raise. It is as much as we have had in cash, and if you will give up that memorandum for it I will pay it you."

"Nonsense! it's for five pund, I tell yer, and five pund I will have."

"No you won't; I cannot get it. So if you

won't take the four, let me out. You may do your worst."

"Come, say four ten."

"You fool, don't you see I am in earnest!" cried Saurin, his suppressed rage bursting out. "Why, I would cut your dirty throat if—" He restrained himself and said, "Fetch the paper if you mean to; I cannot breathe the same air as a man who has threatened me, and I won't stand bargaining here a minute longer."

Josiah Slam knew when he had got his victim in a corner, and desperate to biting pitch; so without another word he fetched the I O U and gave it to Saurin, who simultaneously handed him *two sovereigns and four half-sovereigns.* The fellow took it with a chuckle, for he had never had the slightest intention of getting himself into trouble, which he assuredly would by attempting to make any use of that bit of paper. Call upon Dr. Jolliffe indeed, to get a couple of school-boys, whom he had fleeced, into a shindy! Not worth the trouble for him, indeed. But it occurred to him that the threat might bring cash, and it had.

"Won't yer come in and have something?"

"Let me out!"

"Well, if you must go, here you are. Good-bye, young gent, and better luck next time. And if when yer goes racing, yer wants—" Saurin was out of hearing.

"Bless 'em," continued Mr. Slam, junior, "I should like to know a few more like them two young gents a good bit richer. Well, they are about somewhere, if one could but light on 'em."

Saurin did not return to Weston at once, but walked as fast as he could put foot to ground along the lanes and the highroad, trying by physical exertion to numb thought, and he partly succeeded, now and then, for a short time, but black care soon caught him up again, and brooded over his shoulder.

A voice which did not seem to emanate from his own brain kept repeating, "What you have done can never be undone; never, never. Not if you live to be a hundred; not for all eternity." "It can, it shall," he replied. "Only let me escape suspicion, and I will make it up over and over again." "That would not make what has happened, not to have happened." "It is only one act." "Self-deceiver, you have been growing to it for years, your corruption has been gradual, and this is the natural result. You will go on now; each time it will come easier to you, until you grow to think nothing of it. Read your future—outcast, jail-bird." "No, no; I will lead a new life, work hard, avoid bad company." "Avoid bad company! I like that! What company can be worse than your own *now?*" "I will *not* sink deeper; no one knows." "You forget; one does know, others *may* know, *will* know." "I could not bear that; I would destroy myself and escape the shame." "Destroy yourself indeed! I defy you; you cannot do it. You may kill yourself; it is not at all unlikely; but that is not destruction, but only the commission of another crime."

This inward voice became so real to him that he thought he must be possessed or else going mad. Suppose it were the latter, and he let the truth out in his delirium! He determined to live by rule, to study hard, to be conciliatory, not to draw observation on himself. And to begin with, he must be getting back to Weston; it would never do to be late, and risk questioning.

The first time he had an opportunity of speaking to Edwards alone he said, "I have seen that man as I promised, and there is nothing to fear from him. I have secured his silence."

"At what a price!" sighed Edwards.

"Look here," murmured Saurin, turning on him fiercely; "if it is as you think, you take advantage of it, which is just as bad. We are in the same boat, and must sink or swim together. What is done cannot be undone; don't be a fool.

If your weakness excites suspicion it will be ruin
to both of us."

"I know, I know," said Edwards, turning away
with loathing.

They hated the sight of one another now, these
two inseparables. What revolted Edwards most
of all was the other's insinuation about Crawley.
It was all of a piece with his conduct when Buller
was accused of that poaching business, and showed
his true character. Days went by and they never
spoke to one another of the shameful secret they
shared, and indeed rarely on any other subject.
They would have avoided all association if it had
not been for the fear of exciting suspicion. They
were more attentive to their studies, and at the
same time took a more prominent part in the
school games than either had done for a long time:
Edwards, because it was his natural bent to do
so when freed from other influences; and Saurin,
partly from prudence, partly because he was
making a struggle to escape from the net which he
felt that evil habits had thrown around him. He
was like one who has been walking in a fog along
the brink of a precipice, and discovers his position
by setting a foot on the very edge and nearly falling over. He shrank from the abyss which he
now saw yawning for him. At the same time he
exerted himself to become popular, and since he

was no longer anxious to thrust himself perpetually into the foremost place, he was not without success.

"What a much better fellow Saurin is now he has given up going to that Slam's yard!" said one of his intimates, and his hearers acquiesced. He had never repeated that abominable hint about the possibility of Crawley's not having lost the money at all; but Gould had taken up the idea, and the gossip had spread, as such ill-natured talk about any one who is popular or in a higher position than others, is sure to do. Very few, if any, really believed that there was a grain of truth in the notion, but some thought it clever to talk as if they did, just to be different from the majority. Others might jump to a conclusion, swallowing all that the popular idol chose to tell them, but they withheld their judgment. Unluckily these rumours reached Crawley's ears; some friendly ass "thought he ought to know," as is always the case when anything unpleasant is said, and it fretted and annoyed him exceedingly.

It also had the effect of annulling a movement which was being set on foot to make up the missing money by subscription, the notion of which emanated curiously enough from the same source as the scandal. Saurin had thrown out the hint as a sneer, not a suggestion, but it was taken up by some honest lad in the latter sense. It had been submitted to the masters, who not only approved but were anxious to head the subscription, and the whole thing could have been done at once without anyone feeling it. But Crawley called a special meeting, and the pupil-room was crammed to overflowing this time to hear what he had to say, which was this: " I have asked you to come for a personal and not a public reason. I am told that it is proposed to raise a subscription to make up the four pounds twelve the fund has been robbed of. Now, though I was perhaps not careful enough, I could hardly expect my keys to be taken out of a coat and the box opened during a short absence, and so I should have been very glad not to have to bear this loss, for which, of course, I am solely responsible, alone. But some kind friends (Gould, I believe, started the idea) are pleased to say that I have robbed myself; that is, I have spent the money intrusted to me and invented the story of a robbery." ("Oh! oh! shame! shame!") " Well, yes, I think it was rather a shame, and I am glad you are indignant about it. But the accusation having been once made, of course I cannot accept the kind suggestion to make the loss good."

There was a great hubbub and loud protestations, but Crawley was firm. His honour was at

stake, he said, and he must repay the money himself; then his traducers at all events could not
say that he had profited by holding the office of
treasurer. Those who had indulged in idle inuen-
does were heartily ashamed and sorry, and Gould
for a short time was the most unpopular boy in
the school. Crawley cut him dead.

The day following this special meeting was Saturday, exactly one week after the robbery, and the
day appointed for the football match between the
houses of Head-master and Cookson. I fear that
a detailed account of this match would hardly
interest you, for this reason. The head-master,
whose scholarship and capacity worked up Weston
to that state of prosperity which it has maintained
ever since, was an Etonian, and the games insti-
tuted under his auspices were played according
to Eton rules. Dr. Jolliffe had also been educated
at the same school, and thought everything connected with it almost sacred. So it happened
that the Rugby game of hand-and-football had
never supplanted the older English pastime, which
it has now become so much the fashion to despise,
and which, indeed, if it were not for the Eton
clubs at Oxford, Cambridge, and elsewhere, might
disappear as the national rats did before the
Hanoverian. The Westonians then used round,
not oblong footballs; their object was to work

the ball between the goal posts, not over a bar at the top of them; and it was unlawful to touch it with the hands unless caught in the air, and then only for a drop-kick.

I do not advocate one game more than the other; both to my thinking are excellent, and I have no sympathy with those who would suppress every pastime which is fraught with some roughness and danger. The tendency of civilization is naturally towards softness, effeminacy, and a dread of pain or discomfort; and these evils are far more serious than bruises, sprains, broken collar-bones, or even occasionally a more calamitous accident.

However, the chances are that my reader is all in favour of the Rugby game, and would therefore follow the changes and chances of the present match with but little interest. It was exciting enough, however, to those who were engaged in it, for Cookson's made a better fight of it than their opponents expected. They had been practising with great pains, and their team worked well together and backed each other up excellently. So that, quite early in the match, the ball having been some time at their end, and they acting solely on the defensive, Jolliffe's thought they were going to carry all before them and got a little rash and careless; those who should have kept back to guard their own end pressing too far forwards, when Edwards, who was fleet of foot and really good at seizing chances, got a clear kick at the ball which sent it over the heads of the attackers into the middle of the field, and, getting through to it again, began dribbling it towards the hostile goal with a series of short kicks, having a start of the field, who, seeing their error, were now racing back to their own end. The goal-keeper dashed out and met Edwards in full career, both kicking the ball at the same time; but another on the Cookson side, who had been keeping close in view of such a contingency, got a fair chance at the ball, which slipped sideways from the two, and sent it sheer between the posts, scoring a goal for Cookson's.

The success of such a simple manœuvre was equivalent to a "fools' mate" at chess, and was a lesson to Jolliffe's never to despise their enemy. They were not to be caught napping again, however, and, by dint of steady, persistent, concentrated play, they too got a goal and equalized matters. Then, after a considerable period, during which the advantages fluctuated, they obtained a rooge. If, in the old game, the ball is kicked behind the goal-posts but not between them, there arises a struggle between the contending sides to touch it with the hand. If one of the defenders, those behind whose goal the ball has passed, does so first, nothing has happened, and the ball is kicked off again for renewal of the game. But should one of the opposite side so touch it, a rooge is gained. The rooge is formed close in front of the defenders' goal, they being clustered in a semicircle with their backs to it, and with a big and heavy member of the team for the central pillar, who plants his heel firmly in the ground, the ball being placed against his foot. The opposite side complete the circle, leaving an opening for one of their number to rush in and get a good kick at the ball—they instantly closing upon him and endeavouring to force the whole surging, struggling mass bodily back between the posts, ball and all; if they cannot make an opening they send the ball through alone—the defenders, of course, endeavouring to force the ball out sideways, and either touch it down behind their goal or get it away from their end altogether. One goal counts more than any number of rooges; but when no goal is made at all, or the number of them on each side is equal, the rooges decide the game.

Ends were changed, and after a good deal of play without result Cookson's also scored a rooge, and matters were equal again; after which the Jolliffe team, which was the strongest physically, kept the ball entirely in the neighbourhood of the Cookson goals. For the latter had made great exertions, and were tiring fast. The time fixed for leaving off play was now approaching; and if they could only keep matters as they were a little longer they would make a drawn match of it, which would be of itself a triumph, considering that their opponents, with the redoubtable Crawley at their head, were reckoned so much the stronger.

"Come, we *must* get one more rooge," said the Jolliffe captain, "and weak as they are getting we ought to turn it into a goal." And pursuing his determination he dribbled the ball up close to the base line, sent it behind the goal posts, and rushed forward to touch it down. Edwards ran up to it at the same time to touch it first, and a collision ensued which sent him flying. Near that spot there was a tree with seats round it, and Edwards fell heavily with his side against a corner of this wooden settle. Crawley touched the ball down.

"You have given us all our work to get this!" he called out to the other, laughing; and then seeing that Edwards was lying on the ground, he added, "You are not hurt, old fellow, are you? Only blown?"

But as the other was not in the position in which

any one would lie still a moment to get breath, he went up to him and repeated his question.

"I don't know; I—I feel rather queer," was the reply.

Crawley stooped, and put his arms round his body to raise him up, but Edwards shrieked out, "Ah! don't; that hurts!"

The other players now gathered round, and many offered well-meaning but absurd suggestions. One practical youth ran off, however, to Cookson's house to report what had happened, and then returned with a chair. By the time he got back Edwards had managed to rise, and was sitting on the settle, very faint. They managed to transfer him to the chair, and carried him home in it very gently, and by the time he was laid on his bed, which had been got ready, the doctor arrived. A couple of ribs were broken, he said, after an examination which made poor Edwards groan a good deal; but he did not think there was much more the matter, which words were a great comfort to Crawley, who began to fear that he might have been the cause of the boy's death. He was quite sufficiently sorry and vexed as it was, and would have liked to nurse him if he had been allowed.

It was just as well for his reading that they were not in the same house, for he spent all the hours that he was out of school, and not necessarily in his own tutor's, by Edwards' bedside. You cannot fall with your side against a sharp angle heavily enough to break a couple of ribs without feeling it afterwards, I can tell you, so you had better not try, and Edwards suffered a good deal from pain and difficulty of breathing for a few days, and when the inflammation was got down, and he felt more easy, he was kept back by a great depression of spirits.

"One would say that the boy had something on his mind!" said the doctor to Mr. Cookson, "but that is impossible. At his age we possess no minds worth speaking about to have anything upon;" and so he lost the scent after hitting it off, to go on the trail of a witticism, which after all was not very brilliant.

Edwards was delirious one night, and astonished the housekeeper, a motherly dame who sat up with him, by his talk on the occasion.

"Look here!" he said; and thinking he wanted drink or something she got out of her chair and leaned over him; "let us have five shillings on the black this time; it has gone red four times running, and that can't go on, can it?"

"Certainly not," said Mrs. Blobbs, wondering whatever the boy's distracted fancy was running on. "Don't do it! Don't do it!" he then cried. "I'll have nothing to say to it. Let us stand our chance rather.　Not that way; not that way; no, no, that's making bad worse.　I won't! I won't!"

That was only one night, however, the third after the accident, and he was all right in his head next morning, only so terribly depressed.　Saurin never came near him.

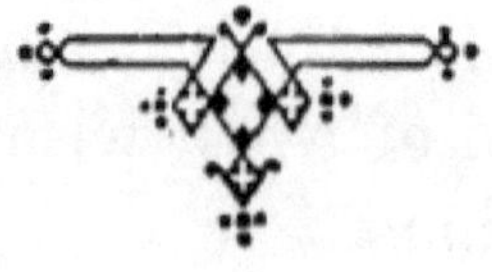

CHAPTER XVII.

COMPOUNDING A FELONY.

 KNOW what is the matter with you,"
said Crawley, replacing the pieces on
a backgammon board at the end of
the game.

"Do you?" replied Edwards, turning if possible
a shade paler, while his heart palpitated under his
sore ribs.

"Yes," continued the other; "you are worrying
because you cannot get on with your reading, and
the prospect of examination is getting uncomfor-
tably distinct.   I hear from Mr. Cookson that you
have been mugging lately, just as I have.   Well,
you will not lose much time, and you will find
yourself all the clearer for lying fallow a little.
And look here, I am a little more forward than
you, and if you will come and stay with us in the
holidays I will read with you; I think I could
help you a bit.   My mother would be very glad

to see you.   Or if that can't be, I'll come to you. I am sure we could more than make up for any lost time."

Edwards was able to sit up now, and Crawley read amusing books, and played games with him whenever he could leave school or pupil room.

"What a kind chap you are!" said Edwards with a broken voice, and with water in his eyes, for he was very weak and nervous; "I—I don't deserve it."

"Not?" exclaimed Crawley.   "Why, surely I ought to do what I can, when it is my fault that you got hurt. I am most unlucky this term; I get robbed, and am suspected of inventing the story of it to cover my misappropriation of the money; and then I wind up with breaking a fellow's ribs!"

"No one thinks for a moment that you were not robbed as you say; I am certain of it!" cried Edwards.

"I don't know about that; some of them said they did, and I would give anything to prove that they did me wrong. It will stick in my gizzard a long time, I can tell you."

Edwards buried his face in his hands and fairly sobbed.

"I can bear it no longer," he cried at last. "You so kind to me and all! I know who robbed you."

"You!" exclaimed Crawley, thinking the boy had gone delirious again.

"Yes, I," repeated Edwards. "I did not see it done, and he never told me he had done it, but I know he did, and—and, I profited by the money and never said anything."

"Come, come, Edwards, you are ill and weak, and exciting yourself too much. We will talk about this another time."

"No, no, now; I must speak; it is killing me."

And then he rapidly told the whole story; how Saurin and he had gambled and lost, and the peril they had brought themselves into; and how Saurin had gone that fatal Saturday afternoon to try and borrow money of Gould—all he knew, in short.

"Saurin!" said Crawley, when he had heard all. "I never thought very much of him, but I had no idea he was so bad as that. But don't you fret, Edwards; you were put in a very queer position, and nobody could say what he would do if he suddenly found it his duty to denounce an intimate friend for a crime which was committed to get out of a scrape in which he himself was implicated. It would be an awful hole to be in! How far have you told me all this in con-fidence?"

"I leave that quite to you. I do not ask to

be spared myself, but if you could be cleared and satisfied without Saurin being publicly tried and sent to prison, I should be very grateful."

"All right! I think I can manage that. And now, don't you bother yourself; you shall not get into any row, that I promise."

"Oh, Crawley, what a good fellow you are!" cried Edwards. "I wish I had got killed, instead of only breaking a couple of ribs!"

"And let me in for being tried for manslaughter!" exclaimed Crawley, laughing. "Thank you for nothing, my boy."

Crawley made up his mind that night what he would do. The next morning he asked Robarts, Buller, and Smith, *alias* "Old Algebra," to come to his room when they came out of school at twelve. Then he made the same request of Gould, who looked surprised and flustered.

"You will condescend to speak to me at last, then?" he said, sulkily.

"I could not suppose that you wished to hold any communication with a defaulter," replied Crawley, "and I am sure I could not trust myself in the company of any fellow who thought me one. I ask you to come to my room now because I have discovered who took the money, and I want to clear myself in your eyes."

"All right! I will come if you wish it."

"Thank you very much."

Having thus arranged for his court of inquiry, the next thing was to secure the attendance of the accused. He found Saurin talking to a knot of boys, and asked if he could speak to him privately for a moment.

"Well, what is up?" Saurin asked. "You look as grave as a mute at a funeral."

"Yes," said Crawley, "what I have to say is rather grave. It is about that four pounds twelve shillings you took out of my box."

"It's a lie!" cried Saurin, turning pale as death.

"And yet the evidence against you is very clear," said Crawley quietly "Do you know a man named Josiah Slam, a son of the fellow who lives near here? Come, I do not wish to prosecute you, unless you force me; I want to give you a chance. Robarts, Buller, Smith, and Gould are coming to my room at twelve o'clock to-day, and I mean to take their advice as to what should be done, if you will come there too, and meet them."

"And if I refuse?" said Saurin.

"In that case I shall go to Dr. Jolliffe, and put the matter in *his* hands," replied Crawley.

"Well, I do not mind coming to hear what cock-and-bull story you have trumped up," muttered Saurin, turning away. He feared lest an unguarded word should betray him.

His anxiety was terrible. What did Crawley know? What was mere conjecture? Of course Edwards had put him on the track; but had he done so distinctly, or had this suspicion been aroused by his wandering talk when delirious? Everything might depend on his exercising calm judgment just now, but his head was in a whirl and he could not collect his wits. Should he make a bolt? Oh, no! that would be confessing himself guilty. Should he defy Crawley? That would bring about a trial, in which he might be found guilty. It seemed safest to go to Crawley's room at twelve and hear what he had to say.

So he went. Robarts and Gould sat on the two chairs with which the room was supplied, Buller perched himself on the table, Smith on a box—all full of curiosity and expectation. Crawley and Saurin remained standing. The door was closed and a mat placed against it, to prevent any sudden entry without warning.

"I am not going to beat about the bush," said Crawley. "I accuse Saurin there of having come to this house, one Saturday when we were all out; of having gone into my room, taken my keys out of the pocket of a coat lying there, opened the cricket and football japanned box, and abstracted

four pounds twelve shillings from a purse inside
it. Then I assert that he put the keys back in
the coat pocket, having first locked the box and
put it back in its place, and ran back to his
tutor's house, where he changed and went out
to play at football. The motive of this theft was
that he had been gambling at Slam's yard, lost
all the money he had or could raise; went on
playing on credit, lost again, and was threatened
with exposure unless he paid up. He had meant
to borrow the money he wanted of you, Gould,
and came to the house with that intention. But
as you were not in, he got it the other way."

"It is all a pack of lies!" cried Saurin. "At
least about robbing, I mean; for it is true that
I lost money playing roulette, and that I meant
to borrow of Gould, only I squared matters with
the man without."

"What day did you come to apply to me for
that loan?" asked Gould.

"I don't know exactly; it was not on a Saturday. I am not sure that I came at all," replied
Saurin, who could not for the life of him help
stammering. "It's all lies; though appearances
might be got up against me."

"They certainly are so already," said Crawley,
"or I should not have accused you. Of course,
if you can prove your innocence, or even if you

are convinced that no one can prove your guilt, you will prefer to stand a trial. Otherwise you might prefer to pay back the money and leave Weston quietly. What do you say?" he added, turning to the others. "Would it not be best for the credit of the school?"

"Yes, yes," said Robarts; "let us wash our dirty linen at home."

"But how am I to leave?" asked Saurin with a groan.

"I don't know; tell your guardian the truth if you like, you must manage that. Only, if you come back next term I shall lay the whole matter before the head-master. And if you leave, and the money does not come, I shall give information to the police."

"That's fair enough," said Buller; "take the chance, Saurin, if you are not a fool." And the others assented.

Not one of them had any doubt as to Saurin's guilt: his confusion and equivocation condemned him.

"What a cool fish you were to suggest that Crawley might have spent the money himself!" said Gould. "You regularly humbugged me."

"You are assuming a good deal, I think," said Saurin bitterly; "making yourselves accusers, juries, judges, executioners, and all. And I am very much in your power, for if this came to a trial, though I should certainly be found innocent of robbery, yet I cannot deny the gambling and having gone to Slam's yard, and I should be expelled for that. So I suppose I had better agree to your terms. I will not come back, and —what sum did you say you demand as the price of your silence? Four pounds ten, or twelve, I think; you shall have it." And turning on his heel with an attempt at swagger which was not very successful, Saurin went out, kicking the mat aside, and banging the door after him.

Of course Edwards had betrayed him, he said to himself; it was not for nothing that Crawley had been constantly with him since his accident. He longed to go to Edwards' room and upbraid him with his treachery, but he durst not trust himself. He was not out of the wood yet; the other three could be trusted, but Gould *must* tattle, and if the story got abroad and reached one of the master's ears, it would no longer be in Crawley's power to hush it up. And then Edwards almost always had some one with him; but if not, and he saw him alone, could he keep his hands off his throat? From the throbbing of his temples when the idea occurred to him he thought it doubtful. No, he must not see him.

"How on earth did you find it out?" cried the

others to Crawley when Saurin's footstep died away on the staircase.

"I have promised not to name my witnesses unless it is necessary to call them forward," replied Crawley. "I am very much obliged to you for coming here, and I feel that it is awfully bad not to take you into full confidence and give up names. But you see I have passed my word and cannot help myself. There's one thing I can tell you, Buller. Saurin was the poacher for whose moonlight excursion you were taken up."

"By Jove!" exclaimed Buller. "Well, I should have imagined that he might have done that, but not such a dirty business as this."

"I suppose he felt himself up a regular tree, poor beggar!" said Robarts.

"Well, Gould," said Crawley, "I hope that your doubts as to my story of having been robbed are set at rest."

"I don't know that I ever had any," replied Gould rather sullenly; "only when a thing like that happens, and nothing can be found out, one puts it in every possible light. Saurin said you were a careless fellow about money matters, and might have mixed up the club money with your own and paid it away without knowing, and then thought you had been robbed. Of course one sees now why he put the idea about; but at the time it looked just possible, and fellows discussed it, I amongst them."

"Well, it was not pleasant for me, as you may easily understand," said Crawley. "However, that is all over, and we will say nothing more about it. And now, of course we will all keep our council about this business for some time. It would be breaking faith with Saurin if we let a word escape before he has left the school; because, if the doctor heard of it, he would insist on expelling him at any rate."

"Yes; and we had better hold our tongues for our own sakes," observed Robarts. "My father's a lawyer, and I have heard him talk about something of the same kind. And I have a strong idea that we have just committed a crime, as that chap in the French play talked prose without knowing it."

"What do you mean?"

"Just this, that to make terms with a thief, by which you agree not to prosecute him, is a legal offence called 'compounding a felony.'"

This notion of Robarts, whether right or wrong, had the useful effect of sealing Gould's lips for some time to come. It only wanted a week to the holidays, so the struggle was not so very prolonged.

Crawley went to see Edwards directly the

council-board broke up, and found him nervous and depressed.

"Perhaps I had no right to speak," he said. "It was not for me to tell. I wouldn't; only you thought yourself under suspicion, and you have been so good to me."

Well, Crawley could not but thank him and tell him he was quite right; but he was not able for the life of him to say so in very cordial tones.

"Look here!" persisted Edwards, noticing this, "tell me honestly; if you had been situated like me, would you have told of him?"

"Not to save my life!" blurted out Crawley; "I mean," he added hastily, "I fear that I should not have had the moral courage."

The week passed, and Weston School once more broke up. What story Saurin told to Sir Richard to induce him to take his name off the boards quietly I do not know, but it had the desired effect; and when the boys reassembled for the summer term Saurin's place was known no longer amongst them. The scandal about him soon began to leak out, and the story ran that but for Crawley's extreme generosity towards him he would have now been in penal servitude at Portland.

Stubbs, too, went away that Easter vacation, taking Topper with him, and the pair went out to China together, Stubbs having lucrative employment in that country. Crawley returned, but that was his last term, and soon afterwards he succeeded in getting into Woolwich.

EPILOGUE.

A young man stood on the platform of the South-Western Railway pointing out his luggage to a porter. There was a good deal of it, and every package had *Serapis* painted upon it. *Serapis*, however, was not the name of that young man; that was inscribed on another part of the trunk, and ran, "Vincent Crawley, R.A." *Serapis* indicated the ship into whose hold all these things were to go. They had other marks, for some were to go to the bottom—absit omen!—the bottom of the hold, I mean, not of the sea, and were to remain there till the end of the voyage. But one trunk was to lie atop, for it contained light clothing to be worn on entering the Red Sea. Minute were the printed directions about these matters which had been sent him directly he got his route. It is the fashion to cry out against red tape, but red tape is a first-rate thing if it only ties up the bundles properly. There is nothing like order, method—routine in short. By following it too closely on exceptional occasions absurd blunders may now and then be committed; but think of the utter confusion that would prevail every hour for the want of it.

With a 'cold March wind blowing how should a young fellow who had never been out of his own country know that in a few days it would be so hot that his present clothes would be unbearable? Or how should he understand the way to meet the difficulty if he did know it? I am all for rules and regulations, and down with the grumblers.

Mrs. Crawley and the girls agreed with me, for the official directions saved them a world of trouble. They wanted to go down to Portsmouth in a body and see him off, but he begged them not.

"I had sooner say good-by here, Mother," he said, "if you don't mind. There's a detachment, and I shall have my men to look after, and if I am with you I shall be bothered. And, well, you know, parting is a melancholy sort of business, and it is better to get it over in private, don't you think?"

Mrs. Crawley saw wisdom in her son's words, and yielded with a sigh, for she yearned to see the very last of him. Ah! we do not half value the love of our mothers until we miss it, and the opportunity for making any return is gone for ever. It seems such a matter of course, like the sun shining, which no one troubles to be grateful for. But if the sun *went out!*

Well, it was a painful business—a good deal worse than a visit to the dentist's—that morning's breakfast, with the table crowded with his favourite dainties, which he could not swallow. And then the final parting, when all the luggage was piled on the cab. It was a relief when it was over, and he found himself alone and trying to whistle. Even now, as he stowed the smaller articles in the carriage, he had a great lump in his throat.

The guard began shutting the doors, so he got in, and as he had fellow-passengers it was necessary to look indifferent, and as if he were accustomed to long journeys. The train moved out of the station, and he found several things to distract his thoughts. Presently on the right they passed the Wimbledon Lawn-tennis Grounds, and he thought of a wonderful rally he had seen there between Renshaw and Lawson. Then further on they came to Sandown on the left, where a steeplechase was in progress. The horses were approaching the water jump, and the travellers put down their newspapers and crowded to the window.

" Something in Tom Cannon's colours leading; he's over. That thing of Lord Marcus is pulling hard. By Jove he is down! No, he has picked him up again. Well ridden, sir!"

"Who is it up?"

"Why, Beresford himself. He will win, too, I think. Oh, hang it, I wish they would stop the train a moment!"

Everybody laughed at this, though it was provoking not to see them over the next fence; but the engine gave a derisive scream, and away they rushed to Farnborough.

"There's Aldershot, and the Long Valley, and that Cocked Hat Wood. British generals would beat creation if they might only let their left rest on Cocked Hat Wood."

They were all army men in the carriage, and the conversation never flagged now it had been started.

"Are you going by the *Serapis?*" asked a gentleman sitting opposite Crawley, seeing *cubin* painted on his busby case in the net overhead.

"Yes," replied Crawley. And then learning that he was bound for India the other inquired the presidency and the station, and it so happened that he had left that district only the year before, and was now settled in Hampshire, having been superannuated, at which he grumbled much, and indeed he was a hale young-looking man to be laid on the shelf. And so the time sped rapidly till they reached Portsmouth harbour, where a conspicuous white vessel, which was pointed out to Crawley as the *Serapis*, lay moored to a quay. Then he superintended the loading of his luggage in a cart, and taking a cab accompanied it through the dock-yard gates to a shed, where he saw it deposited as per regulation. Then he went to the "George," where he had secured a bed, and on entering the coffee-room heard his name uttered in a tone of pleased surprise: "Crawley!"

"What, Buller! How are you, old fellow?"

"All right. Are you going out in the *Serapis?*"

"Yes; and you?"

"Yes."

"That is jolly. What regiment are you in?"

"First Battalion Blankshire. Do you know I got into Sandhurst direct the first time I went up!"

"Of course you did; you would be sure to do anything you really meant; I always said so. I must go and report myself now and see about my detachment, for there are some men going out with me; but we shall meet at dinner."

They dined together at a small table by themselves, and had a long talk afterwards about the old Weston fellows, whom Buller had recent information of through Penrylm, who lived near his people at home.

"I know about Robarts," said Crawley; "he is

in the Oxford eleven; but there is your chum Penryhn, what is he doing?"

"Oh, he is in a government office in Somerset House. Not a large income, but safe, and rounded off with a pension. Better than our line, so far as money goes anyhow."

"I suppose so; but I should not like office work. And Smith, Old Algebra, have you heard of him?"

"Yes, he is mathematical master at a big school."

"And Gould?"

"Why, don't you know? It was in all the papers. Gould's father smashed and died suddenly; did not leave his family a penny. Some friends got Lionel Gould a clerkship in some counting-house; his sister Clarissa, your old friend, you know, supports herself and her mother by the stage."

"Dear, dear, I am sorry for them; it must be precious hard when they were used to such luxury. And that chap Edwards, have you ever heard of him?"

"Oh, yes, he is at Cambridge, and intends to take orders when he gets his degree."

"I hope it will keep him out of mischief; I always fancied he might come to grief, he was such a weak beggar."

"Yes, he was, and is still, I hear. But he has had the luck to get into the clutches of a man who keeps him straight; a fellow as good as gold, and earnest enough to make all the Edwardses in the country believe in him."

"Lucky for Edwards; if he marries a stiffish sort of wife with the same opinions he will live and die a saint. Saurin would have made the other thing of him. By the by, have you ever heard anything of that fellow?"

"Not lately. He had a row with his uncle and guardian, and went to Australia, I believe; but I have heard nothing of him for years.

They chatted late into the night, and when Crawley went to bed his heart smote him to remember how little he had thought of his mother.

The *Serapis* was to sail on the following day at noon, so when Crawley had seen his gunners safely embarked, and the two friends had reported themselves at the little office outside the saloon, had traversed that lofty palatial apartment (how different from the cabins of the old troop-ships!), carefully removing their caps as a placard directed them, had made acquaintance with the little cabin which they were to share together, and had stowed away their minor properties within it, they took a last turn on shore, principally to get one or two little comforts which they had forgotten till then.

As they passed a low public-house on their way back to the ship, a remarkably smart corporal of marines came out of it, and since they were in uniform, saluted. But as he did so, he suddenly turned his head away and quickened his pace.

Crawley and Buller looked at one another.

"Did you recognize him?"

"Yes."

It was Saurin.

THE END.

BLACKIE & SON'S

BOOKS FOR YOUNG PEOPLE.

The New Season's Books.

BY G. A. HENTY.

THE YOUNG CARTHAGINIAN:
A STORY OF THE TIMES OF HANNIBAL.

WITH WOLFE IN CANADA:
OR, THE WINNING OF A CONTINENT.

THE BRAVEST OF THE BRAVE:
OR, WITH PETERBOROUGH IN SPAIN.

A FINAL RECKONING:
A TALE OF BUSH LIFE IN AUSTRALIA.

BY G. MANVILLE FENN.

DEVON BOYS: A TALE OF THE NORTH SHORE.

YUSSUF THE GUIDE:
BEING THE STRANGE STORY OF THE TRAVELS IN ASIA MINOR OF BURNE THE LAWYER, PRESTON THE PROFESSOR, AND LAWRENCE THE SICK.

BY HARRY COLLINGWOOD.

THE LOG OF THE "FLYING FISH":
A STORY OF AERIAL AND SUBMARINE PERIL AND ADVENTURE.

BY ALICE CORKRAN.

DOWN THE SNOW STAIRS;
OR, FROM GOOD-NIGHT TO GOOD-MORNING. *With 60 illustrations by Gordon Browne.*

BY DOUGLAS FRAZAR.

PERSEVERANCE ISLAND:
OR, THE ROBINSON CRUSOE OF THE 19TH CENTURY.

A

By J. PERCY GROVES.
> REEFER AND RIFLEMAN: A Tale of the Two Services.

By JOHN C. HUTCHESON.
> THE WHITE SQUALL: A Story of the Sargasso Sea.
> TEDDY: The Story of a "Little Pickle."

By E. S. BROOKS.
> HISTORIC BOYS:
>> THEIR ENDEAVOURS, THEIR ACHIEVEMENTS, AND THEIR TIMES.

By EVELYN EVERETT GREEN.
> THE EVERSLEY SECRETS.

By R. STEAD.
> THE LADS OF LITTLE CLAYTON.
>> STORIES OF VILLAGE BOY LIFE.

By LAURA E. RICHARDS.
> THE JOYOUS STORY OF TOTO.

TALES OF CAPTIVITY AND EXILE.

By CAROLINE AUSTIN.
> DOROTHY'S DILEMMA: A Tale of the Time of Charles I.

By ROSA MULHOLLAND.
> THE LATE MISS HOLLINGFORD.

By AMY WALTON.
> THE HAWTHORNES.
> OUR FRANK, AND OTHER STORIES.

GORDON BROWNE'S SERIES OF OLD FAIRY TALES.
> HOP O' MY THUMB.
> BEAUTY AND THE BEAST.

Also, New Books in the Shilling, Ninepenny, and Sixpenny Series.
By F. BAYFORD HARRISON,
Mrs. GEO. CUPPLES, MARY C. ROWSELL, ANNIE S. FENN,
EMMA LESLIE, and other favourite Authors.

DOWN THE SNOW STAIRS·

Or, From Good-night to Good-morning. By ALICE CORKRAN. With 60 character Illustrations by GORDON BROWNE. Square crown 8vo, cloth elegant, gilt edges, 6s.

This is a remarkable story: full of vivid fancy and quaint originality. In its most fantastic imaginings it carries with it a sense of reality, and derives a singular attraction from that combination of simplicity, originality, and subtle humour which is so much appreciated by lively and thoughtful children. Children of a larger growth will also be deeply interested in Kitty's strange journey: and her wonderful experiences amidst the extraordinary people whom she meets. The work is profusely illustrated by an artist whose facile pencil has portrayed alike the graceful and the grotesque, the images of goblin and fairy land and the semblances of child life.

BY PROFESSOR CHURCH.

TWO THOUSAND YEARS AGO:

Or, The Adventures of a Roman Boy. By Professor A. J. Church, Author of "Stories from the Classics." With 12 full-page Illustrations by Adrien Marie, in black and tint. Crown 8vo, cloth elegant, olivine edges, 6s.

Prof. Church has in this story sought to revivify that most interesting period, the last days of the Roman Republic. The hero of the story, Lucius Marius, is a young Roman who has a very chequered career, being now a captive in the hands of Spartacus, again an officer on board a vessel detailed for the suppression of the pirates, and anon a captive once more, on a pirate ship. He escapes to Tarsus, is taken prisoner in the war with Mithradates, and detained by the latter in Pontus for a number of years.

While boys will follow with the deepest interest the career of Lucius, they will gain a clear insight into the history and life of the ancient Roman world.

"Adventures well worth the telling. The book is extremely entertaining as well as useful, and there is a wonderful freshness in the Roman scenes and characters."—*The Times.*

"Entertaining in the highest degree from beginning to end, and full of adventure which is all the livelier for its close connection with history."—*Spectator.*

"We know of no book which will do more to make the Romans of that day live again for the English reader."—*Guardian.*

BY PROFESSOR POUCHET.

THE UNIVERSE:

Or the Infinitely Great and the Infinitely Little. A Sketch of Contrasts in Creation, and Marvels revealed and explained by Natural Science. By F. A. Pouchet, M.D. Illustrated by 273 Engravings on wood. 9th Edition, medium 8vo, cloth elegant, gilt edges, 7s. 6d.; morocco antique, 16s.

The object of this Work is to inspire and extend a taste for natural science. It is not a learned treatise, but a simple study. The title adopted indicates that the author has gathered from creation at large, often contrasting the smallest of its productions with the mightiest.

"We can honestly commend this work, which is admirably, as it is copiously illustrated."—*Times.*

"As interesting as the most exciting romance, and a great deal more likely to be remembered to good purpose."—*Standard.*

"Scarcely any book in French or in English is so likely to stimulate in the young an interest in the physical phenomena."—*Fortnightly Review.*

"The volume, and it is a splendid one, will serve as a good pioneer to more exact studies."—*Saturday Review.*

BY G. A. HENTY.

"Surely Mr. Henty should understand boys' tastes better than any man living."
— *The Times.*

THE YOUNG CARTHAGINIAN:

A Story of the Times of Hannibal. By G. A. HENTY. With 12 full-page Illustrations by C. J. STANILAND, R.I. Crown 8vo, cloth elegant, olivine edges, 6s.

When boys at school read of the history of the Punic Wars their appreciation of the merits of the struggle between the Romans and Carthaginians is usually slight. That it was at first a struggle for empire, and afterwards one for existence on the part of Carthage, that Hannibal was a great and skilful general, that he defeated the Romans at Trebia, Lake Trasimenus, and Cannæ, and all but took Rome, and that the Romans behaved with bad faith and great cruelty at the capture of Carthage, represents pretty nearly the sum total of their knowledge.

To let them know more about this momentous struggle for the empire of the world Mr. Henty has written this story, which not only gives in graphic style a brilliant description of a most interesting period of history, but is a tale of exciting adventure sure to secure the interest of the reader.

THE LION OF THE NORTH.

A Tale of Gustavus Adolphus and the Wars of Religion. By G. A. HENTY. With 12 full-page Illustrations by JOHN SCHÖNBERG, in black and tint. Crown 8vo, cloth elegant, olivine edges, 6s.

In this story Mr. Henty gives the history of the first part of the Thirty Years' War, a struggle unprecedented in length, in the fury with which it was carried on, and in the terrible destruction and ruin which it caused. The issue had its importance, which has extended to the present day, as it established religious freedom in Germany. The army of the chivalrous King of Sweden, the prop and maintenance of the Protestant cause, was largely composed of Scotchmen, and among these was the hero of the story. The chief interest of the tale turns on the great struggle between Gustavus and his chief opponents Wallenstein, Tilly, and Pappenheim.

"As we might expect from Mr. Henty the tale is a clever and instructive piece of history, and as boys may be trusted to read it conscientiously, they can hardly fail to be profited as well as pleased."—*The Times.*

"A praiseworthy attempt to interest British youth in the great deeds of the Scotch Brigade in the wars of Gusta-vus Adolphus. Mackay, Hepburn, and Munro live again in Mr. Henty's pages, as those deserve to live whose disciplined bands formed really the germ of the modern British army."—*Athenæum.*

"A stirring story of stirring times. This book should hold a place among the classics of youthful fiction."—*United Service Gazette.*

BY G. A. HENTY.

"Mr. Henty as a boy's story-teller stands in the very foremost rank."
—*Glasgow Herald.*

WITH WOLFE IN CANADA:

Or, The Winning of a Continent. By G. A. HENTY. With
12 full-page Illustrations by GORDON BROWNE. Crown 8vo,
cloth elegant, olivine edges, 6s.

In the present volume Mr. Henty has endeavoured to give the details
of the principal events in the struggle between Britain and France for
supremacy on the North American continent. The importance of this
struggle can scarcely be overrated, as on the issue of it depended not
only the destinies of North America, but to a large extent those of the
mother countries themselves. The fall of Quebec decided that the Anglo-
Saxon race should predominate in the New World, that Britain, and not
France, should take the lead among the nations, and that English com-
merce, the English language, and English literature, should spread right
round the globe. While thus of the greatest significance, this episode from
the world's history lends itself pre-eminently to the romantic style of treat-
ment of which Mr. Henty is master.

WITH CLIVE IN INDIA:

Or the Beginnings of an Empire. By G. A. HENTY. With
12 full-page Illustrations by GORDON BROWNE, in black and
tint. Crown 8vo, cloth elegant, olivine edges, 6s.

The period between the landing of Clive as a young writer in India and
the close of his career was critical and eventful in the extreme. At its
commencement the English were traders existing on sufferance of the
native princes. At its close they were masters of Bengal and of the greater
part of Southern India. The author has given a full and accurate account
of the events of that stirring time, and battles and sieges follow each other
in rapid succession, while he combines with his narrative a tale of daring
and adventure, which gives a lifelike interest to the volume.

"In this book Mr. Henty has contrived
to exceed himself in stirring adventures
and thrilling situations. The pictures add
greatly to the interest of the book."—
Saturday Review.

"Among writers of stories of adventure
for boys Mr. Henty stands in the very
first rank, and Mr. Gordon Browne occu-
pies a similar place with his pencil. . . .
Those who know something about India
will be the most ready to thank Mr.
Henty for giving them this instructive
volume to place in the hands of their children."—*Academy.*

"He has taken a period of Indian History of the most vital importance, and he
has embroidered on the historical facts
a story which of itself is deeply interesting. Young people assuredly will be delighted with the volume."—*Scotsman.*

BY G. A. HENTY.

"The brightest of all the living writers whose office it is to enchant the boys."
—Christian Leader.

THROUGH THE FRAY:

A Story of the Luddite Riots. By G. A. HENTY. With 12 full-page Illustrations by H. M. PAGET, in black and tint. Crown 8vo, cloth elegant, olivine edges, 6s.

The author in this story has followed the lines which he worked out so successfully in *Facing Death*. As in that story he shows that there are victories to be won in peaceful fields, and that steadfastness and tenacity are virtues which tell in the long run. The story is laid in Yorkshire at the commencement of the present century, when the high price of food induced by the war and the introduction of machinery drove the working-classes to desperation, and caused them to band themselves in that wide-spread organization known as the Luddite Society. There is an abundance of adventure in the tale, but its chief interest lies in the character of the hero, and the manner in which by a combination of circumstances he is put on trial for his life, but at last comes victorious "through the fray."

"Mr. Henty inspires a love and admiration for straightforwardness, truth, and courage. This is one of the best of the many good books Mr. Henty has produced, and deserves to be classed with his *Facing Death.*"—*Standard.*

"The interest of the story never flags. Were we to propose a competition for the best list of novel writers for boys we have little doubt that Mr. Henty's name would stand first."—*Journal of Education.*

TRUE TO THE OLD FLAG:

A Tale of the American War of Independence. By G. A. HENTY. With 12 full-page Illustrations by GORDON BROWNE, in black and tint. Crown 8vo, cloth elegant, olivine edges, 6s.

In this story the author has gone to the accounts of English officers who took part in the conflict, and lads will find that in no war in which British soldiers have been engaged did they behave with greater courage and good conduct. The historical portion of the book being accompanied with numerous thrilling adventures with the redskins on the shores of Lake Huron, a story of exciting interest is interwoven with the general narrative and carried through the book.

"Does justice to the pluck and determination of the British soldiers during the unfortunate struggle against American emancipation. The son of an American loyalist, who remains true to our flag, falls among the hostile redskins in that very Huron country which has been endeared to us by the exploits of Hawkeye and Chingachgook."—*The Times.*

"Mr. G. A. Henty's extensive personal experience of adventures and moving incidents by flood and field, combined with a gift of picturesque narrative, make his books always welcome visitors in the home circle."—*Daily News.*

"Very superior in every way. The book is almost unique in its class in having illustrative maps."—*Saturday Review.*

BY G. A. HENTY.

"Mr. Henty's books never fail to interest boy readers."—*Academy.*

IN FREEDOM'S CAUSE:

A Story of Wallace and Bruce. By G. A. HENTY. With 12 full-page Illustrations by GORDON BROWNE, in black and tint. Crown 8vo, cloth elegant, olivine edges, 6s.

In this story the author relates the stirring tale of the Scottish War of Independence. The extraordinary valour and personal prowess of Wallace and Bruce rival the deeds of the mythical heroes of chivalry, and indeed at one time Wallace was ranked with these legendary personages. The researches of modern historians have shown, however, that he was a living, breathing man—and a valiant champion. The hero of the tale fought under both Wallace and Bruce, and while the strictest historical accuracy has been maintained with respect to public events, the work is full of "hair-breadth 'scapes" and wild adventure.

"Mr. Henty has broken new ground as an historical novelist. His tale is full of stirring action, and will commend itself to boys."—*Athenæum.*

"It is written in the author's best style. Full of the wildest and most remarkable achievements, it is a tale of great interest, which a boy, once he has begun it, will not willingly put on one side."—*The Schoolmaster.*

"Scarcely anywhere have we seen in prose a more lucid and spirit-stirring description of Bannockburn than the one with which the author fittingly closes his volume."—*Dumfries Standard.*

UNDER DRAKE'S FLAG.

A Tale of the Spanish Main. By G. A. HENTY. Illustrated by 12 full-page Pictures by GORDON BROWNE, in black and tint. Crown 8vo, cloth elegant, olivine edges, 6s.

A story of the days when England and Spain struggled for the supremacy of the sea, and England carried off the palm. The heroes sail as lads with Drake in the expedition in which the Pacific Ocean was first seen by an Englishman from a tree-top on the Isthmus of Panama, and in his great voyage of circumnavigation. The historical portion of the story is absolutely to be relied upon, but this, although very useful to lads, will perhaps be less attractive than the great variety of exciting adventure through which the young adventurers pass in the course of their voyages.

"A stirring book of Drake's time, and just such a book as the youth of this maritime country are likely to prize highly."—*Daily Telegraph.*

"Ned in the coils of the boa-constrictor is a wonderful picture. A boy must be hard to please if he wishes for anything more exciting."—*Pall Mall Gazette.*

"A book of adventure, where the hero meets with experience enough one would think to turn his hair gray."—*Harper's Monthly Magazine.*

BY G. A. HENTY.

"Mr. Henty is the prince of story-tellers for boys."—Sheffield Independent.

THE BRAVEST OF THE BRAVE:

Or, With Peterborough in Spain. By G. A. HENTY. With 8 full-page Illustrations by H. M. PAGET. Crown 8vo, cloth elegant, 5s.

There are few great leaders whose lives and actions have so completely fallen into oblivion as those of the Earl of Peterborough. This is largely due to the fact that they were overshadowed by the glory and successes of Marlborough. His career as General extended over little more than a year, and yet, in that time, he showed a genius for warfare which has never been surpassed, and performed feats of daring worthy of the leaders of chivalry.

Round the fortunes of Jack Stilwell, the hero, and of Peterborough, Mr. Henty has woven an interesting and instructive narrative descriptive of this portion of the War of the Spanish Succession (1705–6).

THE DRAGON AND THE RAVEN:

Or, The Days of King Alfred. By G. A. HENTY. With 8 full-page Illustrations by C. J. STANILAND, R.I., in black and tint. Crown 8vo, cloth elegant, 5s.

In this story the author gives an account of the desperate struggle between Saxon and Dane for supremacy in England, and presents a vivid picture of the misery and ruin to which the country was reduced by the ravages of the sea-wolves. The hero of the story, a young Saxon thane, takes part in all the battles fought by King Alfred, and the incidents in his career are unusually varied and exciting. He is driven from his home, takes to the sea and resists the Danes on their own element, and being pursued by them up the Seine, is present at the long and desperate siege of Paris.

"Perhaps the best story of the early days of England which has yet been told."—*Court Journal.*

"A well-built superstructure of fiction on an interesting substratum of fact. Treated in a manner most attractive to the boyish reader."—*Athenæum.*

"A story that may justly be styled remarkable. Boys, in reading it, will be surprised to find how Alfred persevered, through years of bloodshed and times of peace, to rescue his people from the thraldom of the Danes. We hope the book will soon be widely known in all our schools."—*Schoolmaster.*

"We know of no popular book in which the stirring incidents of the reign of the heroic Saxon king are made accessible to young readers as they are here. Mr. Henty has made a book which will afford much delight to boys, and is of genuine historic value."—*Scotsman.*

BY G. A. HENTY.

"Mr. Henty is one of the best of story-tellers for young people."—*Spectator.*

A FINAL RECKONING:

A Tale of Bush Life in Australia. By G. A. HENTY. With 8 full-page Illustrations by W. B. WOLLEN. Crown 8vo, cloth elegant, 5*s.*

In this book Mr. Henty has again left the battlefields of history and has written a story of adventure in Australia in the early days of its settlement, when the bush-rangers and the natives constituted a real and formidable danger.

The hero, a young English lad, after rather a stormy boyhood, emigrates to Australia, where he gets employment as an officer in the mounted police.

A few years of active work on the frontier, where he has many a brush with both natives and bush-rangers, gain him promotion to a captaincy. In that post he greatly distinguishes himself, and finally leaves the service and settles down to the peaceful life of a squatter.

ST. GEORGE FOR ENGLAND:

A Tale of Cressy and Poitiers. By G. A. HENTY. With 8 full-page Illustrations by GORDON BROWNE, in black and tint. Crown 8vo, cloth elegant, 5*s.*

No portion of English history is more crowded with great events than that of the reign of Edward III. Cressy and Poitiers laid France prostrate at the feet of England; the Spanish fleet was dispersed and destroyed by a naval battle as remarkable in its incidents as was that which broke up the Armada in the time of Elizabeth. Europe was ravaged by the dreadful plague known as the Black Death, and France was the scene of the terrible peasant rising called the Jacquerie. All these stirring events are treated by the author in *St. George for England.* The hero of the story, although of good family, begins life as a London apprentice, but after countless adventures and perils, becomes by valour and good conduct the squire, and at last the trusted friend of the Black Prince.

"A story of very great interest for boys. In his own forcible style the author has endeavoured to show that determination and enthusiasm can accomplish marvellous results; that courage is generally accompanied by magnanimity and gentleness, and that it is the parent of nearly all the other virtues, since but few of them can be practised without it."—*Pall Mall Gazette.*

"Mr. Henty has developed for himself a type of historical novel for boys which bids fair to supplement, on their behalf, the historical labours of Sir Walter Scott in the land of fiction."—*Standard.*

"Mr. Henty as a boy's story-teller stands in the very foremost rank. With plenty of scope to work upon he has produced a strong story at once instructive and entertaining."—*Glasgow Herald.*

BY G. A. HENTY.

"Among writers of stories of adventure for boys Mr. Henty stands in the very first rank."—*Academy.*

FOR NAME AND FAME:

Or, Through Afghan Passes. By G. A. HENTY. With 8 full-page Illustrations by GORDON BROWNE, in black and tint. Crown 8vo, cloth elegant, 5s.

This is an interesting story of the last war in Afghanistan. The hero, after being wrecked and going through many stirring adventures among the Malays, finds his way to Calcutta, and enlists in a regiment proceeding to join the army at the Afghan passes. He accompanies the force under General Roberts to the Peiwar Kotal, is wounded, taken prisoner, and carried to Cabul, whence he is transferred to Candahar, and takes part in the final defeat of the army of Ayoub Khan.

"Mr. Henty's pen is never more effectively employed than when he is describing incidents of warfare. The best feature of the book—apart from the interest of its scenes of adventure—is its honest effort to do justice to the patriotism of the Afghan people."—*Daily News.*

"Here we have not only a rousing story, replete with all the varied forms of excitement of a campaign, but an instructive history of a recent war, and, what is still more useful, an account of a territory and its inhabitants which must for a long time possess a supreme interest for Englishmen, as being the key to our Indian Empire."—*Glasgow Herald.*

BY SHEER PLUCK:

A Tale of the Ashanti War. By G. A. HENTY. With 8 full-page Illustrations by GORDON BROWNE, in black and tint. Crown 8vo, cloth elegant, 5s.

The Ashanti Campaign seems but an event of yesterday, but it happened when the generation now rising up were too young to have made themselves acquainted with its incidents. The author has woven, in a tale of thrilling interest, all the details of the campaign, of which he was himself a witness. His hero, after many exciting adventures in the interior, finds himself at Coomassie just before the outbreak of the war, is detained a prisoner by the king, is sent down with the army which invaded the British Protectorate, escapes, and accompanies the English expedition on their march to Coomassie.

"Mr. Henty keeps up his reputation as a writer of boys' stories. 'By Sheer Pluck' will be eagerly read."—*Athenæum.*

"The book is one which will not only sustain, but add to Mr. Henty's reputation."—*The Standard.*

"Written with a simple directness, force, and purity of style worthy of Defoe. Morally, the book is everything that could be desired, setting before the boys a bright and bracing ideal of the English gentleman."—*Christian Leader.*

BY G. A. HENTY.

"Mr. Henty's books are always welcome visitors in the home circle."—*Daily News.*

FACING DEATH:

Or the Hero of the Vaughan Pit. A Tale of the Coal Mines. By G. A. HENTY. With 8 full-page Illustrations by GORDON BROWNE, in black and tint. Crown 8vo, cloth elegant, 5*s.*

"Facing Death" is a story with a purpose. It is intended to show that a lad who makes up his mind firmly and resolutely that he will rise in life, and who is prepared to face toil and ridicule and hardship to carry out his determination, is sure to succeed. The hero of the story is a typical British boy, dogged, earnest, generous, and though "shamefaced" to a degree, is ready to face death in the discharge of duty. His is a character for imitation by boys in every station.

"The tale is well written and well illustrated, and there is much reality in the characters."—*Athenæum.*

"If any father, godfather, clergyman, or schoolmaster is on the look-out for a good book to give as a present to a boy who is worth his salt, this is the book we would recommend."—*Standard.*

YARNS ON THE BEACH.

By G. A. HENTY. With 2 full-page Illustrations. Crown 8vo, cloth extra, 1*s.* 6*d.*

"This little book should find special favour among boys. The yarns are spun by old sailors, and while full of romance and adventure, are admirably calculated to foster a manly spirit."—*The Echo.*

BY GEORGE MANVILLE FENN.

IN THE KING'S NAME:

Or the Cruise of the *Kestrel.* By G. MANVILLE FENN. Illustrated by 12 full-page Pictures by GORDON BROWNE, in black and tint. Crown 8vo, cloth elegant, olivine edges, 6*s.*

"In the King's Name" is a spirited story of the Jacobite times, concerning the adventures of Hilary Leigh, a young naval officer in the preventive service off the coast of Sussex, on board the *Kestrel.* Leigh is taken prisoner by the adherents of the Pretender, amongst whom is an early friend and patron who desires to spare the lad's life, but will not release him. The narrative is full of exciting and often humorous incident.

"Mr. Fenn has won a foremost place among writers for boys. 'In the King's Name' is, we think, the best of all his productions in this field."—*Daily News.*

"Told with the freshness and verve which characterize all Mr. Fenn's writings and put him in the front rank of writers for boys."—*Standard.*

BY GEORGE MANVILLE FENN.

"Mr. Manville Fenn may be regarded as the successor in boyhood's affections of Captain Mayne Reid."—*Academy*.

DEVON BOYS:

A Tale of the North Shore. By GEORGE MANVILLE FENN. With 12 full-page Illustrations by GORDON BROWNE. Crown 8vo, cloth elegant, olivine edges, 6s.

The adventures of Sep Duncan and his school friends take place in the early part of the Georgian era, during the wars between England and France. The scene is laid on the picturesque rocky coast of North Devon, where the three lads pass through many perils both afloat and ashore. Fishermen, smugglers, naval officers, and a stern old country surgeon play their parts in the story, which is one of honest adventure with the mastering of difficulties in a wholesome manly way, mingled with sufficient excitement to satisfy the most exacting reader. The discovery of the British silver mine and its working up and defence take up a large portion of the story.

BROWNSMITH'S BOY.

By GEORGE MANVILLE FENN. With 12 full-page Illustrations by GORDON BROWNE, in black and tint. Crown 8vo, cloth elegant, olivine edges, 6s.

The career of "Brownsmith's Boy" embraces the home adventures of an orphan, who, having formed the acquaintance of an eccentric old gardener, accepts his offer of a home and finds that there is plenty of romance in a garden, and much excitement even in a journey now and then to town. In a half-savage lad he finds a friend who shows his love and fidelity principally by pretending to be an enemy. In "Brownsmith's Boy" there is abundance of excitement and trouble within four walls.

"'Brownsmith's Boy' excels all the numerous 'juvenile' books that the present season has yet produced."—*Academy*.

"Mr. Fenn's books are among the best, if not altogether the best, of the stories for boys. Mr. Fenn is at his best in 'Brownsmith's Boy.' The story is a thoroughly manly and healthy one."—*Pictorial World*.

"'Brownsmith's Boy' must rank among the few undeniably good boys' books. He will be a very dull boy indeed who lays it down without wishing that it had gone on for at least 100 pages more."—*North British Mail*.

"In every way a charming book for young people. The author has much of the inventiveness of the well-known French writer Jules Verne; indeed, he is in the front rank of writers of stories for boys. Parents especially ought to be very thankful to him for providing their sons with so much wholesome and fascinating amusement in the way of literature."—*Liverpool Mercury*.

BY GEORGE MANVILLE FENN.

"There is a freshness, a buoyancy, a heartiness about Mr. Fenn's writings."—*Standard.*

THE GOLDEN MAGNET:

A Tale of the Land of the Incas.   By G. MANVILLE FENN. With 12 full-page Pictures by GORDON BROWNE, in black and tint.   Crown 8vo, cloth elegant, olivine edges, 6*s.*

The tale is of a romantic lad, who leaves home to seek his fortune in South America by endeavouring to discover some of that treasure which legends declare was ages ago hidden to preserve it from the Spanish invaders.   He is accompanied by a faithful companion, who, in the capacity both of comrade and henchman, does true service, and shows the dogged courage of the English lad during the strange adventures which befall them.

"Told with admirable force and strength.   Few men other than Mr. Fenn have the capacity for telling such stories as this."—*Scotsman.*

"There could be no more welcome present for a boy.   There is not a dull page, and many will be read with breathless interest."—*Journal of Education.*

BUNYIP LAND:

The Story of a Wild Journey in New Guinea.   By G. MANVILLE FENN.   With 12 full-page Illustrations by GORDON BROWNE.   Crown 8vo, cloth elegant, olivine edges, 6*s.*

"Bunyip Land" is the story of an eminent botanist, who ventures into the interior of New Guinea in his search for new plants.   Years pass away, and he does not return; and though supposed to be dead, his young wife and son refuse to believe it; and as soon as he is old enough young Joe goes in search of his father, accompanied by Jimmy, a native black.   Their adventures are many and exciting, but after numerous perils they discover the lost one, a prisoner among the blacks, and bring him home in triumph.

"Mr. Fenn deserves the thanks of everybody for 'Bunyip Land' and 'Menhardoc,' and we may venture to promise that a quiet week may be reckoned on whilst the youngsters have such fascinating literature provided for their evenings' amusement."—*Spectator.*

"One of the best tales of adventure produced by any living writer, combining the inventiveness of Jules Verne, and the solidity of character and earnestness of spirit which have made the English victorious in so many fields of labour and research."—*Daily Chronicle.*

A TERRIBLE COWARD.

By G. MANVILLE FENN.   With 2 full-page Illustrations in black and tint.   Crown 8vo, cloth extra, 1*s.* 6*d.*

The tale of a lad who never bounced, bragged, or bullied.   When the testing time came, however, the "coward" was found to be the one who distanced all by his cool unflinching English courage.

"Just such a tale as boys will delight to read, and as they are certain to profit by."—*Aberdeen Journal.*

BY GEORGE MANVILLE FENN.

"Mr. Fenn is in the front rank of writers of stories for boys."—*Liverpool Mercury.*

YUSSUF THE GUIDE:

Being the Strange Story of the Travels in Asia Minor of Burne the Lawyer, Preston the Professor, and Lawrence the Sick. By G. MANVILLE FENN. With 8 full-page Illustrations by JOHN SCHÖNBERG. Crown 8vo, cloth elegant, 5*s.*

Deals with the stirring incidents in the career of Lawrence Grange, a lad who has been almost given over by the doctors, but who rapidly recovers health and strength in a journey through Asia Minor with his guardians "The Professor" and "The Lawyer." Yussuf is their guide; and in their journeyings through the wild mountain region in search of the ancient cities of the Greeks and Romans they penetrate where law is disregarded, and finally fall into the hands of brigands. Their adventures in this rarely-traversed romantic region are many, and culminate in the travellers being snowed up for the winter in the mountains, from which they escape while their captors are waiting for the ransom that does not come.

MENHARDOC:

A Story of Cornish Nets and Mines. By G. MANVILLE FENN. With 8 full-page Illustrations by C. J. STANILAND, R.I., in black and tint. Crown 8vo, cloth elegant, 5*s.*

The scene of this story of boyish aspiration and adventure is laid among the granite piles and tors of Cornwall. Here amongst the hardy, honest fishermen and miners the two London boys are inducted into the secrets of fishing in the great bay, they learn how to catch mackerel, pollack, and conger with the line, and are present at the hauling of the nets, although not without incurring many serious risks. Adventures are pretty plentiful, but the story has for its strong base the development of character of the three boys. There is a good deal of quaint character throughout, and the sketches of Cornish life and local colouring are based upon experience in the bay, whose fishing village is called here Menhardoc. This is a thoroughly English story of phases of life but little touched upon in boys' literature up to the present time.

"They are real living boys, with the virtues and faults which characterize the transition stage between boyhood and manhood. The Cornish fishermen are drawn from life, they are racy of the soil, salt with the sea-water, and they stand out from the pages in their jerseys and sea-boots all sprinkled with silvery pilchard scales."—*Spectator.*

"Mr. Fenn has written many books in his time; he has not often written one which for genuine merit as a story for young people will exceed this."—*Scotsman.*

BY GEORGE MANVILLE FENN.

"No one can find his way to the hearts of lads more readily than Mr. Fenn."—Nottingham Guardian.

PATIENCE WINS:

Or, War in the Works. By G. MANVILLE FENN. With 8 full-page Illustrations by GORDON BROWNE, in black and tint. Crown 8vo, cloth elegant, 5s.

This is a graphic narrative of factory life in the Black Country. The hero, Cob, and his three uncles, engineers, machinists, and inventors, go down to Arrowfield to set up "a works." They find, however, that the workmen, through prejudice and ignorance, are determined to have no new-fangled machinery. After a series of narrow escapes and stirring encounters, the workmen by degrees find that no malice is borne against them, and at last admiration takes the place of hatred. A great business is built up, and its foundation is laid on the good-will of the men.

"An excellent story, the interest being sustained from first to last. This is, both in its intention and the way the story is told, one of the best books of its kind which has come before us this year."—*Saturday Review.*

"Mr. Fenn is at his best in 'Patience Wins.' It is sure to prove acceptable to youthful readers, and will give a good idea of that which was the real state of one of our largest manufacturing towns not many years ago."—*Guardian.*

"Mr. Fenn has written many a book for boys, but never has he hit upon a happier plan than in writing this story of Yorkshire factory life. The whole book, from page 1 to 352, is all aglow with life, the scenes varying continually with kaleidoscopic rapidity."—*Pall Mall Gazette.*

NAT THE NATURALIST:

A Boy's Adventures in the Eastern Seas. By G. MANVILLE FENN. Illustrated by 8 full-page Pictures by GORDON BROWNE, in black and tint. Crown 8vo, cloth elegant, 5s.

This is a pleasant story of a lad who has a great desire to go abroad to seek specimens in natural history, and has that desire gratified. The boy Nat and his uncle Dick go on a voyage to the remoter islands of the Eastern seas, and their adventures there are told in a truthful and vastly interesting fashion, which will at once attract and maintain the earnest attention of young readers. The descriptions of Mr. Ebony, their black comrade, and of the scenes of savage life, are full of genuine humour.

"Mr. Manville Fenn has here hit upon a capital idea. . . . This is among the best of the boys' books of the season."—*The Times.*

"This sort of book encourages independence of character, develops resource, and teaches a boy to keep his eyes open."—*Saturday Review.*

"We can conceive of no more attractive present for a young naturalist."—*Land and Water.*

"The late Lord Palmerston used to say that one use of war was to teach geography; such books as this teach it in a more harmless and cheaper way."—*Athenæum.*

BY HARRY COLLINGWOOD.

"Mr. G. A. Henty has found a formidable rival in Mr. Collingwood."—*Academy.*

THE LOG OF THE "FLYING FISH:"

A Story of Aerial and Submarine Peril and Adventure. By HARRY COLLINGWOOD. With 12 full-page Illustrations by GORDON BROWNE. Crown 8vo, cloth elegant, olivine edges, 6s.

In this story the aim of the author has been, not only to interest and amuse, but also to stimulate a taste for scientific study. He has utilized natural science as a peg whereon to hang the web of a narrative of absorbing interest, interweaving therewith sundry very striking scientific facts in such a manner as to provoke a desire for further information.

Professor Von Schalckenberg constructs a gigantic and wonderful ship, appropriately named the *Flying Fish*, which is capable of navigating not only the higher reaches of the atmosphere, but also the extremest depths of ocean; and in her the four adventurers make a voyage to the North Pole, and to a hitherto unexplored portion of Central Africa.

In common with all this author's stories, "The Log of the Flying Fish" is thoroughly healthy and unexceptionable in tone, and may be unhesitatingly placed in the hands of "our boys," who will enjoy in its perusal a literary treat entirely after their own hearts.

THE CONGO ROVERS:

A Tale of the Slave Squadron. By HARRY COLLINGWOOD. With 8 full-page Illustrations by J. SCHÖNBERG, in black and tint. Crown 8vo, cloth extra, 5s.

The scene of this tale is laid on the west coast of Africa, and in the lower reaches of the Congo; the characteristic scenery of the great river being delineated with wonderful accuracy and completeness of detail. The hero of the story—a midshipman on board one of the ships of the slave squadron—after being effectually laughed out of his boyish vanity, develops into a lad possessed of a large share of sound common sense, the exercise of which enables him to render much valuable service to his superior officers in unmasking a most daring and successful ruse on the part of the slavers.

"Mr. Collingwood carries us off for another cruise at sea, in 'The Congo Rovers,' and boys will need no pressing to join the daring crew, which seeks adventures and meets with any number of them in the forests and pestilential fogs of the Congo."—*The Times.*

"We can heartily recommend it as one that boys will be sure to read throughout with pleasure, and with advantage, also, to their morals and their imaginations."—*Academy.*

"No better sea story has lately been written than the *Congo Rovers*. It is as original as any boy could desire."—*Morning Post.*

BY HARRY COLLINGWOOD.

"Mr. Collingwood has established his reputation as a first-rate writer of sea-stories."—*Scotsman.*

THE PIRATE ISLAND:

A Story of the South Pacific. By HARRY COLLINGWOOD. Illustrated by 8 full-page Pictures by C. J. STANILAND and J. R. WELLS, in black and tint. Crown 8vo, cloth elegant, 5s.

This story details the adventures of a lad who was found in his infancy on board a wreck, and is adopted by a fisherman. By a deed of true gallantry his whole destiny is changed, and, going to sea, he forms one of a party who, after being burned out of their ship in the South Pacific, and experiencing great hardship and suffering in their boats, are picked up by a pirate brig and taken to the "Pirate Island." After many thrilling adventures, they ultimately succeed in effecting their escape. The story depicts both the Christian and the manly virtues in such colours as will cause them to be admired—and therefore imitated.

"A capital story of the sea; indeed in our opinion the author is superior in some respects as a marine novelist to the better known Mr. Clarke Russell."—*The Times.*

"The best of these books. . . . The events are described with minuteness and care. The result is a very amusing book."—*Saturday Review.*

"Told in the most vivid and graphic language. It would be difficult to find a more thoroughly delightful gift-book."—*The Guardian.*

"One of the very best books for boys that we have seen for a long time: its author is thoroughly at home in maritime matters, and stands far in advance of any other writer for boys as a teller of stories of the sea."—*The Standard.*

"There is enough to make any boy dream of all that is strange and wild. But bravery and gentleness and helpfulness are shown in all their beauty; and so we should like as many boys as possible to read the story and admire the daring deeds."—*Christian Leader.*

BY DOUGLAS FRAZAR.

PERSEVERANCE ISLAND:

Or the Robinson Crusoe of the 19th Century. By DOUGLAS FRAZAR. With 12 full-page Illustrations. Crown 8vo, cloth elegant, 5s.

This story shows the limitless ingenuity and invention of man, and portrays the works and achievements of a castaway, who, thrown ashore almost literally naked upon a desert isle, is able, by the use of his brains, the skill of his hands, and a practical knowledge of the common arts and sciences, to far surpass the achievements of all his predecessors, and to surround himself with implements of power utterly beyond the reach of the original Robinson Crusoe.

"One of the best issues, if not absolutely the best, of Defoe's work which has ever appeared."—*The Standard.*

THE LIFE AND SURPRISING ADVENTURES OF ROBINSON CRUSOE.

BY DANIEL DEFOE.

Beautifully Printed, and Illustrated by above 100 Pictures Designed by Gordon Browne.

Crown 8vo, cloth elegant, olivine edges, 6s.

There have been countless editions of *Robinson Crusoe,* and they have mostly been imperfect, inasmuch as they have been so largely altered from the original text that the language in many instances has not been that of Defoe but of his revisers. The present volume has been carefully printed from the original edition, and all obsolete or little-known terms and obscure phrases are explained in brief foot-notes. The "Editing" is not a corruption or pretended improvement of Defoe's great work.

"Of the many editions of Defoe's immortal story that have passed through our hands in recent years, we are inclined to rank this the most desirable as a present for a good boy."—*The Academy.*

GULLIVER'S TRAVELS.

A NEW EDITION, beautifully printed, and illustrated by more than 100 Pictures from designs by GORDON BROWNE. In crown 8vo, cloth elegant, olivine edges, 5s.

The wonderful travels of Gulliver "into several remote regions of the world" are still as fresh and entertaining as when they were first presented to the public more than a hundred and fifty years ago. In this edition the text has been judiciously curtailed by the omission of several passages quite unsuited for the perusal of the young or for family reading; and foot-notes to the text have been added to explain and throw light on those allusions, references, &c., which a young reader would not understand.

"Mr. Gordon Browne is, to my thinking, incomparably the most artistic, spirited, and brilliant of our illustrators of books for boys, and one of the most humorous also, as his illustrations of 'Gulliver' amply testify."—*Truth.*

"By help of the admirable illustrations, and a little judicious skipping, it has enchanted a family party of ages varying from six to sixty. Which of the other Christmas books could stand this test?"—*Journal of Education.*

BY ASCOTT R. HOPE.

STORIES OF OLD RENOWN:

Tales of Knights and Heroes. By Ascott R. Hope. With nearly 100 Illustrations by Gordon Browne. Crown 8vo, cloth elegant, olivine edges, 5s.

A Series of the best of the Stories of Noble Knighthood and Old Romance, told in refined and simple language, and adapted to young readers. A book possessing remarkable attractions for boys.

"The stories are admirably chosen. It is a book to be coveted by all young readers."—*Scotsman.*

"One of the best, if not the best, boys' book of the season."—*Truth.*

THE WIGWAM AND THE WAR-PATH:

Stories of the Red Indians. By Ascott R. Hope. With 8 full-page Pictures by Gordon Browne, in black and tint. Crown 8vo, cloth elegant, 5s.

"The Wigwam and the War-path" consists of stories of Red Indians which are none the less romantic for being true. They are taken from the actual records of those who have been made prisoners by the red men or have lived among them, joining in their expeditions and taking part in their semi-savage but often picturesque and adventurous life.

"Mr. Hope's volume is notably good: it gives a very vivid picture of life among the Indians."—*Spectator.*

"All the stories are told well, in simple spirited language and with a fulness of detail that makes them instructive as well as interesting."—*Journal of Education.*

BY J. PERCY GROVES.

REEFER AND RIFLEMAN:

A Tale of the Two Services. By J. Percy Groves, late 27th Inniskillings, author of "From Cadet to Captain," &c. With 6 full-page Illustrations by John Schönberg. Crown 8vo, cloth elegant, 3s. 6d.

A tale of the naval and military services in the early part of the present century. The hero enters the Royal Navy just after the rupture of the Peace of Amiens. After a short but eventful career afloat he returns home, and subsequently joins the sister service, being appointed to a second lieutenancy in the old 95th Rifles. The ex-"reefer" takes an active part in the opening scenes of the Peninsular War, and meets with varied adventures in Portugal and Spain. After the battle of Coruña he once more returns to England. The story has an historical interest as well as a plot of exciting adventure, and a spice of humour which will commend it to the attention of lads who admire the stories of Captain Marryat.

BY JOHN C. HUTCHESON.

"Mr. Hutcheson bids fair to take a prominent place among our best writers of boys' books."—*The Academy.*

THE WHITE SQUALL:

A Story of the Sargasso Sea. By JOHN C. HUTCHESON. With 6 full-page Illustrations by JOHN SCHÖNBERG. Crown 8vo, cloth elegant, 3s. 6d.

Commencing amid the fairy-like scenes and surroundings of a West Indian home, this story passes to Tom Eastman's setting sail from the Windward Islands on a voyage to England. At first the good ship *Josephine* glides buoyantly through the balmy waters of the Caribbean Sea, but getting out into the broad Atlantic, calm and whirlwind are succeeded by a gale which drives her to the confines of the Sargasso Sea, that meadow-like portion of the ocean, between the Azores and Bermuda, which is constantly covered with the fibrous tentacles of the gulf-weed. Here a sudden and unexpected "white squall" assails her—the *Josephine* is turned over on her beam-ends, and the captain and crew climb up on the ship's keel for shelter. How they extricate themselves from this terrible predicament, and how the *Josephine* is righted and pursues her voyage safely to the English Channel, the reader will discover in the book.

THE WRECK OF THE NANCY BELL:

Or, Cast Away on Kerguelen Land. By JOHN C. HUTCHESON. Illustrated by 6 full-page Pictures by FRANK FELLER, in black and tint. Crown 8vo, cloth extra, 3s. 6d.

This is a book after a boy's own heart. The story narrates the eventful voyage of a vessel from the port of London to New Zealand, and the haps and mishaps that befell her, culminating in the wreck of the *Nancy Bell* on Kerguelen Land. There is no lack of incident. From the opening chapter, with the cowardly steward's alarm of "a ghost in the cabin," to the end of the story, which details the rescue of the shipwrecked passengers, one engrossing narrative holds the attention of the reader.

"A full circumstantial narrative such as boys delight in. The ship so sadly destined to wreck on Kerguelen Land is manned by a very life-like party, passengers and crew. The life in the Antarctic Iceland is well treated."—*Athenæum.*

TOM FINCH'S MONKEY

And other Yarns. By JOHN C. HUTCHESON. With 2 full-page Illustrations in black and tint. Crown 8vo, cloth extra, 1s. 6d.

"Short stories of an altogether unexceptionable character, with adventure sufficient for a dozen books of its size."—*United Service Gazette.*

BY JOHN C. HUTCHESON.

"Mr. Hutcheson is master of a capital style for boy readers."—*Scotsman.*

PICKED UP AT SEA:

Or the Gold Miners of Minturne Creek; and other Stories. By JOHN C. HUTCHESON. With 6 full-page Pictures in tints. Crown 8vo, cloth extra, 3s. 6d.

The story of a young English lad, rescued in mid Atlantic from a watery grave, and taken out west by a party of gold-diggers to the wild regions of the Black Hills in Dakota. Here, after warring with the elements during months of unceasing toil in their search for the riches of the earth, and having the result of their indefatigable labour well-nigh torn from their grasp when on the verge of victory, success at last rewards the efforts of the adventurous band.

"A capital book; full of startling incident, clever dialogue, admirable descriptions of sky and water in all their aspects, and plenty of fun."—*Sheffield Independent.*

"This is the first appearance of the author as a writer of books for boys, and the success is so marked that it may well encourage him to further efforts. The description of mining life in the Far-west is true and accurate."—*Standard.*

TEDDY

The Story of a "Little Pickle." By JOHN C. HUTCHESON. With 3 full-page Illustrations. Crown 8vo, cloth extra, 2s.

This is the story of a little fellow, who, while brave and fearless, is always in mischief, and a torment to everyone connected with him, by reason of his natural exuberance of animal spirits. As Teddy cannot manage to steer clear of hot water on shore he is sent to sea, in the hope that discipline and duty will tame down the rough points of his character, and teach him to be a noble and good man. Although a "little pickle" at the beginning of his career, Teddy turns out a little hero at the close of the story, as the reader will find out if the wonderful adventures of the "young torment" be followed to the end.

THE PENANG PIRATE,

And THE LOST PINNACE. By JOHN C. HUTCHESON. With 3 full-page Illustrations. Crown 8vo, cloth extra, 2s.

Deals with the pirates who infest the great water-highways of the East, and tells how a party of Malayan freebooters were caught in their own toils and how the gallant ship *Hankow Lin* voyaged from the Canton river through the straits of Sunda. Both stories are founded on fact.

"A book which most boys will thoroughly enjoy. It is rattling, adventurous, and romantic, and the stories are thoroughly healthy in tone, and written by a skilful hand."—*Aberdeen Journal*

BY MRS. R. H. READ.

SILVER MILL:

A Tale of the Don Valley. By Mrs. R. H. READ. With 6 full-page Illustrations by JOHN SCHÖNBERG, in black and tint. Crown 8vo, cloth elegant, 3s. 6d.

The story of a girl and boy. The chief interest centres around Ruth, who is supposed to be the orphan child of a working-man, but who eventually turns out to be the daughter of the cynical, though essentially kind-hearted, owner of Silver Mill. In tracing the character of Ruth as she develops from an impulsive girl to noble womanhood, the author has drawn a picture at once pleasing and suggestive.

"Another of those pleasant stories which are always acceptable, especially perhaps to girls standing on the debatable ground between girlhood and young ladyhood."—*The Guardian.*

"A good girl's story-book. The plot is interesting, and the heroine, Ruth, a lady by birth, though brought up in a humble station, well deserves the more elevated position in which the end of the book leaves her. The pictures are very spirited."—*Saturday Review.*

DORA:

Or a Girl without a Home. By Mrs. R. H. READ. With 6 full-page Illustrations. Crown 8vo, cloth elegant, 3s. 6d.

The story of a friendless orphan girl, who is placed as pupil-teacher at the school in which she was educated, but is suddenly removed by hard and selfish relatives, who employ her as a menial as well as a governess. Through a series of exciting adventures she makes discoveries respecting a large property which is restored to its rightful owners, and at the same time she secures her escape from her persecutors.

"It is no slight thing, in an age of rubbish, to get a story so pure and healthy."—*The Academy.*

' One of the most pleasing stories for young people that we have met with of late years. There is in it a freshness, simplicity, and naturalness very engaging."—*Harper's Magazine.*

FAIRY FANCY:

What she Heard and what she Saw. By Mrs. R. H. READ. With many Woodcut Illustrations in the text, and a Frontispiece printed in colours. Crown 8vo, cloth elegant, 2s.

The tale is designed to show the influence of character even among little children, and the narrative is such as to awaken and sustain the interest of the younger readers.

"The authoress has very great insight into child nature."—*Glasgow Herald.*

" All is pleasant, nice reading, with a little knowledge of natural history and other matters gently introduced and divested of dryness."—*Practical Teacher.*

BY MRS. R. H. READ.

OUR DOLLY:

Her Words and Ways. By Mrs. R. H. READ. With many Woodcuts, and a Frontispiece in colours. Cr. 8vo, cloth extra, 2s.

A story showing the growth and development of character in a little girl; with a series of entertaining small adventures suitable for very juvenile readers.

"Prettily told and prettily illustrated."—*Guardian.*

"Sure to be a great favourite with young children."—*School Guardian.*

BY ALICE BANKS.

CHEEP AND CHATTER:

Or, LESSONS FROM FIELD AND TREE. By ALICE BANKS. With 54 Character Illustrations by GORDON BROWNE. Small 4to, cloth, handsome design on cover, 3s. 6d.; gilt edges, 4s.

About a dozen highly dramatic sketches or little stories, the actors in which are birds, beasts, and insects. They are instructive, suited to the capacities of young people, and very amusing.

"The real charm of the volume lies in the illustrations. Every one is a success. With birds and mice and insects the artist is equally at home; but his birds above all are inimitable."—*Academy.*

"The author has done her work extremely well, and has conveyed very many admirable lessons to young people. The illustrations are capital—full of fun and genuine humour."—*Scotsman.*

BY LEWIS HOUGH.

DR. JOLLIFFE'S BOYS:

A Tale of Weston School. By LEWIS HOUGH. With 6 full-page
Pictures in black and tint. Crown 8vo, cloth extra, 3s. 6d.

A story of school life which will be read with genuine interest, especially
as it exposes some of the dangers which may beset lads who are ill in-
structed at home or have been thrown among unscrupulous companions.
The descriptions of the characters of the boys are vivid and truthful. The
narrative throughout is bright, easy, and lighted by touches of humour.

"Young people who appreciate 'Tom Brown's School-days' will find this story a worthy companion to that fascinating book. There is the same manliness of tone, truthfulness of outline, avoidance of exaggeration and caricature, and healthy morality as characterized the masterpiece of Mr. Hughes."—*Newcastle Journal.*

BY MRS. EMMA RAYMOND PITMAN.

"Mrs. Pitman's works are all to be prized for their ennobling character—pure,
elevating, interesting, and intellectual."—*Christian Union.*

GARNERED SHEAVES.

A Tale for Boys. By Mrs. E. R. PITMAN. With 4 full-page
Illustrations in black and tint. Crown 8vo, cloth extra, 3s. 6d.

"This book is of unusual merit. It breathes out good thoughts in earnest and true tones that speak to the heart." —*Schoolmistress.*

LIFE'S DAILY MINISTRY.

A Story of Everyday Service for Others. By Mrs. PITMAN. With
4 full-page Illustrations. Crown 8vo, cloth extra, 3s. 6d.

"Full of stirring interest, genuine pic- tures of real life, and pervaded by a broad and active sympathy for the true and good."—*Christian Commonwealth.*

FLORENCE GODFREY'S FAITH.

A Story of Australian Life. By MRS. E. R. PITMAN. With 4
full-page Illustrations. Crown 8vo, cloth extra, 3s. 6d.

"This is a clever, and what is better still, a good book, written with a fresh- ness and power which win the reader's sympathies."—*Christian Globe.*

MY GOVERNESS LIFE:

Or Earning my Living. By MRS. E. R. PITMAN. With 4 full-page
Illustrations in black and tint. Crown 8vo, cloth extra, 3s. 6d.

"Told in the author's usual winsome style, which holds the reader spell-bound
from first to last."—*Christian Union.*

BY HENRY FRITH.

THE SEARCH FOR THE TALISMAN:

A Story of Labrador. By HENRY FRITH. With 6 full-page Illustrations by JOHN SCHÖNBERG, in black and tint. Crown 8vo, cloth elegant, 3*s.* 6*d.*

A stirring tale of adventure. Four youths and two elder relatives proceed in search of a "talisman" left by the father of two of the young explorers when an officer in the Hudson's Bay Company's service. On an exploring expedition they are separated, and various adventures result until they unite again and land amongst the Esquimaux. After suffering many vicissitudes they succeed in recovering the talisman.

"A genial and rollicking tale. It is a regular boys' book, and a very cheery and wholesome one."—*Spectator.*

"Is everything that a boy's book should be—healthy in teaching, instructive, yet never dull. Mr. Frith is a thorough master of boy nature."—*Glasgow Herald.*

JACK O' LANTHORN:

A Tale of Adventure. By HENRY FRITH. With 4 full-page Illustrations in black and tint. Crown 8vo, cloth elegant, 2*s.* 6*d.*

A story of the days when George the Third was king. The hero gets into certain scrapes, and at the sea-coast makes the acquaintance of Jack o' Lanthorn. Drifting out to sea in an open boat they discover in a singular manner the approach of the Spanish fleet, and Jack accompanies the hero of the tale to report what they have seen. Seized by a press-gang they are taken off to sea, and eventually take part in the defence of Gibraltar.

"'Jack o' Lanthorn' will hold its own with the best works of Mr. Henty and Mr. Fenn."—*Morning Advertiser.*

"The narrative is crushed full of stirring incident, and is sure to be a prime favourite with boys."—*Christian Leader.*

BY F. BAYFORD HARRISON.

BROTHERS IN ARMS:

A Story of the Crusades. By F. BAYFORD HARRISON. With 4 Illustrations by GORDON BROWNE. Cr. 8vo, cloth extra, 2*s.* 6*d.*

A story which, while it provides exciting incidents and vivid descriptions, will be of real value to the young reader because of its containing accurate historical information on the subject of the Crusades and the doings of Richard the Lion-heart and his army in the Holy Land.

"Full of striking incident, is very fairly illustrated, and may safely be chosen as sure to prove interesting to young people of both sexes."—*Guardian.*

"One of the best accounts of the Crusades it has been our privilege to read. The book cannot fail to interest boys."—*Schoolmistress.*

BY MARY C. ROWSELL.

TRAITOR OR PATRIOT?

A Tale of the Rye-House Plot. By MARY C. ROWSELL. With 6 full-page Pictures by C. O. MURRAY and C. J. STANILAND, R.I. Crown 8vo, cloth elegant, 3s. 6d.

A romantic tale of the later days of Charles II. The main theme of the story is the conspiracy for the assassination of the king and the Duke of York, which was to be effected on their return from Newmarket. The hero of the story, Lawrence Lee, a young farmer, accidentally learns the truth, and starts on horseback for Newmarket to warn the king. After a series of adventures, the young man succeeds in his loyal enterprise, and duly receives his reward for his conspicuous share in the frustration of the "Rye-House Plot."

"A romantic love episode, whose true characters are life-like beings, not dry sticks as in many historical tales."—*Graphic.*

"The character of the heroine, Ruth, is singularly pretty and attractive: we thank the author for so charming a creation."—*Bristol Mercury.*

THE PEDLAR AND HIS DOG.

By MARY C. ROWSELL. With 2 Illustrations by GEORGE CRUIKSHANK, in black and tint. Crown 8vo, cloth extra, 1s. 6d.

A story of English life in the time of Good Queen Bess. Accompanying John Pennycuick and his dog Shock in their wanderings, we get a pleasant view of rural England, quiet and peaceful then, as it is now, and of London with its quaint old streets and houses.

"The opening chapter, with its description of Necton Fair, will forcibly remind many readers of George Eliot.

The style is clear and attractive, and taken altogether it is a delightful story."—*Western Morning News.*

BY ELIZABETH J. LYSAGHT.

BROTHER AND SISTER:

Or the Trials of the Moore Family. By ELIZABETH J. LYSAGHT. With 6 full-page Illustrations. Cr. 8vo, cloth extra, 3s. 6d.

An interesting story for young people, showing by the narrative of the vicissitudes and struggles of a family which has "come down in the world," and of the brave endeavours of its two younger members, how the pressure of adversity is mitigated by domestic affection, mutual confidence, and hopeful honest effort.

"A pretty story, and well told. The plot is cleverly constructed, and the moral is excellent."—*Athenæum.*

"'Brother and Sister' is a charming story, admirably adapted for young people."—*Society.*

BY E. S. BROOKS.

HISTORIC BOYS:

Their Endeavours, their Achievements, and their Times. By
E. S. Brooks. With 12 full-page Illustrations by R. B. Birch
and John Schönberg. Crown 8vo, cloth extra, 3s. 6d.

The careers of a dozen young fellows of different lands and epochs, such
as show that, from the earliest ages, manliness and self-reliance have ever
been the chief groundwork of character.

"We may safely predict that this book
will be voraciously read by every boy
into whose hands it may come: and no
boy will read it without being thereby
better fitted to fight the battle of life."
—*Literary World.*

BY JANE ANDREWS.

TEN BOYS

Who lived on the Road from Long Ago till Now. By Jane
Andrews. With 20 Illustrations. Cr. 8vo, cloth extra, 2s. 6d.

Introduces the stories of Kablu the Aryan Boy, Darius the Persian Boy,
Cleon the Greek Boy, Horatius the Roman Boy, Wulf the Saxon Boy,
Gilbert the Page, Roger the English Lad, Ezekiel Fuller the Puritan Boy,
Jonathan Dawson the Yankee Boy, Frank Wilson the Boy of 1885, and
gives much entertaining and instructive reading on the manners and
customs of the different nations from Aryan age to now.

BY EVELYN EVERETT GREEN.

THE EVERSLEY SECRETS.

By Evelyn Everett Green. With 4 full-page Illustrations by
J. J. Proctor. Crown 8vo, cloth elegant, 2s. 6d.

This is a story of family life, and deals with the effects of the influence of
one member of the family upon another. The story is told in the easy but
deeply engaging style for which the author has attained a high reputation.

BY R. STEAD.

THE LADS OF LITTLE CLAYTON:

Stories of Village Boy Life. By R. Stead. With 4 full-page
Illustrations. Crown 8vo, cloth elegant, 2s. 6d.

These stories show that humble country boys are often as well worth
writing about as the young gentlemen of the public school or academy.
The stories will be found interesting and even exciting, and most of them
have the advantage of being founded on fact. A healthy moral tone pervades the tales.

FAMOUS DISCOVERIES BY SEA AND LAND.

With 4 full-page Illustrations by A. Monro Smith, in black and tint.   Crown 8vo, cloth elegant, 2s. 6d.

Narratives of the stirring times when the great achievement of Columbus had shown that beyond the Atlantic there were new worlds and oceans to discover and explore—stories of bold adventure and heroic effort which, while strictly historical, are invested with all the charm of romance.

"Either of these volumes will be a gift beyond price for studious lads."—*Norwich Mercury*.

"Such a volume may providentially stir up some youths by the divine fire kindled by these 'great of old' to lay open other lands, and show their vast resources."—*Perthshire Advertiser*.

STIRRING EVENTS OF HISTORY.

With 4 full-page Illustrations by John Schönberg.   Crown 8vo, cloth elegant, 2s. 6d.

The incidents in this volume have been drawn from times and countries wide apart, the aim having been to present the young reader with a series of historical pictures instructive in themselves, and thus to induce a taste for further reading in the same direction.

"The volume will fairly hold its place among those which make the smaller ways of history pleasant and attractive. It may safely be selected as a gift-book, in which the interest will not be exhausted with one reading."—*Guardian*.

STORIES OF THE SEA IN FORMER DAYS:

Narratives of Wreck and Rescue.   With 4 full-page Illustrations by Frank Feller.   Crown 8vo, cloth elegant, 2s. 6d.

While no attempt is made in "Stories of the Sea" to paint the sailor's life in glowing colours, or invest it with a glamour of romance, the narratives selected are full of such thrilling incidents of peril, suffering, and shipwreck, as are always deeply interesting to the young reader.

"Next to an original sea-tale of sustained interest come well-sketched collections of maritime peril and suffering which awaken the sympathies by the realism of fact. 'Stories of the Sea,' are a very good specimen of the kind."—*The Times*.

ADVENTURES IN FIELD, FLOOD, & FOREST:

Stories of Danger and Daring.   With 4 full-page Illustrations by Frank Feller.   Crown 8vo, cloth elegant, 2s. 6d.

These narratives of real personal experience in "Field, Flood, and Forest," while in no sense fictitious, will be found quite as exciting and more truly interesting than the most cunningly devised fables.

"The editor has beyond all question succeeded admirably. . . . It cannot fail to be read with interest and advantage."—*Academy*.

"All admirably told. It will be counted one of the best of the story-books that Christmas produces."—*Scotsman*.

TALES OF CAPTIVITY AND EXILE.

With 4 full-page Illustrations by W. B. FORTESCUE. Crown 8vo, cloth elegant, 2s. 6d.

A volume of stories of men and women in many lands, who in prison or in exile have suffered for their conscientious convictions, or have been the victims of irresponsible tyranny. The walls of many a dungeon in ancient as well as modern times could tell of heroic endurance of wrong, and of marvellous patience and ingenuity in devising means of lightening the horrors of the prison or effecting deliverance from it. In this volume will be found authentic records of many of these more notable life-stories.

THE JOYOUS STORY OF TOTO.

By LAURA E. RICHARDS. With 30 humorous and fanciful Illustrations by E. H. GARRETT. Crown 8vo, cloth extra, 2s. 6d.

Toto is a little boy who finds his friends among the birds and the animals, who tell him many wonderful stories in a bright, quaint, humorous fashion. The fun is genuine and cheerful, and the illustrations give a delightful personality to the characters.

"A very delightful book for children, which deserves to find a place in every nursery."—*Lady's Pictorial*.

"An excellent book for children, which should take its place beside Lewis Carroll's unique works."—*Birmingham Gaz*.

BY EMMA LESLIE.

GYTHA'S MESSAGE:

A Tale of Saxon England. By EMMA LESLIE, author of "Glaucia the Greek Slave," &c. With 4 full-page Pictures by C. J. STANILAND, R.I. Crown 8vo, cloth extra, 2s. 6d.

This is a story of the time of "Harold, the last of the Saxon Kings." Though mainly a domestic tale, we yet get a glimpse of the stirring events taking place in the country at that period. A good deal is learned of Saxon manners and customs, and both boys and girls will delight to read of the home life of Hilda and Gytha, and of the brave deeds of the impulsive Gurth and the faithful Leofric.

"This is a charmingly told story. It is the sort of book that all girls and some boys like, and can only get good from."—*Journal of Education.*

"The book is throughout most interesting, and shows in a very natural manner the rough habits and usages in Saxon England."—*Schoolmistress.*

BY M. A. PAULL.

MY MISTRESS THE QUEEN:

By Miss M. A. PAULL. With 4 full-page Illustrations by C. T. GARLAND. Crown 8vo, cloth extra, 2s. 6d.

"My Mistress the Queen" is Mary, daughter of James II., into whose service the narrator, a girl of 16, enters just before the marriage of Mary to William III. The descriptions of persons and manners at the courts of Charles II. and William III. are life-like and accurate. The language is simple, and imitative of the quaint quiet style of that period.

"The style is pure and graceful, the presentation of manners and character has been well studied, and the story is full of interest."—*Scotsman.*

"This is a charming book. The old-time sentiment which pervades the volume renders it all the more alluring."—*Western Mercury.*

BY DARLEY DALE.

THE FAMILY FAILING.

By DARLEY DALE, author of "Spoilt Guy," &c. With 4 full-page Illustrations. Crown 8vo, cloth elegant, 2s. 6d.

This is a lively and amusing account of a family, the members of which while they lived in affluence were remarkable for their discontent, but who, after the loss of fortune has compelled them to seek a more humble home in Jersey, become less selfish, and develop very excellent traits of character under the pressure of comparative adversity.

"'The Family Failing' is at once an amusing and an interesting story, and a capital lesson on the value of contentedness."—*Aberdeen Journal.*

BY ROSA MULHOLLAND.

HETTY GRAY:

Or Nobody's Bairn. By Rosa Mulholland. With 4 full-page Illustrations in black and tint. Cr. 8vo, cloth extra, 2s. 6d.

"Hetty Gray" is the story of a girl who, having been found as an infant by a villager, is brought up by his wife, and is a kind of general pet, till an accident causes a rich widow to adopt her. On the death of her adoptive mother Hetty, who is left unprovided for, is taken by the widow's relatives to be educated with a view to her gaining her livelihood as a governess, an event which is prevented by a rather remarkable discovery.

"A pleasantly told story for girls, with a happy ending."—*Athenæum.*

"A charming story for young folks.

Hetty is a delightful creature—piquant, tender, and true—and her varying fortunes are perfectly realistic."—*World.*

FOUR LITTLE MISCHIEFS.

By Rosa Mulholland. With 3 full-page Pictures in colours by Gordon Browne. Crown 8vo, cloth extra, 2s.

The history of Kitty, Jock, Bunko, and Ba, who, after successfully weathering the mumps in their London nursery, are sent to the country to recruit. The book is full of innocent fun and attractive incident.

"Will be read with absorbing interest by the youngsters."—*Land and Water.*

"A charming bright story about real children."—*Watchman.*

THE LATE MISS HOLLINGFORD.

By Rosa Mulholland. With 2 full-page Illustrations. Crown 8vo, cloth extra, 1s. 6d.

This story, which was a great favourite of Charles Dickens, and originally appeared in *All the Year Round,* is of an orphan girl, who, leaving the gaiety and frivolity of London life, goes to live with an old friend of her mother at a farm-house. A delightful picture is given of the peaceful country life; but there is a strangely pathetic drama running through the quiet narrative, and the troubles which Marjory narrates as having been her portion in youth are sure to interest all who have sympathetic hearts.

NAUGHTY MISS BUNNY:

Her Tricks and Troubles. By Clara Mulholland. With 3 Illustrations in colours. Crown 8vo, cloth extra, 2s.

The story consists of small incidents such as please small listeners, who will be interested not only in Miss Bunny's naughtiness, but in her reformation.

"This naughty child is positively delightful. Papas should not omit 'Naughty

Miss Bunny' from their list of juvenile presents."—*Land and Water.*

BY KATE WOOD.

WINNIE'S SECRET:

A Story of Faith and Patience. By KATE WOOD. With 4 full-page Pictures in black and tint. Crown 8vo, cloth extra, 2s. 6d.

Tells the story of two orphan girls, who, at an early age, are left in a miserable den of London to struggle for a living. The vicissitudes of the little sisters are narrated with touching sympathy, at times sad enough; but relieved by flashes of fun and gleams of genuine humour.

"One of the best story-books we have read. Girls will be charmed with the tale."—*Schoolmaster*.

"A very pretty tale, with great variety of incident and subtle character study, written precisely in the style that is surest to win the hearts of young folks."—*Pictorial World*.

A WAIF OF THE SEA:

Or, the Lost Found. By KATE WOOD. With 4 full-page Illustrations in black and tint. Crown 8vo, cloth extra, 2s. 6d.

"A Waif of the Sea" deals very pathetically with the sorrows and trials of children, and of mothers who are separated from their children. The narrative is full of human interest, and the lives and struggles of the people of a poor London neighbourhood are well portrayed.

"A very touching and pretty tale of town and country, full of pathos and interest, embodied in a narrative which never flags, and told in a style which deserves the highest praise for its lucid and natural ease."—*Edinburgh Courant*.

BY ANNIE S. SWAN.

WARNER'S CHASE:

Or the Gentle Heart. By ANNIE S. SWAN. With 3 Illustrations printed in colours. Crown 8vo, cloth extra, 2s.

"Warner's Chase" is a domestic story, in which we see the failure of an essentially self-seeking and self-assertive nature to secure happiness to itself or bestow it upon others, and the triumph of gentleness, love, and unselfish service, in the person of a feeble girl.

"A good book for boys and girls. There is nothing sentimental in it, but a tone of quiet and true religion that keeps its own place."—*Perth Advertiser*.

"In Milly Warren, the heroine, who unwittingly restores the family fortunes, we have a fine ideal of real womanly goodness."—*Schoolmaster*.

INTO THE HAVEN.

By ANNIE S. SWAN. With 2 Illustrations printed in colours. Crown 8vo, cloth extra, 1s. 6d.

"No story more attractive, by reason of its breezy freshness and unforced pathos, as well as for the practical lessons it conveys."—*Christian Leader*.

BY CAROLINE AUSTIN.

DOROTHY'S DILEMMA:

A Tale of the Time of Charles I. By CAROLINE AUSTIN. With 3 full-page Illustrations. Crown 8vo, cloth extra, 2*s.*

This is a story of the time of Charles I., and the opening scenes are laid in a remote country district through which the king passes in his flight to the north. A little Puritan maiden, Dorothy Hardcastle, is induced to afford a night's shelter to his majesty unknown to her father, who has fought on the side of the Parliament. In the event, her deception costs her father his life, and she is removed to London, whither her only brother John also goes. The story follows them both through their strange adventures in the great city, and leaves them setting sail for the New World, full of sorrow for past mistakes and with an earnest desire to lead a true, unselfish life on the other side of the sea.

MARIE'S HOME:

Or, A Glimpse of the Past. By CAROLINE AUSTIN. With 3 full-page Illustrations. Crown 8vo, cloth extra, 2*s.*

This record of an early life, spent partly in an old English home and partly amid stirring scenes of the French revolution, teaches just such lessons of unselfish love as are of value to English maidens of to-day.

"An exquisitely told story. The heroine is as fine a type of girlhood as one could wish to set before our little British damsels."—*Christian Leader.*

"A pure, fresh story of what is the result in a young girl's life when it is governed by unselfishness and a sense of duty."—*Bradford Observer.*

BY AMY WALTON.

THE HAWTHORNES.

By AMY WALTON. With 3 full-page Illustrations by J. J. PROCTOR. Crown 8vo, cloth extra, 2*s.*

Describes in eight chapters the joys and troubles of five children living in a country rectory—their faults, fancies, pets, and amusements, written in simple language, and fit for children who love the country.

OUR FRANK.

By AMY WALTON. With 2 full-page Illustrations. Crown 8vo, cloth extra, 1*s.* 6*d.*

Six stories suitable for young readers. "Our Frank," which is the longest, describes the fortunes of a runaway boy in the Buckinghamshire woods—how he met with a tramp, how they travelled together, and how, after all, Frank found that "From East to West, At Home is best."

BY THOMAS ARCHER.

LITTLE TOTTIE,

And Two Other Stories. By THOMAS ARCHER. With 3 full-page Illustrations by J. J. PROCTOR. Crown 8vo, cloth extra, 2s.

A thrilling little drama of the life of a poor neighbourhood, and perhaps fuller of suggestion than many more pretentious tales.

"We can warmly commend all three stories, and the attractive binding and pleasing illustrations combine with the contents to render the book a most alluring prize for the younger ones."—*Schoolmaster.*

MISS GRANTLEY'S GIRLS,

And the Stories She Told Them. By THOMAS ARCHER. With 2 Illustrations by GORDON BROWNE. Cr. 8vo, cloth ex., 1s. 6d.

Stories that are likely to prove attractive to the girls in other schools. They are small romances of real life with a good deal of genuine pathos and exciting incident in them.

"For fireside reading more wholesome and, at the same time, highly entertaining reading for young people could not be found."—*Northern Chronicle.*

MISS FENWICK'S FAILURES:

Or "Peggy Pepper-Pot." By ESMÉ STUART. With 4 full-page Illustrations. Crown 8vo, cloth extra, 2s. 6d.

A pleasing narration of the failures of Peggy Fenwick, who, before her sixteenth birthday, had to assume the responsible position of head of her father's house. The story abounds in capitally told domestic adventures; and while it has an excellent moral purpose, it is brimful of fun.

"Esmé Stuart may be commended for producing a girl true to real life, who will put no nonsense into young heads." —*Graphic.*

"There is not a dull page in it; while it is graphically written and abounds in touches of genuine humour and innocent fun."—*Freeman.*

THE BALL OF FORTUNE:

Or Ned Somerset's Inheritance. By CHARLES PEARCE. With 4 full-page Illustrations. Crown 8vo, cloth extra, 2s. 6d.

A story of London life, founded on the strange bequest left by a sea captain, and the endeavours of some unscrupulous persons to obtain possession of it before the discovery of the true heir in the person of a street Arab.

"The most exciting of them all."— *The Times.*

"A bright genial story, which boys will thoroughly enjoy."—*Birmingham Post.*

BY ALICE CORKRAN.

ADVENTURES OF MRS. WISHING-TO-BE.

By ALICE CORKRAN, author of "Latheby Towers," &c. With 3 full-page Pictures in colours. Crown 8vo, cloth extra, 2s.

The strange adventures of a very young lady, showing how she met with the wonderful people of nursery legend and the manner of her introduction to them.

"Simply a charming book for little girls."—*Saturday Review.*

"Well worth buying for the frontispiece alone."—*Times.*

THE WINGS OF COURAGE,

AND THE CLOUD-SPINNER. Translated from the French of GEORGE SAND, by MRS. CORKRAN. With 2 coloured Illustrations. Crown 8vo, cloth extra, 2s.

These stories are among the most attractive of the many tales which the great French novelist wrote for her grandchildren. They are full of fancy, of vivid description, and of a keen appreciation of the best way to arouse the interest of juvenile readers.

"Mrs. Corkran has earned our gratitude by translating into readable English these two charming little stories."—*Athenæum.*

" Ranks with the writings of Erckmann - Chatrian for finish, beauty, and naturalness. The whole story is delightful."—*Dundee Advertiser.*

MAGNA CHARTA STORIES:

Or Struggles for Freedom in the Olden Time. Edited by ARTHUR GILMAN, A.M. With 12 full-page Illustrations. Crown 8vo, cloth extra, 2s.

These stories of heroic deed in the cause of national liberty, from Marathon and Thermopylæ to the times of King Alfred and the *Magna Charta,* are designed to stimulate a love of history, and add to the inspiration of freedom, which should be the heritage of every boy and girl.

"A book of special excellence, which ought to be in the hands of all boys. It

is as readable as it is instructive, and as elevating as it is readable."—*Educ. News.*

THE PATRIOT MARTYR:

And other Narratives of Female Heroism in Peace and War. With 2 Coloured Illustrations. Cloth extra, 1s. 6d.

"It should be read with interest by every girl who loves to learn what her

sex can accomplish in times of difficulty and danger."—*Bristol Times.*

BY GREGSON GOW.

NEW LIGHT THROUGH OLD WINDOWS:

A Series of Stories illustrating Fables of Æsop. By GREGSON
Gow. With 3 Pictures in colours. Cloth extra, 2s.

Stories designed to bring before the young mind, in a new and entertaining form, some of the shreds of wit and wisdom which have come down
to us from ancient times in the guise of fables.

"The most delightfully-written little stories one can easily find in the litera- ture of the season. Well constructed and brightly told."—*Glasgow Herald.*

DOWN AND UP AGAIN:

Being some Account of the Felton Family, and the Odd People
they Met. By GREGSON Gow. With 2 Illustrations in colours.
Crown 8vo, cloth extra, 1s. 6d.

A story of city life, in which, though the chief aim is to amuse through
the recital of interesting events and the exhibition of original and humorous character, the reader may see something of the spirit in which mis-
fortune should be met, and receive an impulse towards kindliness of deed
and charity of thought.

"The story is very neatly told, with some fairly dramatic incidents, and cal- culated altogether to please young boys." —*Scotsman.*

TROUBLES AND TRIUMPHS OF LITTLE TIM.

A City Story. By GREGSON Gow. With 2 Illustrations in
colours. Crown 8vo, cloth extra, 1s. 6d.

"An undercurrent of sympathy with the struggles of the poor, and an ability to describe their feelings under various circumstances, eminently characteristic of Dickens, are marked features in Mr. Gow's story."—*North British Mail.*

THE HAPPY LAD:

A Story of Peasant Life in Norway. From the Norwegian of
Björnson. With Frontispiece in colours. Cloth extra, 1s. 6d.

"This pretty story has a freshness and natural eloquence about it such as are seldom met with in our home-made tales. It seems to carry us back to some of the love stories of the Bible."—*Aberdeen Free Press.*

BOX OF STORIES.

Packed for Young Folk by HORACE HAPPYMAN. A Series of
interesting Tales for the Young. With 2 Illustrations printed
in colours. Crown 8vo, cloth extra, 1s. 6d.

One Shilling each.   Others to follow.

1. *HOP O' MY THUMB.*

2. *BEAUTY AND THE BEAST.*

Each book contains 32 pages 4to, and is illustrated by over 30 pictures in the text, and 4 full-page plates.

The pictures are by Gordon Browne, whose name is a guarantee for the artistic quality of the work. They are graphic character illustrations of a quaint and humorous kind which will be equally relished by young and old. Almost every page is illustrated, and the little reader can thus follow the story step by step by the pictures, and will be able to relate the tale to the younger members of the nursery by the aid of the illustrations alone. The stories are retold by LAURA E. RICHARDS in a manner that will charm children.

THE SHILLING SERIES OF BOOKS FOR YOUNG PEOPLE.

Square 16mo, neatly bound in cloth extra. Each book contains 128 pages and a Coloured Illustration.

"Quality is not sacrificed to quantity, the stories one and all being of the highest, and eminently suited for the purposes of gift books for either day or Sabbath schools."—*Schoolmaster.*

ALF JETSAM: or Found Afloat. By Mrs. GEORGE CUPPLES.

Alf Jetsam is a little boy who is cast ashore from a wreck on the coast of England. He is adopted and brought up by a kind old fisherman and his wife. Eventually he goes to sea, and after many voyages finds his parents. The story of his adventures is charmingly told.

THE REDFORDS: An Emigrant Story. By Mrs. GEORGE CUPPLES.

The story of an English family forced to leave their pleasant country home and face the hardships of pioneer life in New Zealand. The many haps and mishaps which befell them will excite the deepest interest in youthful readers, who will learn in the perusal many a lesson of patience and fortitude.

MISSY. By F. BAYFORD HARRISON.

A tale of joyous child-life in the country. The pranks of Missy and Ernest Dacre with their dog Don are sure to please the "little ones," while the story of Missy's fault will teach the lesson of sincerity and truthfulness.

HIDDEN SEED: or a Year in a Girl's Life. By EMMA LESLIE.

A brightly told story of a girl who on her fifteenth birthday resolves to make herself useful in the world; but who, forgetting that her home where she is needed is her proper sphere of action, is betrayed into worldliness, while her simple loving cousin Isabel, without pretension or self-consciousness, delights in serving those near her and in making them happy.

URSULA'S AUNT. By ANNIE S. FENN.

The fresh and simple narrative of the troubles of two girls, who make a not uncommon mistake in thinking they are not beloved by their guardian, and of the manner in which they discover the truth by means of a great sorrow, which, however, turns to as great a joy.

JACK'S TWO SOVEREIGNS. By ANNIE S. FENN.

A story which will interest the young reader in the fortunes of a poor and very peculiar family, the members of which show great diversity of character, but are united by the troubles that befall them, and by the singular events which at last lead to their being relieved from serious difficulties.

THE SHILLING SERIES—Continued.

OLIVE MOUNT. By ANNIE S. FENN.

A bright and sparkling story about a family of boys and girls left, through the death of both parents, to the charge of their eldest brother. For a time the children fairly run riot in the pleasant country-side at Olive Mount; till the wholesome discipline of sorrow and the gentle influence of their governess lead them to find enjoyment in doing what is right.

A LITTLE ADVENTURER. By GREGSON GOW.

Tells how little Tommy Treffit started off to search for his father in Australia. How he hid himself on board a vessel bound for Madeira, and how, after many adventures, he at last found his father, not in Australia, but safe at home.

TOM WATKINS' MISTAKE. By EMMA LESLIE.

Tom Watkins, having given way to the temptation to commit acts of petty pilfering in the carpenter's shop where he is apprenticed, ultimately suffers the consequences of his wrong-doing, and not only learns that honesty is the best policy, but comes to see the sinfulness of his conduct.

TWO LITTLE BROTHERS. By HARRIET M. CAPES.

This is a pleasant account of some of the incidents which befell two little brothers, whose home was in a seaside village. It tells of their adventures on the shore and of the wonderful sights they saw during a trip to London, and how a kind father taught them to practise at all times self-control and courtesy.

THREE LITTLE ONES: Their Haps and Mishaps. By CORA LANGTON.

A simple tale of home life. Children are sure to love and admire bright Mabel, affectionate Eddie, and sad little Lucy, while the story of Mabel's sin and Lucy's sorrow will teach them truthfulness and obedience.

THE NEW BOY AT MERRITON. By JULIA GODDARD.

"A story of English school life. It is an attempt to teach a somewhat higher code of honour than that which prevails among the general run of schoolboys, and the lesson makes a very good story."—*School Board Chronicle.*

THE BLIND BOY OF DRESDEN.

"This is a family story of great pathos. It does not obtrusively dictate its lesson, but it quietly introduces, and leaves it within the heart."—*Aberdeen Journal.*

JON OF ICELAND: A True Story.

"'Jon of Iceland' is a sturdy, well-educated young Icelander, who becomes a successful teacher. It gives children a clear idea of the chief physical features of the island, and of the simple and manly character of its inhabitants."—*School Guardian.*

STORIES FROM SHAKESPEARE.

"The stories are told in such a way that young people having read them will desire to study the works of Shakespeare in their original form."—*The Schoolmistress.*

THE SHILLING SERIES—Continued.

EVERY MAN IN HIS PLACE. The Story of a City Boy and a Forest Boy.

"This is the history of the son of a wealthy Hamburg merchant, who wished to follow in the steps of Robinson Crusoe. He was put to the test, and became convinced in the end that it is better to live the life of a wealthy merchant in a great city than to endure hardship by choice."—*School Board Chronicle.*

FIRESIDE FAIRIES AND FLOWER FANCIES: Stories for Girls.

"Nine stories are included, all for girls, encouraging them to try and do their duty. Young servants would find this book very interesting."—*The Schoolmistress.*

TO THE SEA IN SHIPS: Stories of Suffering and Saving at Sea.

"*To the Sea in Ships* records several noted disasters at sea, such as the foundering of the *London* and the wreck of the *Atlantic.* It also contains narratives of successful rescues. This is a capital book for boys."—*School Guardian.*

JACK'S VICTORY: Stories about Dogs.

"Every boy, and some girls, take great delight in reading about dogs. Well, Jack was a dog; a famous and wonderful one, too. He became leader of a team in Greenland, and some rare exploits he took part in."—*The Schoolmistress.*

THE STORY OF A KING, Told by one of his Soldiers.

"This book recounts the boyhood and reign of Charles XII. of Sweden. The wars *in* which he was engaged and the extraordinary victories he won are well described, and equally so are the misfortunes which latterly came on him and his kingdom through his uncontrollable wilfulness."—*Aberdeen Journal.*

LITTLE DANIEL: A Story of a Flood on the Rhine.

"A simple and touching story of a flood on the Rhine, told as well as George Eliot so graphically wrote of *The Mill on the Floss.*"—*Governess.*

PRINCE ALEXIS: A Tale of Old Russia.

This is a legend wrought into a story, rendering a fiction of Life in Russia, something more than a hundred years ago; a state of things which, as the author says, "is now impossible, and will soon become incredible."

SASHA THE SERF: And other Stories of Russian Life.

The stories in the volume comprise:—The Life of Sasha, a poor boy who saved the life of his lord, and finally rose to wealth and gained his freedom,—Incidents of remarkable personal bravery in the army, &c. &c.

TRUE STORIES OF FOREIGN HISTORY. A Series of Interesting Tales.

The book contains stories—How Quentin Matsys the Antwerp smith became a great painter,—The rise and fall of Jean Ango the fisherman of Dieppe,—The heroism of Casabianca the little French midshipman, &c. &c.

THE NINEPENNY SERIES OF BOOKS FOR CHILDREN.

Neatly bound in cloth extra.   Each contains 96 pages and a Coloured Illustration.

ABOARD THE MERSEY: or Our Youngest Passenger. By Mrs. GEO. CUPPLES.

A tale of the sea, told in the simple and fascinating style in which few writers can equal Mrs. Cupples.   Little Miss Matty, our youngest passenger, is a dear little girl, who, by her tender devotion, sustains many of the rough sailors in time of danger, and leads them to a knowledge of the better life.   Boys will appreciate the story for its incident, and girls because the chief actor is a little maiden.

SEPPERL THE DRUMMER-BOY. By MARY C. ROWSELL.

The story is of a drummer-boy, who, by courage and patience, became a great musician, and whose name is remembered with reverence and admiration.   The narrative and the style are both simple enough for very young readers, but yet so interesting that a good many "grown up" people will take real pleasure in making the little ones listeners, and reading the story to them.

A BLIND PUPIL. By ANNIE S. FENN.

This is a strikingly original tale, which will deeply interest both girls and boys, for it is full of simple but exciting incidents; and though the hero of the story is a blind boy, whose unhappy disposition is improved and at last quite changed by the influence of a firm and kindly friendship, the descriptions of external objects are remarkably picturesque and vivid.

LOST AND FOUND: or Twelve Years with Bulgarian Gypsies. By Mrs. CARL ROTHER.

Tells of how the young heir of Wolfsburg on the Rhine was entrapped and carried off by a gang of Bulgarian gypsies; how for years he wandered with them through Austria and Bulgaria; how he eventually joined the Bulgarian army and fought against the Servians, and how at last he found his father's home.   The wandering life through the fertile valleys of the Rhine and Danube is pleasantly depicted.

FISHERMAN GRIM. By MARY C. ROWSELL.

May be called a historical romance in a nutshell.   The scene is laid in Saxon times on the north-east coast of England, where Grimsby now stands, and the story of Hablok the little Danish Prince, and Grim the rough English fisherman with his cat Tib, is told with a simplicity and vivacity that will delight children.

THE SIXPENNY SERIES FOR CHILDREN.

Neatly bound in cloth extra.   Each book contains 64 pages and a Coloured Illustration.

NEW VOLUMES.

Little Mop: and other Stories. By Mrs. CHARLES BRAY.

The Tree Cake: and other Stories. By W. L. ROOPER.

Nurse Peggy, and Little Dog Trip. Two Stories by Two Sisters.

Wild Marsh Marigolds. By DARLEY DALE.

Fanny's King. By DARLEY DALE.

Kitty's Cousin. By HANNAH B. MACKENZIE.

Cleared at Last. By JULIA GODDARD.

Little Dolly Forbes. By ANNIE S. FENN.

A Year with Nellie. By ANNIE S. FENN.

The Little Brown Bird: a Story of Industry.

The Maid of Domremy: and other Tales.

Little Eric: a Story of Honesty.

Uncle Ben the Whaler: and other Stories.

The Palace of Luxury: and other Stories.

The Charcoal-Burner: or, Kindness Repaid.

Willy Black: a Story of Doing Right.

The Horse and his Ways: Stories of Man and his best Friend.

The Shoemaker's Present: a Legendary Story.

Lights to Walk by: Stories for the Young.

The Little Merchant: and other Stories.

Nicholina: a Story about an Iceberg.

"The whole of the set will be found admirably adapted for the use of the young."—*Schoolmaster.*

"A very praiseworthy series of Prize Books. Most of the stories are designed to enforce some important moral lesson, such as honesty, industry, kindness, helpfulness, &c."—*School Guardian.*

A SERIES OF FOURPENNY REWARD BOOKS.

Each 64 pages, 18mo, Illustrated, in Picture Boards.

Holidays at Sunnycroft. By ANNIE S. SWAN.

Worthy of Trust. By H. B. MACKENZIE.

Maudie and Bertie. By GREGSON GOW.

Phil Foster. By J. LOCKHART.

Brave and True. By GREGSON GOW.

Poor Tom Olliver. By JULIA GODDARD.

The Children and the Water-Lily. By JULIA GODDARD.

Johnnie Tupper's Temptation. By GREGSON GOW.

Fritz's Experiment. By LETITIA M'LINTOCK.

Climbing the Hill. By ANNIE S. SWAN.

A Year at Coverley. By Do.

Lucy's Christmas-Box.

**** These little books have been specially written with the aim of inculcating some sound moral, such as obedience to parents, love for brothers and sisters, kindness to animals, perseverance and diligence leading to success, &c. &c.

"Any one who wishes to send a dainty packet of story-books to a household blessed with little children will find in these exactly what he wants. They are issued with the prettiest of all the coloured covers we have yet seen."—*Christian Leader.*

VERE FOSTER'S
WATER-COLOR DRAWING-BOOKS.

The Times says:—"We can strongly recommend the series to young students."

PAINTING FOR BEGINNERS.

FIRST STAGE. Teaching the use of ONE COLOR. Ten Facsimiles of Original Studies in Sepia by J. CALLOW, and numerous Illustrations in pencil. With full Instructions in easy language. 4to, cloth elegant, 2s. 6d.

"Sound little books, teaching the elements of 'washing' with much clearness by means of plain directions and well-executed plates."—*Academy.*

PAINTING FOR BEGINNERS.

SECOND STAGE. Teaching the use of SEVEN COLORS. Twenty Facsimiles of Original Drawings by J. CALLOW, and many Illustrations in pencil. With full Instructions in easy language. 4to, cloth elegant, 4s.

"The rules are so clear and simple that they cannot fail to be understood even by those who have no previous knowledge of drawing. The letterpress of the book is as good as the illustrations are beautiful."—*Birmingham Gazette.*

SIMPLE LESSONS IN FLOWER PAINTING.

Eight Facsimiles of Original Water-Color Drawings, and numerous Outline Drawings of Flowers, after various artists. With Instructions for Drawing and Painting. 4to, cloth elegant, 3s.

"Everything necessary for acquiring the art of flower painting is here: the *facsimiles* of water-color drawings are very beautiful."—*Graphic.*

"Such excellent books, so carefully written and studied, cannot fail to have great advantage in the creation and fostering of a taste for art."—*Scotsman.*

SIMPLE LESSONS IN LANDSCAPE PAINTING.

Eight Facsimiles of Original Water-Color Drawings, and Thirty Vignettes, after various artists. With full Instructions by an experienced Master. 4to, cloth elegant, 3s.

"As a work of art in the book line we have seldom seen its equal; and it could not fail to be a delightful present, affording a great amount of pleasurable amusement and instruction, to young people."—*St. James's Gazette.*

SIMPLE LESSONS IN MARINE PAINTING.

Twelve Facsimiles of Original Water-Color Sketches. By EDWARD DUNCAN. With numerous Illustrations in pencil, and Practical Lessons by an experienced Master. 4to, cloth elegant, 3s.

"The book must prove of great value to students. Nothing could be prettier or more charming than the marine sketches here presented."—*Graphic.*

VERE FOSTER'S DRAWING-BOOKS—Continued.

STUDIES OF TREES

In Pencil and in Water-Colors. By J. Needham. A Series of Eighteen Examples in Colors, and Thirty-three Drawings in pencil. With descriptions of the Trees, and full Instructions for Drawing and Painting. First Series, cloth elegant, 5s.; Second Series, cloth elegant, 5s.

"We commend them most heartily to all persons of taste who may be wanting to cultivate the great accomplishment of Water-color Drawing, or who want a gift-book for a lad or girl taking up the study."—*Schoolmaster*.

ADVANCED STUDIES IN FLOWER PAINTING

By Ada Hanbury. A Series of Twelve beautifully finished Examples in Colors, and numerous Outlines in pencil. With full Instructions for Painting, and a description of each plant by Blanche Hanbury. 4to, cloth elegant, 7s. 6d.

"Apart from its educational value in art training this is a lovely book: we have seen nothing to equal the coloured plates."—*Sheffield Independent*.

"The handsomest and most instructive volume of the series yet produced."—*Daily Chronicle*.

"Coloured sketches of flowers which it is literally no exaggeration to term exquisite."—*Knowledge*.

EASY STUDIES IN WATER-COLOR PAINTING

By R. P. Leitch and J. Callow. A Series of Nine Pictures executed in Neutral Tints. With full Instructions for drawing each subject, and for sketching from Nature. 4to, cloth elegant, 6s.

SKETCHES IN WATER-COLORS

By T. M. Richardson, R. P. Leitch, J. A. Houston, T. L. Rowbotham, E. Duncan, and J. Needham. A Series of Nine Pictures executed in Colors. With full Instructions for drawing, by an experienced Teacher. 4to, cloth elegant, 5s.

"To those who wish to become proficient in the art of water-color painting no better instructor could be recommended than these two series."—*Newcastle Chronicle*.

ILLUMINATING.

Nine Examples in Colors and Gold of ancient Illuminating of the best periods, with numerous Illustrations in Outline, Historical Notes and full descriptions and instructions by Rev. W. J. Loftie, B.A., F.S.A. 4to, cloth elegant, 6s.

"The illuminations are admirably reproduced in colour. Mr. Loftie's practical instructions enhance the value of an excellent handbook."—*Saturday Review*.

BOOKS FOR YOUNG PEOPLE.

Classified according to Price.   Elegantly Bound in Extra Cloth.

Books at 7s. 6d.

The Universe; or The Infinitely Great and Infinitely Little. By F. A. POUCHET, M.D.
Advanced Studies in Flower Painting.

Books at 6s.

The Young Carthaginian. By G. A. HENTY.

With Wolfe in Canada. By G. A. HENTY.

Down the Snow Stairs. By ALICE CORKRAN.

The Lion of the North. By G. A. HENTY.

Through the Fray. By G. A. HENTY.

In Freedom's Cause. By G. A. HENTY.

With Clive in India. By G. A. HENTY.

True to the Old Flag. By G. A. HENTY.

Under Drake's Flag. By G. A. HENTY.

Two Thousand Years Ago. By Prof. A. J. CHURCH.

The Log of the "Flying Fish." By HARRY COLLINGWOOD.

Devon Boys. By G. MANVILLE FENN.

Brownsmith's Boy. By G. MANVILLE FENN.

Bunyip Land. By G. MANVILLE FENN.

The Golden Magnet. By G. M. FENN.

In the King's Name. By G. M. FENN.

Robinson Crusoe. Over 100 Illustrations by GORDON BROWNE.

Lessons in the Art of Illuminating.

Easy Studies in Water-Colors.

Books at 5s.

Bravest of the Brave. By G. A. HENTY.

A Final Reckoning. By G. A. HENTY.

For Name and Fame. By G. A. HENTY.

The Dragon and the Raven. By G. A. HENTY.

St. George for England. By G. A. HENTY.

By Sheer Pluck. By G. A. HENTY.

Facing Death. By G. A. HENTY.

The Congo Rovers. By H. COLLINGWOOD.

The Pirate Island. By H. COLLINGWOOD.

Gulliver's Travels. Over 100 Illustrations by GORDON BROWNE.

Yussuf the Guide. By G. MANVILLE FENN.

Patience Wins. By G. MANVILLE FENN.

Menhardoc. By G. MANVILLE FENN.

Nat the Naturalist. By G. M. FENN.

Perseverance Island. By DOUGLAS FRAZAR.

The Wigwam and War-Path. By ASCOTT R. HOPE.

Stories of Old Renown. By. A. R. HOPE.

Studies of Trees in Pencil and Water-Colors. Two Series.

Sketches in Water-Colors.

Book at 4s.

Painting for Beginners, 2nd Stage.

Books at 3s. 6d.

Reefer and Rifleman. By PERCY GROVES.

The White Squall. By J. C. HUTCHESON.

The Search for the Talisman. By HENRY FRITH.

Silver Mill. By Mrs. R. H. READ.

The Wreck of the Nancy Bell. By J. C. HUTCHESON.

Picked up at Sea. By J. C. HUTCHESON.

Dr. Jolliffe's Boys. By LEWIS HOUGH.

Historic Boys. By E. S. BROOKS.

Traitor or Patriot? By M. C. ROWSELL.

Brother and Sister. By Mrs. LYSAGHT.

Dora. By Mrs. R. H. READ.

Cheep and Chatter. By ALICE BANKS.

Garnered Sheaves. By Mrs. PITMAN.

Life's Daily Ministry. By Mrs. PITMAN.

Florence Godfrey's Faith. By Do.

My Governess Life. By Mrs. PITMAN.

Books at 3s.

Simple Lessons in Flower Painting.

Simple Lessons in Marine Painting.

Simple Lessons in Landscape Painting.

Books at 2s. 6d.

The Eversley Secrets. By E. E. Green.
The Lads of Little Clayton. By R. Stead.
Ten Boys. By Jane Andrews.
The Joyous Story of Toto. By Laura E. Richards.
Gytha's Message. By Emma Leslie.
My Mistress the Queen. By M. A. Paull.
Brothers in Arms: A Story of the Crusades. By F. Bayford Harrison.
Miss Fenwick's Failures. By E. Stuart.
Winnie's Secret. By Kate Wood.
A Waif of the Sea. By Kate Wood.
Jack o' Lanthorn. By Henry Frith.
Hetty Gray. By Rosa Mulholland.
The Ball of Fortune. By Chas. Pearce.
The Family Failing. By Darley Dale.
Famous Discoveries by Sea and Land.
Stirring Events of History.
Stories of the Sea in Former Days.
Adventures in Field, Flood, and Forest.
Tales of Captivity and Exile.
Painting for Beginners, 1st Stage.

Books at 2s.

Dorothy's Dilemma. By Caroline Austin.
The Hawthornes. By Amy Walton.
Teddy. By J. C. Hutcheson.
The Penang Pirate. By J. C. Hutcheson.
Little Tottie. By Thomas Archer.
Marie's Home. By Caroline Austin.
Warner's Chase. By Annie S. Swan.
The Wings of Courage. By George Sand.
Mrs. Wishing-to-be. By Alice Corkran.
Four Little Mischiefs. By Rosa Mulholland.
Magna Charta Stories. By A. Gilman.
New Light through Old Windows. By Gregson Gow.
Our Dolly. By Mrs. R. H. Read.
Fairy Fancy. By Mrs. R. H. Read.
Naughty Miss Bunny. By Clara Mulholland.

Books at 1s. 6d.

The Late Miss Hollingford. By Rosa Mulholland.
Our Frank. By Amy Walton.
A Terrible Coward. By G. M. Fenn.
Yarns on the Beach. By G. A. Henty.
Miss Grantley's Girls. By T. Archer.
The Pedlar and his Dog. By Mary C. Rowsell.
Tom Finch's Monkey. By J. C. Hutcheson.
Down and Up Again. By Gregson Gow.
Little Tim. By Gregson Gow.
The Happy Lad. By Björnson.
Into the Haven. By Annie S. Swan.
Box of Stories. By H. Happyman.
The Patriot Martyr: and other Narratives.

Books at 1s.

Alf Jetsam. By Mrs. Geo. Cupples.
Jack's Two Sovereigns. By A. S. Fenn.
Ursula's Aunt. By A. S. Fenn.
Missy. By F. B. Harrison.
The Redfords. By Mrs. Geo. Cupples.
Hidden Seed. By Emma Leslie.
A Little Adventurer. By Gregson Gow.
Olive Mount. By A. S. Fenn.
Two Little Brothers. By H. M. Capes.
Three Little Ones. By Cora Langton.
Tom Watkins' Mistake.
The New Boy at Merriton.
The Blind Boy of Dresden.
Jon of Iceland: A True Story.
Stories from Shakespeare.
Every Man in His Place.
Fireside Fairies.
To the Sea in Ships.
Little Daniel: a Story of the Rhine.
Jack's Victory: Stories about Dogs.
The Story of a King.
Prince Alexis.
Sasha the Serf: Stories of Russia.
True Stories of Foreign History.

For Series at 9d., 6d., and 4d. see pages 43 and 44.

LONDON: BLACKIE & SON, 49 OLD BAILEY, E.C.
GLASGOW, EDINBURGH, AND DUBLIN.